AUTUMN STORM

The Rebel & the Witch

A paranormal historical romance

Magpie
Press

First published by Magpie Press 2022

Copyright © 2022 by Autumn Storm

This novel is entirely a work of fiction. The names, characters and incidents portrayed in it are the work of the author's imagination. Any resemblance to actual persons, living or dead, events or localities is entirely coincidental.

Autumn Storm has no responsibility for the persistence or accuracy of URLs for external or third-party Internet Websites referred to in this publication and does not guarantee that any content on such Websites is, or will remain, accurate or appropriate.

First edition

ISBN: 978-1-7345602-5-1

This book was professionally typeset on Reedsy. Find out more at reedsy.com

Contents

Chapter 1	1
Chapter 2	7
Chapter 3	11
Chapter 4	17
Chapter 5	21
Chapter 6	27
Chapter 7	31
Chapter 8	34
Chapter 9	40
Chapter 10	44
Chapter 11	51
Chapter 12	57
Chapter 13	61
Chapter 14	68
Chapter 15	73
Chapter 16	77
Chapter 17	81
Chapter 18	88
Chapter 19	92
Chapter 20	98
Chapter 21	102
Chapter 22	105
Chapter 23	109
Chapter 24	118

Chapter 25   124

Chapter 26   128

Chapter 27   135

Chapter 28   139

Chapter 29   143

Chapter 30   146

Chapter 31   151

Chapter 32   156

Chapter 33   162

Chapter 34   167

Chapter 35   172

Chapter 36   178

Chapter 37   182

Chapter 38   188

Chapter 39   194

Chapter 40   197

Chapter 41   199

Chapter 42   203

Chapter 43   205

Chapter 44   211

Chapter 45   215

Chapter 46   219

Chapter 47   221

Chapter 48   226

Chapter 49   230

Chapter 50   235

Chapter 51   239

Chapter 52   242

Chapter 53   244

Chapter 54   252

Chapter 55   256

Chapter 56   262
Chapter 57   265
Chapter 58   267
Chapter 59   270
Chapter 60   273
Chapter 61   278
Chapter 62   281
Chapter 63   286
Forthcoming from Autumn Storm...   290
Chapter 1   291
Chapter 2   296
About the Author   299
Also by Autumn Storm   300

Chapter 1

D uke Channing had a love affair with the West. So, when he rolled into that dusty Kansas Territory trading post of Warren in the summer of 1855, he wasn't looking for anything other than a cool drink of water and a place to lay his head for the night. And he certainly wasn't looking for a wife.

And maybe later in the week, he'd find those border ruffians who were rumored to be hiding out in the hills north of town. Give them some trouble from a U.S. Marshal's business end of a pistol and send them back south where they'd come from.

But for now, he'd catch his breath, rest his horse, find a bath. He checked his six-shooters in their holsters and leaned his rifle against a stool as he sat down in the saloon.

Gooseflesh crawled up his arms, and he snapped his head up. A pair of green eyes on the landing upstairs caught his. No, they had *commanded* him to look. Their intensity and forthrightness were singular. Their depths stirred him, so frank and questioning were they.

And he sensed something else: Magic. The air snapped with it just as her eyes did.

Though he had no magic of his own, he knew the western wilderness was a place for things that defied common knowledge. It was a place for people to hide, whether from persecution or the law. And it was a place for the fantastic to flourish.

He had the briefest impression of the rest of her form before it was eclipsed by the enormous crimson skirts that followed. Dark hair piled up on her head. A long, graceful neck. He wondered what a woman of her status was doing in this dusty, Godforsaken territory. He hadn't seen store clothes like that for many a year. Surely she was only moving through, as he was.

He tipped his hat to the sweep of skirts that had disappeared into a door upstairs. The green eyes stayed with him. Their incredible intensity and intelligence were not lost on him, nor was the snap of magic he saw living within their depths, even from that distance. A man would have to be blind to not sense something fantastic about the woman.

"Who was that?" he asked the man sitting next to him.

"That's Isaac Goodnight's daughter. I'm surprised she's out of her rooms at all."

Duke sipped at his whiskey and considered that. He knew the way of things here. This stop on the prairie had a reputation for a firm hand with lawbreakers, and they weren't afraid to punish to the law's fullest extent. Another reason why it had surprised him to be sent here to help rid the area of border ruffians. That Isaac Goodnight hadn't dispatched with them yet meant there might be more trouble that Duke had expected.

The man next to him hadn't quit studying him. "Ain't you that brokeneck cowboy? Duke, isn't it?"

Duke scoffed. He wasn't surprised his likeness had reached

this place. Though he had hoped for a reprieve in a new town. Most thought him an outlaw because his business as a U.S. Marshal was better kept hush-hush. He frowned into his whiskey, then he regarded the man next to him more carefully. For all the dust and dirt on the man's clothes, Duke knew fine clothes when he saw them. Fine cloth, fine stitching, fine, tailored cut. The man's buckles were pure silver, and the two matching pieces in his chest holster were new, oiled, gleaming. His skin wasn't baked enough to be used to rough riding on scorching days. No, this was no traveling man, no man just passing through.

Duke sipped at his whiskey again and leaned back in his chair. The dust that had gotten inside his shirt irritated his skin, and his muscles ached from being on the trail so long. He'd pay a pretty penny for a hot bath just about now. Depending on how the next few minutes went, he'd either be taking one in Warren or hightailing it out of there for the next dot on the map. "I take it you're Isaac Goodnight, heavy hand of the law in this town?"

The man seemed surprised, then recovered himself. "Would the good marshal care for ice in that whiskey of his?"

It was Duke's turn to be surprised. How would Isaac Goodnight know that? But the ice was a bargaining chip, and a good one it was. He hadn't seen ice in a month of Sundays, and that was one luxury he missed. "I imagine that would help me shake the dust off rather faster."

Goodnight motioned for the bartender, who took a sharp pick over to an inconspicuous-looking box behind the bar. The barkeep returned with a new whiskey over ice for Goodnight and a sizeable sliver for Duke. Duke watched the ice slide into the amber liquid and felt almost giddy at even the thought of the coolness.

"I don't know a man who would turn that down," Goodnight said with a smile. While no trail hard ruffian, Duke saw the strength in the man seated next to him. Men didn't make it in the West for nothing.

Duke sipped at his cooling whiskey. Oh, yes. This would do a fine job of knocking the dust off. "The Devil might, just to spite us."

Goodnight set his drink down and settled in his chair. But not relaxed, Duke realized. Waiting, alert, with the pretense of relaxation. "I take that as you're not the devil I hear you are."

Duke held back a scoff. He knew better than to laugh at a man who offered him ice before he offered him trouble. "I suppose that depends on which side of the pistol you end up on."

Goodnight didn't seem perturbed by the statement. "Spoken like the true rebel marshal I hear you to be. Out here shooting ruffians for God and country. Outside of the reach of men in an office where their boots never get dusty. Outside of the law."

Duke felt the prickle of annoyance at this man knowing his business, though he didn't know much of Goodnight's aside from the rumors which preceded him.

Goodnight continued. "I may seem a hard man, Mr. Channing, but I assure you I'm fair. You've done nothing to me or my town except get spit out here by the West. I'd prefer you stay here and spend your money, get comfortable. With the McLaury brothers around, your name might keep some of the trouble out. So long as you aren't set on making some of your own."

"I never set out to cause trouble."

"It seems to find you easily enough," Goodnight replied, keeping his eyes on Duke. A challenge, Duke knew, but he wasn't afraid. And he was glad Goodnight wasn't either. This stop might prove more profitable than he'd realized.

"Men don't like to run into the quickest draw in the West, but the trouble often seeks me. They think my title is a bluff. I won't wait for them to shoot first, in any case."

"Self-defense, then. It's a shame there aren't often witnesses."

"If you were a man bent on a challenge, would you want another to see you lose?"

Goodnight nodded but didn't respond. There was another flurry of skirts on the landing far above them, and Duke didn't miss the look the man next to him sent upward. It was a warning.

"She must be your daughter," Duke said casually.

"She is," Goodnight replied. Another warning.

Duke stepped carefully with his next words. "And you let her run loose like that? I've seen a heavy hand taken for less than that."

"She does as she wishes. I never needed raise a hand to her when I reared her, and I don't aim to start now. There is a dance down at the public hall tonight, Mr. Channing," he continued. "I'd appreciate your presence as I hear the McLaury boys aim to come and cause a ruckus."

"Will she be there?" Magic, Duke thought, would be why the girl did as she pleased. Likely running about keeping others at her beck and call. He found himself drawn to it, curious. What he'd caught in glimpses across the West in others—witching for water, seeking out gold, conjuring things he'd sworn he'd not seen the moment before—now felt closer than ever. He knew good and well what happened to moths and night bugs when they drew too close to a campfire, but he could be more careful than they.

There wasn't even a beat of hesitation from Goodnight. "She will."

Long had it been since he'd been in good company. Even knowing he wouldn't stay in town, Duke could appreciate the value of a night spent with finer folk. "Does she dance?"

Duke was surprised when Goodnight's response was laughter instead of derision. "You may hold conversation with her, but she dances with no man."

Duke couldn't help himself. He didn't know the girl, but he knew that too firm a hand made a rebel of any child. He should know. His father had been the hardest on him. "I've heard that's the way to make a girl wild."

Mirth spread across Goodnight's face before he laughed. "That is her choice, Duke Channing. A grown woman may make her own decisions. You would be wise to heed that advice."

"I'll keep that in mind." And with that warning, Duke took that and his traveling dust with him to find a room and suitable clothes for that night's adventure.

Chapter 2

The dance that night was to be well-attended by Warren's higher society. Relatively speaking. That meant perhaps twenty and five men, a handful of ladies, plus the rest of the town.

While that should have mattered to Cheyenne Goodnight, it only served to remind her that someday, this place might too be filled with people as Boston had been. Already that summer, a dozen more well-to-do families had come in by boat on the river along with barges full of timber. Most were in the throes of building their homes on the prairie. She had several offers for tea that she needed to answer before her delay was considered rude. She was trying to work out how to say no without letting her father know she'd gotten invitations. She would have to accept them if he did. She had struggled in a larger city to find people with whom she had much in common, and she wasn't eager to begin that disappointing process over again on the prairie.

Cheyenne didn't miss the big city. Boston had pressed in around her, had shown her little charm save its few green spaces, had forced her to hide her magic, who she truly was. She had no love for the wharf and the smell of fish and waste coming in off the water, and she longed for the wide-open skies of the West she had heard her father speak of. The wide-open skies her mother had been born under.

So when the Emigrant Aid Committee had sent them to the Kansas Territory to establish it as a Free State, Cheyenne knew she had come home. No matter that there weren't the conveniences of the city here. No matter that there was hardly any society. No matter that her finest clothes were dusty and disheveled by the day's end.

She felt free.

The green hills which opened up onto the vast prairie and the wilder West beyond called to her heart and dove deeply into her soul. Here she could breathe freely of the wild air, here she could keep her own schedule. Even the snows and harsh winds of winter couldn't hold back her joy for this land.

Here where survival trumped decorum any day.

Here where she could practice her magic without fear.

Here where she would meet her destiny.

Cheyenne did not think she was an unusual girl because she knew how to do magic. Cheyenne felt she was unusual because she remembered her birth and every moment since that time. And because she remembered her birth, she remembered the last thing her mother spoke before she left this world and passed on to the next.

She closed her eyes and remembered, feeling the rush of emotion that recalling that moment always brought upon her.

A man will come in from the West for you. He will be tall and strong and steel-eyed, and his heart will be full of rebellion.

And Cheyenne had wailed at the brightness she had been thrust into and cried when she was taken from her mother's cold arms and wailed when her father held her close and

8

shushed her gently while his hot tears fell on her newborn head. She had not understood then. She grew to understand. She understood more now.

And she yearned to fully understand what it meant to live, to love, to share the passion of life with another soul.

As a child and beyond, Father had encouraged her to learn, to cultivate both skills of the home and skills of the mind. They had money enough for hired help, but the West dealt out its hardships equally.

She had felt him before she saw him, the way she'd known he'd walked into the taproom below her rooms. He'd been dusty then, beat hard on the trail.

She'd seen Duke Channing's likeness in every town west of the Mississippi, had heard tales of his sharpshooting amongst her father's friends in law enforcement, his taking the law into his hands in the West. And here was Duke Channing, surest shot in the West, walking into her prairie town to shake off the dust.

And, she supposed, he wouldn't expect her to know that he was a U.S. Marshal. Having that card up her sleeve was how she planned to capture his attention, should she need to. She wasn't the sort who made designs as they had always seemed like an exhausting waste of time, but in this case, she felt having a plan would be in her best interest.

She felt nerves where she hadn't before. No gentleman in Boston had ever caught her eye as this man had. And certainly none in Warren, though it wasn't because she felt herself above any of the men here. It was simply because none of them were the man she was seeking. The man whom her mother said would come for her from the West.

He was tall and strong and full of confidence. She knew he'd tower over her, and she felt a thrill run through her, knowing that soon, she would know the strength of that form. Father seemed to like him, though she thought that might change should the man show interest in her.

That first look into his steely eyes from her spot about the taproom floor had seen straight through her, and there had been so much fire in his eyes that she nearly lost her breath. Not one to run from a challenge and someone who preferred to meet fire with fire, she surprised even herself by running back to her rooms as quickly as she could.

"Mother," she'd breathed once back in the safety of her room. "This is he, isn't it?"

Her answer had been in the scream of a hawk soaring outside.

She readied for the dance that night with trembling fingers. Would he know? Was she ready for this? She had felt yearning before, knew what it was to want, but how would it happen with this man? Would it be instant or take time?

Cheyenne took a deep breath and calmed herself in front of her mirror. Tonight she would finally meet the man who would change the course of her life.

Chapter 3

She waited in the dance hall as she had done countless times before, attending on Father's wishes, but this time was different. Now, she looked to the door when others entered, anticipated seeing the dusty frame once more.

The room quieted, and Cheyenne knew.

But the man who filled the doorway with the same eyes of steel didn't look like a dusty rebel just off the highway. He'd cleaned up, somehow found a suitable evening dress—his dark coat and trousers didn't have a speck of dust on them, and his shoes gleamed with a recent shining. She was taken aback by his dress and felt almost that she should inspect her own to be certain *she* wouldn't get dust on *him*!

He strode to her confidently, the sureness of his gait so undeniably male. Powerful, he was. And handsome, now that she could see his face without the peculiar wide-brimmed felt hat he'd worn before. He hadn't been tanned by the sun as much as the rest of the men who came through, and he carried himself with more grace than she would've expected from a rebel on the run. This man played the role of a wealthy man well. Cheyenne had seen his likeness as far as Iowa, the sharpshooter unafraid to fell a man for pulling his pistol. A man of the law masquerading as a rebel to draw those to him who sought to make the West a place of lawlessness. She could keep his secret. She wondered if he could keep hers.

When he reached her, his bow was as perfect as she would have expected from a gentleman in Boston. Intrigued, she held out her gloved hand for him, which he barely grazed with lips so warm, she could feel their heat through the black silk. She shivered at the shock which passed through her at his touch. Cheyenne was certain the man did not know of his own magic, and yet his entire being pulsed with the power of it.

"Mr. Duke Channing," she said quietly.

He hid his surprise well, recovering with a smile that was more mischievous than she'd expected. Having had all these years to wonder what he might look like, this ruggedly handsome man was not quite what she had been imagining. And why had she thought he would be polished from head to toe? Perhaps because that was all she had known in Boston.

"While you may already have the honor of my name, I do not yet have yours," he said politely.

"Cheyenne Goodnight."

His lips curled into a tantalizing smile. "Well met, Miss Cheyenne. Your father tells me you do not dance." His tone hovered somewhere between bored and challenging, though she could not for the life of her tell which he meant, which meant she would have to ask.

She had never had to ask a man to clarify his words or his intentions.

Miffed, she held her hand out. "I imagine he told you I am a woman who makes her own choices."

Unperturbed, he offered her a crooked smile that lit his steel eyes aflame again. Cheyenne couldn't stop looking at his lips. "I'd think it'd be in your best interest to dance. With me."

"Pardon me?" She asked. Mr. Duke Channing wasn't saying anything he was supposed to.

"You must make exceptions to your rule."

"Only when forced.," she sputtered.

That set a gleam in his eyes which was positively sadistic.

"I mean when my father says I must," she said quickly to covering the rising embarrassment which she could feel creeping up her chest and neck. She was out of step here, thinking the conversation with this man would be easy.

Mr. Channing raised an eyebrow at her, which only served to make her angry. Who did this man think he was to make her dance with him? However had she thought him handsome only moments before? No man had ever flustered her so, and so quickly.

"You are very rude, Mr. Channing, to come challenge me in my father's house. You seem to not know your place as a visitor."

"Then let me try again," Mr. Channing said, a gentleness spreading across his features. "I'd like to dance with you."

"No," Cheyenne said, mostly to see what Mr. Channing would do with such a forward statement from her.

To her surprise, he laughed, loudly enough to draw the attention of several groups nearby. Cheyenne surprised herself with a quiet noise of pleasure at his reaction, and a smile pulled her lips.

"Let me dance with you," he said, the mirth and gentleness turning his heat and steel into honeyed warmth. Playing or not, he was good with words. "I want to hear about how you and your family have come to be here."

Wary still, but game to find out more about this man who could be a dusty cowboy one moment and a gentleman the next, she nodded.

"I will dance with you," she said demurely, lifting her hand for him again.

And Mr. Channing took her hand without another word and guided her toward the dance floor, where the band was readying for the next song.

She would dance with him and let him step on her toes when she spun them into a dance he surely would not know. Then let him see about his domineering attitude then.

And to her enduring surprise, he fell into the dance with fluid grace so that *she* nearly stumbled to keep up with the precision of his steps. Wherever this rebel marshal had learned to dance, they had taught him well.

He pulled her just closer than was appropriate, and she could feel the heat of him near her through her silks. Her hand on his arm told of hard-won muscle beneath his shirt and jacket, and skin so hot it would sear her. She imagined what sort of work had molded his body, and her stomach fluttered. Other men had been forward with her, and she had hit them with the sting of rejection. Other men had proposed, and she had said no. She had felt the flutterings of desire for a handsome face before, but she had not felt it quite so keenly as this. This desire to dive deep into the rawness of the feeling blossoming for this stranger who was fated to meet her on her path.

So close to him, she could see that there were green flecks in his gray eyes. His eyes which missed nothing, she noticed. She would not look away. She would rise to his challenge.

"How did you come to this place?" he asked as he turned

14

gracefully with her across the floor.

"The usual way," she replied gamely.

"No wonder you don't dance," Mr. Channing said. "You would knock over any man with your words at fifty yards."

Cheyenne smiled. This was a compliment to her, and while she suspected Mr. Channing had meant it as such, she forged ahead warily.

"Were you aboard the *Hartford*?" she asked, trying to temper the fire within her with cool conversation, knowing what his answer would be.

He shook his head. "I rode in from farther West in the Kansas Territory, New Mexico Territory."

"I love the West," she said simply. And it was true. The thought of that vast wilderness sent a thrill through her.

"The West is dangerous," he replied, and the smoldering look in his deep eyes told her that it wasn't only the land which held snares and traps. She was used to the stares of men, and though this one was more handsome than most, she knew it would be best to tread carefully.

"Existing in this world is dangerous. Far more so, I would think, if one sits still and does not venture beyond one's own front door," Cheyenne replied, and when she felt the middle finger of his left hand trace a little circle at the small of her back, the suggestive touch sent a wave of desire through her. Men had been more forward with her, but never so out in the open where anyone in the dance might see.

But Duke's eyes gave nothing away of his game. "You would not have so romantic a view of it were you on the trail. No one's life is worth a pin's fee out there."

She threw back her head and laughed, the thrill of pleasure still filling her. Laughter and pleasure—that was not how she had expected to spend her evening. "How do you think I arrived here, Mr. Channing? Do you think I transformed into a bird and flew? I took dusty trails—same as you."

She was keenly aware that he kept twirling her into the next dance—more dances than was proper. She felt her father's eyes at her back during the third dance with him, and she knew just as she had known that he had come from the West that he was spinning her into each dance with the knowledge that it was improper.

But if he wanted her to comment on it, he would be disappointed.

"What's your claim to fame, Mr. Channing?"

His lips curled into that sinuous smile again, a smile which might have ignited flames within her had she not been so keen on attempting to step on his toes. "I can kill a man at thirty-five yards. I have yet to meet a man faster on the draw."

He wasn't boasting. He simply told the truth. And she knew that in these parts, a sure shot, a quick shot, was the difference between life and death. "Well, that is sensational, Mr. Channing."

Yes, she had said the right thing then, for his eyes smiled at her, even for the glint of sparks on steel they still held.

Chapter 4

O ver the strings, a familiar sound reached Duke's ears. Gunfire. When he locked eyes with Cheyenne, he knew she'd heard it too.

"I must get you somewhere safe," he said, expecting her to wilt into his arms once she understood what the sound was.

Instead, she laughed, green eyes sharp and sparkling. "My dear Mr. Channing, did I not just make it clear that I am familiar with the dangers of the West? Of even going out one's door?"

Duke had known loose women to carry guns to protect themselves from aggressive customers, but to not be afraid of gunfire?

"I'm certain it's the McLaurys come to intimidate us. Whatever shall you do?" she asked. It sounded like a challenge. His ire rose.

"You stay here," he said, grasping for control of the situation.

She had the audacity to laugh again. "Come, this way," she grabbed his hand and pulled him toward an inconspicuous side door hidden behind a decorative curtain at the far side of the room. Opposite the direction everyone else ran. There, she slid a slim key into the lock and pulled them both into a hallway that ran the length of the building.

A hall that was full of supplies. Wooden crates stacked upon wooden crates with trade names stamped on the side. Cheyenne rushed him by them so quickly, he was only able to catch some of the names. But he'd seen enough—the names he recognized were those of arms and ammunitions manufacturers.

"What is all this?" he asked, interest piqued.

"'The West is dangerous,'" she repeated his own words back to him, eyes glittering with something that looked like excitement. And in her crimson silk dress and wide skirts, dark hair in curls pinned close about her face, a face and skin which, should it see more sun, he had seen on his scouts of Indian encampments, she looked positively feral, a woman ready for anything the West could throw at her. Ready to throw her own magic right back at anything which dared come for her.

Who was this woman?

He had to know, but he had to get control of the situation first. She could be leading them straight into the arms of the enemy for all he knew.

"Where are you going?" he hissed. "You'll get yourself killed. Or worse."

There was the haughty gleam in her eyes again. "I fear no man." And then she pulled him through another door and out into the night, the sound of gunfire on the opposite side of the building. Loud voices and a single cry broke the silence between gunshots.

He might've thought her a fool had he not felt the sheer force of her already, seen the intelligence glittering in her perfect green eyes. She was scintillating even in the confines of the modesty in the dance hall. And now, out alone in the darkness with her, she moved with the grace and confidence of any number of night creatures he'd seen on his travels. Coyotes, wolves, owls, mountain lions. Even encumbered by her dress and layers of frivolity every woman wore, she moved quietly and confidently.

With a wry grin, he wondered how well she moved out of all that. It was a dangerous though to be having about a woman of her class, but he'd had women of her status before. But that thought made him uneasy, for it was clear that Cheyenne Goodnight was in a class of her own. He would have to think long and hard about whether he wanted any more than stealing a kiss with her.

Cheyenne gave him a look in the dim light that told him she must've already said something, and he hadn't responded. "We're going to see what's going on. Or would you rather stay put and see if they set the building afire with people still in it?"

She had a point, but she didn't have to be so forward about it. Even the women in brothels pretended to be demure and ladylike. Cheyenne Goodnight affected neither, though it was clear that she was still a lady. "Lead on," he said.

Curious and intrigued by her confidence, he followed her as she led him through the dark. She was sure-footed even for the inky darkness which played tricks on his eyes as they walked. He was grateful that she knew the area so well she could walk it in the near total darkness.

"We should have grabbed a lantern at least," Duke whispered, keenly aware that the sound of the troublemakers was growing louder.

"I can see where we're going. Just stay with me," Cheyenne

replied, and when she looked at him, he could have sworn her eyes glowed a faint green. He shivered. Just another trick of the darkness.

Chapter 5

They passed a man lying in the summer prairie grasses at the far end of the street. The first shot they'd heard, surely. Cheyenne didn't react when she saw the man, only hoisted her skirts higher and picked up her pace. Candlelit windows of far-off farmhouses were barely visible, and the rising moon had only just begun giving him enough light to see well.

And he knew what they were seeking. He'd quit scouting for Indians when his conscience told him better to start scouting these troublemakers near the boundary with Missouri instead. Here where trouble arose in the form of men who thought they could lord over other men, he'd found more of his purpose. And roughing up border ruffians had become easy pickings for a sharpshooter.

In the cover of night, he was still a sure shot, but at shorter distances. If they could find these men before they found more trouble, it would save this town from much unneeded strife.

If *he* could find these men, that was. Cheyenne might know the lay of the town, but Duke knew the lay of these men's actions better than most. She was just a woman, if a pretty, smart-mouthed woman.

He patted an 1851 Colt Ranger in both side holsters, grateful he'd not left them in his room. Some fools had started calling it the Colt Navy, but it would always be a Ranger to him. Once a scout, always a scout, but damned if he would get lumped in with the men used that title for atrocities.

Noise ahead stilled them, and Duke reached out to grab Cheyenne's arm and still her. She shot a sharp look at him, and he had the same feeling that her green eyes were glowing faintly. Slightly uneasy, he let go of her arm and turned to assess what was before them. He reminded himself that he had seen magic in her earlier in the day, and he would do well to respect that.

"We need to get under cover," he whispered.

She nodded, and they left the soft dirt path, still warm from the day, and settled into the prairie grasses and limestone and scrubby brush at the side of the road.

"I have a plan," she whispered, her eyes sparkling with the same intelligence and mischief as they had at the dance.

Duke held up his pistols. "I assume it involves my pistols?"

He swore she grinned. "It can if you wish."

Not far ahead, a group of men on horseback came into view. They must've ridden away to regroup and reload, Duke reckoned, and now they were fixing to ride back into town and cause more chaos. Light from their lanterns threw strange shadows around them. Duke felt a chill. He shouldn't have let Cheyenne come out here with him, no matter that she'd led them straight to the trouble. As sure a shot as he was, they were outnumbered. He saw at least seven horses, and more might be just beyond the lanternlight.

The moon had risen enough that he could see more than the

outline of the woman next to him. She seemed as keen on this drama as he did. Unless she had a brace of pistols under those skirts of hers, though, they were apt to find more trouble than they could handle.

Cheyenne knelt in the dust, and her vibrant skirts seemed to shift color before his eyes, to become camouflage. He was about to ask her what she was doing when she pressed her hands into the dusty road, but her chanting stopped him cold.

She whispered words which he knew he would never understand, while a cool wind picked up around them.

The hair on his arms and neck rose, and he felt the same lightning sizzle like what had passed between them during the dance. Only this time, it felt as though it came straight from *her*.

The ground ahead of them began to steam. Behind their limestone shelf cover, Duke watched, rapt. As much as he didn't want to tear his eyes from the enigmatic woman next to him, he had to see what happened. The ruffians had readied themselves and their horses and were extinguishing their lanterns in favor of torches. The ring of light around the group grew as Cheyenne's chanting intensified

When the first dark tendril of smoke sprouted from the ground, Duke's first instinct was to shoot at it, but he held himself back.

And the tendrils become shapes of fog, shapes like tree branches with long, gnarled fingers on the ends. More smoke speared out of the ground, became what looked like the antlers of a great deer. Duke couldn't look away from the fantastic sight before him. And all while the woman next to him continued to mutter in a language which might've even been English, but he was so focused on the sight before him, the words didn't matter. But it did matter that *she* was the reason for these magnificent and terrifying spirits.

The dark figures rose from the ground, stretching taller into the night sky, taller than the tallest trees. Their hazy bodies bore the head and antlers of a deer, a long misshapen torso of a man and arms and legs which were far too long for their body. Half a dozen of the creatures rose from the soil, which remained undisturbed despite their enormous size. Together they strode to the men who had caused the ruckus, coming upon them before the men could even utter noises of terror.

They seemed to be made of dark smoke, of soot, of stuff which would blow away with the wind, but one reached out and plucked a would-be rioter from his saddle as easily as a cat would snatch up a mouse.

And then everyone and everything was in motion. Men screamed, cursed the Devil, some simply fell from their horses and lay still on the ground, dead from the terror. Duke, sensing his moment, whipped his guns from their holsters and fired into the frenzy. Just as quickly, he was reholstering, waiting to see what happened next.

Duke tore his eyes from the chaos to look at the woman next to him.

Cheyenne chanted through it all, hands pressed into the dirt, head bent, eyes squeezed shut. A preternatural wind tousled her hair and stirred her skirts. She was beautiful and terrifying at once, a feral creature he had no name for. He knew most men would run from the sight of such a creature, but he'd always been one to run into danger instead of away from it. She thrilled him more than anything he had experienced before.

Duke clenched his fists and remained still at Cheyenne's

side. The unnatural wind swirled around them still, stirring her hair and his clothes in the night. It moved like the wind of a dust devil, though no dust was lifted from where they hid.

Cheyenne's creatures cried out with a screech like that of a hawk and gave chase to the few rabble rousers who dared stand against them. When the shadow creatures drew near, they turned their horses and fled.

They chased the remaining men until Duke lost them to the darkness. The two men he'd shot lay still in the road. The still forms of men slain by fear lay further off. Goodnight and the rest wouldn't be far behind.

He prayed the creatures didn't return to their mistress, who had turned to regard him with something like humor. Her eyes glowed that soft green again, daring him to speak, to move, to say something which would get his tongue in a bind.

He had heard tales, had seen things in the West which defied all of God's reason, had experienced the other end of it during his disastrous time as a scout.

He stared at Cheyenne, working hard to school his features, to control his words. He wouldn't turn into a bumbling idiot just because he'd seen something so fantastic happen right before him.

"I wanted to help," Cheyenne said, misunderstanding the look on his face.

"It seems you have," Duke said.

"Yes, but it's not enough," Cheyenne replied.

Duke understood the not enough part. That's why he'd left to become a marshal in the first place. Life was rough on the trail. Life was rough fighting with ruffians. But life was infinitely rougher at home where he would never escape his guilt. Not that he had done a good job of escaping it anyway.

It followed him wherever he went.

"I am enamored with what you do," Cheyenne said. "I can't ever imagine becoming bored. So many exciting sights to see. I long to feel that rush myself, to feel the wind in my hair as my horse races across the prairie."

Duke scoffed, "You understand it's much more dangerous than that. I risk my life every day under the burning sun."

"Better to die having done something under the burning sun than waste away indoors over embroidery," Cheyenne said.

Chapter 6

She felt his eyes on her, could feel the questions he wanted to ask searing into her skin. But she was tired of hiding from everyone, was tired of pretending she was someone she wasn't in front of polite society. So perhaps she could share this with another rebel, another who lived outside the laws of the land and survived.

"Where did you learn that?" Duke asked.

She knew he didn't mean her pretty words.

"I was born with it," she replied to the simple question. Relief washed over her, and she sighed, which her corset appreciated.

Duke recovered himself and found that his relief at winning the night was outpaced by the advantage they had. "It seems you should hold the advantage in every situation. You are a boon for this town, even if your advantage was unfair."

The statement surprised her. She would have expected fear or judgment or calling upon the wrath of God, but this? She didn't stay silent long. Words had always come easily to her, especially in the face of a challenge. She knew who she was, knew her own worth, knew that while the world owed her nothing, she wanted more of it than it would have given her in a quiet life of marriage and children in Boston. "I am not all-powerful. I am mortal just like you. Would you have rather I walked up to them, breasts bared, and let them have me?"

Duke sputtered, and he was not a man who sputtered. "No, but..."

"Would you consider it a fair fight when you are the surest shot west of the Mississippi? When your likeness is advertised in every town and men ready themselves to go to death before your pistols?"

"Cheyenne," he said on a growl, even as he liked the way her name fell from his lips.

The way he said her name was at once sensual and annoying. "I do not know what you would have me do, then, but protect this town with what power I have at my disposal."

"Goddamn, woman! Can you take a breath so I can get a word in?"

She carelessly wiped the sweat from her hands on the grass, losing patience. Conjuring took the wind from her, and she'd never had to converse so soon after. This man had gone from guarding her back and assisting her in a fight to annoying her in nearly a single breath. How was this supposed to be her one true match? She held her tongue, though, to see what else might fall from this man's mouth.

"You are a witch, Cheyenne."

Somedays, she loathed the term. "I have a gift. I would not be so quick to put a name on it."

But Duke was unfazed, excited even for his quick judgement of her. "I have seen things in the West, you know. There are some tribes in the southwest who conjure, but nothing like I have seen from you."

"I am a witch—your term, Mr. Channing—because my father's mother was. Your misconceptions about the native peoples of this continent betray your ignorance. A *witch* to them is evil."

"But your mother must've been an Indian."

"My mother was a woman who loved my father," she said, and the wind rose around her, snapping at her hair. A dust devil kicked up a few paces from them. Duke stood his ground. He'd seen enough of wild animals to know you didn't turn your back on them, and you dare not run.

"Then why isn't she here with you?"

"She died giving birth to me. Her last words were my name." And others which she couldn't bring herself to tell him. Not him, not now. How this had gotten away from her control so quickly, she didn't understand.

"I want to know more about you."

Her eyes flashed in the night. "Then you must ask the right questions."

Duke stepped toward her, and she stepped back. "Every time I move to you, you move away." He imagined his hand on the small of her back, her arched against him in an embrace. The wariness in Cheyenne's eyes, the way her breathing quickened, told him she, too, thought of more with him

"My grandmother was Sioux, as your mother was," he pressed on.

"And you wish us to be cousins, do you?" The wind died as her humor rose again.

"I do wish us to quit this place before your father arrives. And to find more time to know more about you." And that was honest, he knew. He wanted to know what those lips felt like, but he wanted to hear them tell their story, too.

She seemed to consider that. "Yes, that would be smart. He prefers I not do that, you know. He fears I'll draw attention

29

to myself eventually."

Even in the moonlight, she was captivating. Her skirts were their glorious crimson again, and the sight of her made him want as he'd never wanted before. She was at once exotic and familiar, something that was at once out of reach and near him just the same. "You'd draw attention regardless."

They stole back into town, and Cheyenne was careful to keep her distance from the man walking beside her. She could feel his eyes on her still, asking questions that she was not yet certain how to answer.

Chapter 7

Cheyenne paced her room, unable to sleep. Her soft chair by the hearth was uncomfortable, the dwindling fire was too hot, her rooms too stuffy. She stood before her mirror and bared her teeth at her reflection, willing the tension coursing through her to release.

She craved the wind from the open fields, the pockets of cool air in the low areas near the creek. She craved the moonlight. The way the moon felt on her skin, how it restored her. How had she spent so much of her life away from this freedom, chained to a city which offered little escape into nature, into the places which brought her to life?

But she knew. She had done it for her father and her mother, both of whom loved her dearly and wanted only the best for her. Her father had done his best to keep himself upbeat and happy for her, but she knew how much of a toll her mother's death had taken on him. How much it had done to her, too. How much it continued to do.

And she had thought that when she met the man her mother spoke of with her last words, everything would fall into place. But after the whirlwind of being next to him in the night, of seeing the ease with which he used his pistols, of his odd acceptance despite judgement of her abilities, she felt only confused.

And what had she thought? That this man would fall into her arms and pledge undying love for her? Is that what she truly had thought?

She had.

The realization churned her stomach. Everything in life had come easy for her, despite knowing that life was not easy. It humbled her in a manner which she had not expected.

And now that she was supposed to have what she wanted, she didn't know what to do with it. She had thought so long about coming west and simply having it, that she didn't know what to do now. Were they to court each other? Would he come to know that they were meant to be? It was clear he wanted her, wanted to embrace her, but love her? How did that work?

Cheyenne turned away her from reflection in the mirror. It was her mother's face she saw there, the face which she had looked into when she had first opened her eyes. That black silk hair, the golden skin. Her hair and skin Cheyenne had gotten. Her eyes, the almost unnatural green, had come from her father's side, and from his mother before him, the woman who had passed her gifts onto Cheyenne.

And what good she could do with those gifts now, here, in this place.

She had to admit that she'd conjured partially to see if it would frighten Duke Channing. And it hadn't. He hadn't run, he hadn't said she was of the Devil, he hadn't so much as flinched. Certainly, he had seemed in awe of her power once they were safe, but frightened?

She wondered what it would take to frighten Duke Channing. Would it take turning him into a rabbit? To show him how powerful she truly was?

Cheyenne frowned. This was not how she had been raised. She scolded herself. Her grandmother would have had stern words with her granddaughter about how to conduct herself and her power sooner than later should she continue those thoughts. Grandmother would probably know anyway, would say something to her in the coming days about it. Well, Cheyenne would have to answer for her thoughts then.

And she had not done anything *wrong* by conjuring in his presence, per say, but her conscience would not settle and nor could she.

He hadn't been what she'd expected. A heart full of rebellion? The man was domineering and arrogant. And while she could feel the heat of a lustful man radiating from him, she felt no desire from him for anything else save base desire and an open curiosity for her abilities.

She would find an answer to this problem. Mother would not be wrong. She couldn't be. Not when she had given her last breath to tell Cheyenne of her fate. It was too important.

With a huff, she made certain that Father was abed, then she stole out into the night. Duke Channing or not, she could go find her own peace under the moonlight.

Chapter 8

J ust as he had been compelled to look up at her when he had first seen her, he felt pushed to leave his room and go out into the moonlight.

After the raucous events of earlier that night, the simple hum of crickets soothed nerves frayed by the evening's altercation. He hated killing a man, but if it meant keeping his own life, he was prepared to do whatever it took. By God, that was his right as a man, and he wasn't going to lie down and take it.

He wandered toward the river, moonlight his guide through the tall grasses just off the beaten path taken by steamboat passengers arriving for their new life on the prairie. With the water still a way's off, he swerved further off the path and into the trees. Something there waited for him. He felt the pull deep in his belly, deep within the place inside him which was all man.

He followed a deer trail through a thicket. When he saw a dim light in the clearing ahead, he slowed his steps. Memories of every man he had hunted floated behind his eyes. Moving soundlessly through sand and cacti in the southwest. Crawling on his belly through scrubby brush of the West so near the mountains, he could smell them. Shifting silently through the prairie, hoping the Indian didn't hear him before he drew his pistol.

He frowned. That last memory tormented him, turned his belly sour every time he thought of it. The scouts with him hadn't cared who they shot on their assignment. The only good Indian was a dead one to them. And their superiors had thought much the same, though the way they phrased the assignments were with the stiff formality of wars long gone.

Duke had vowed never to kill another Indian again after that day. That had been no noble cause. So he became a U.S. Marshal and set his sights on the men causing trouble in Kansas and Missouri. Kansas would have their free election. He would see to it.

He took a deep breath and shook the dread from his person. This was no time for unpleasant memories. He knew what must lay in the clearing ahead.

He pressed ahead through a path of trees which seemed to part for him. He steeled himself. This was no time to be frightened like a boy. He recognized a predator when he saw one, and he was very certain Cheyenne could smell fear if he let it control him.

She was nearly naked in the moonlight, dancing in a clearing. And she very clearly thought she was alone. Good, she hadn't sensed him. Only a thin shift covered her skin which seemed to throw moonlight back into the night, lighting the world around her. He pitied the men who thought they could walk into this town and take it. They had no idea what they were up against. But he aimed to find her out.

As he watched, she lifted her arms and let down her hair, scattering the pins to the wind with a flick of her wrists. Then she lifted her shift and cast it to the ground too. Even from his distance, he saw the glory that was her body. Her skin was deeply golden even for the pearl moonlight playing over her.

Fireflies rose up out of the grass to spin around her, drawn to her even as he was. If he had been enchanted, he was a willing participant. He would've had to be dead to not feel quickened by her sensual form, to not feel the lust which uncurled from that place deep within him and wrapped around him.

The memory of her at the dance, of his first impression of her as a striking and singular woman, had only crystalized from there. Her conjuring which had driven away the ruffians and now this, this reckless display of her self, which he knew he was intruding upon, though he couldn't turn his own self away.

Even as he knew that desire was a thing to be controlled, he wanted her with a primal urge which nearly unseated him. He wanted her as a man wanted a woman. No, he wanted her as an animal, to couple with her in a frenzy of bared teeth and indelicate movements.

But he checked himself.

Control was a man's greatest weapon. Control was what made his hand so sure on the trigger. Control was what made him the quickest shot. Control was what made him.

When he strode into the clearing, she did not start, nor did she race to her clothes. He had seen loose women less comfortable with themselves. He didn't miss the coolness in her eyes when he approached, though. She finally reached for her shift, though, and he found himself remiss. He wanted to keep drinking in the sight of her.

"If you try to run, I'll turn you into rabbit," she said with a wicked smile.

He was uncertain enough that he didn't want to push her too much. Just yet, anyway. "You're a witch, Cheyenne. And even if I haven't come here of my own free will, I wanted to see what pulled me."

Those green eyes challenged him to speak again. He didn't satisfy her by saying anything else. "You think I'll turn you into a toad, or do you seek a love potion?"

"I have my great love already."

He could have sworn there was hurt and shock in her eyes, but it was quickly replaced by fire that snapped and sparked at him. "Then why are you in a clearing at midnight with a lewd woman and not with her?"

He chuckled and reached for her. She stepped back just as smoothly, leaving him to only catch the briefest touch of the ends of her silken locks. "You are anything but a hoyden, Miss Cheyenne."

"You don't know me well enough to say."

"Your looks tell me you are no stranger to a man's touch."

He didn't miss the hurt this time. "My innocence is intact, but do not take me for a fool. I know my worth. I will give myself to the pleasure of a man should I choose. I want to see the fire which is kindled between two souls, but I've yet to see if such a man exists who can entice me both mind and body."

"We'll see about that." He closed the distance between them and pulled her roughly against him, the way he'd imagined doing half the night with her already. The dance, the skirmish with rebels in the night, their conversations, coursed between them. He could feel her hummingbird heart racing beneath her full breasts, saw the starlight in her eyes and the half open mouth that didn't know if it should curse him or let him continue. He settled the matter by crushing his lips to hers, claiming that smart mouth before it could say something else.

He didn't expect her to respond like she did. He expected the same as he'd found in every town he'd stopped in. The women he'd seen were either meek or desperate and neither way left him feeling comfortable with himself. He didn't expect her to return his kiss with a passion that rivaled his own, a passion that spoke of a zest for life, of a knowledge of her own mortality, of a desire for more than what life offered those who did not reach for what they wanted.

And he knew what power was, the great sight of twisters on the prairie. It was power that hummed between them. The wind rushed up around them, though the night had been still, the skies clear.

She gave and gave with her mouth, threading her own hands up his shoulders and into his hair. She tipped his hat off his head so she could angle her mouth to better nip at each lip in turn. Her head spun with his magic, spun with the sudden feeling of desire which sprung up between them.

Something pulled them closer, had his hands skimming over the light cotton shift which covered her. Over the sinuous curve where her back met her hips, over the curve of her waist, made defined by years of corsets and perfect posture. Just touching her there without so many layers of fabric between them nearly snapped his control.

Heat for her burned through him and onto her skin. His hands found the swells of her breasts, and she cried out with such want, that he kept exploring, kept discovering that he needed to feel her skin against his. And great God, her breasts fit so perfectly in his hands…

He stopped.

An alarm sounded within him. Of course she felt perfect. She was a witch. She could make him think or believe anything she wanted. He hesitated. Those pleading eyes didn't seem to think she held all the power, but he couldn't stop thinking that perhaps this wasn't all he believed it to be. All that he felt it to be.

Chapter 9

"**H**ave you enchanted me?" he asked, breathless. The words fell from his lips from somewhere in the fog he felt near her. Great God, it was as though he couldn't taste her enough. He was a man starving, wanting, needing her. And when she gave in to him, becoming molten and liquid under his touch, the more he drank, the more he wanted.

She responded with laughter which cracked the night apart. The crickets and cicadas stilled. The grasses in which they stood stilled. He swore the night air itself stopped breathing.

"Would you care?" she asked, the green glow from earlier in the night back again.

The kiss they had shared still sparked between them. "No. Even if it's an unfair advantage," he continued with a sly grin.

She felt him goading her, and oh, how it nipped at her. But this time it wasn't with annoyance. It was with something far hotter. She had imagined a man who would complete her, but Duke? She hadn't imagined a man who would challenge her, who would push her to be better and do more. She hadn't imagined that he would appear like this, like a rebel on the wind, but she wanted it. Wanted it more than she knew.

He leaned in to take her lips again, and she pressed herself against him, giving her kiss to him willingly. His hands roamed, but this time they were slower, more measured. This was a man who had known pleasure before. And why should he not? Cheyenne wondered. A man who knew what he was doing was far less dangerous than a man who didn't. Or so she thought.

His hands found her hair, and they ran wild in her own untamed locks. Gone was the hair piled on her head during the day, pins stabbing her every which way. She felt wild and free out here in the grasses with him, beneath the big night sky which promised them everything and nothing all at once.

Somewhere in the distance, a chorus of coyotes began their night song. Had the wild woman before him turned into one and run off into the darkness, he wasn't certain he would have been surprised.

He wondered as he tasted the skin of her inner wrist if she could transform herself as she promised to transform him should he irk her. He smiled as he drew his teeth gently across her wrist, drawing a sigh from her.

It seemed she was made of pieces of the night. For just another stop on the prairie, he was glad to have found the brightest jewel it had to offer.

He nipped at the smooth skin of her jaw. There he tasted the rosewater she must have splashed her face with before she'd stepped out into the night. And another taste, something far more exotic, the taste of a woman, tantalized his roving lips and teeth even more.

"Don't you miss Boston?" he asked between tastes of her exquisite neck.

Her eyes fluttered open and closed, then open. She looked

like she was struggling to keep them open. Good. For some reason, he liked that he could wield this kind of power over her.

"I miss only the little conveniences that it offered," she said on the next intake of breath. "That I may have walked down the street for a new dress or paper or a million other things. I can live without those things for a time, though."

"For a time? Do you expect to return?" And here he drew his fingers down her neck, which was golden tan even under the moonlight, but had the sheen of pearl. Fitting, he thought, that in one fleeting thought he would think her the night and the next she would shift, and he would see her as rare stones and precious metals. He had never considered himself a poet, but he'd read enough during his school years to remember those who were. And he might not know her well, but he'd bet his life that she'd laugh in his face if he told her either of those things.

"I hope not," Cheyenne sighed, then visibly shook off the melancholy thought. Interesting. Most women would take that as an opening to speak about what they wanted out of life, to tell the man they were dancing with—or in this case, stealing kisses with—so as to see how they measured up to his plans. She wasn't stupid. She had avoided the question on purpose.

"I've never kissed a rebel cowboy before," she said with a smirk, pushing them even further from the question.

If only she knew. He fought a frown. If she knew, she'd know that he was from much grander stock than the rebel cowboy she took him for.

"I'm curious about whom you have kissed, though," he said as he trailed his own kisses down her neck. Her head fell back in ecstasy.

"You wish me to kiss and tell? No gentleman would ever deign to ask such a question."

He pressed a smoldering kiss against the swell of her breast through her nightgown. "I am no gentleman, Miss Cheyenne. I'm a bad man."

He felt her shiver against him. "And do you think me a bad woman, for the things I do, for the things I know?"

His answer was not direct. "You are quite trusting to be out here alone. Out here with me," he said. "That is either a woman who is loose with her morals or quite certain of herself and her person."

"I can fend for myself. As you've seen."

"And what if I overpowered you here, had my way with you?"

Something dark came into her eyes, and perhaps her eyes changed, then, grew black. He wouldn't have been surprised. "Why, I'd have to turn you into a rabbit, Mr. Channing. Are you trying to frighten me?"

"Even with your hands pinned under you?"

The dark look turned more sensual. "You certainly know how to charm a lady."

He captured her lips with his, and they spoke no more for a time.

Chapter 10

When Cheyenne woke the next morning, she was determined to go about her day as though Duke Channing weren't in town and very likely sleeping in a bed at the hotel next door. She had given too much of herself the night before, had been overeager. And while part of her was elated, she found the other part of herself to be terrified. The confidence she had affected in front of him had sizzled out by the morning. What he had said about having his great love already bothered her. If that were true, then he must not be the man meant to be with her. So why did she feel so certainly that he was?

The conflict warring within her, she listened as her father spoke with the sheriff and his deputies about what had occurred the night before. And while she was pleased to know that no one had seen or heard of her conjuring, she knew there was much more work to be done before they rid themselves of this threat.

Duke Channing slipped in the back of the meeting room, listening but not participating. He wanted to hear about the night's events as much as he wanted to get a look at Miss

Goodnight in the light of day. And there she sat, back straight, hair curled and pinned, her dark blue silks a bright jewel amongst the drab scenery around her.

A grin pulled at his lips. More poetic words for the bright bird who had settled on the prairie. He left silently before Miss Goodnight could see him.

Cheyenne turned around when she felt the air in the room change. The door was just closing shut. A charge was still in the air, though, and she wondered about Mr. Channing. Even for the bellyache she had wondering about his words, she did still want to see him.

After the meeting, she changed and followed the feeling to the stables. She had an itch to ride out onto the prairie, and there he was, tending to his own animal. There was a gentleness about his person as he stood there talking softly to the beautiful mare, stroking the animal's fetlock and brushing her neck with straw until she gleamed.

He took one look at her in her riding habit and then went back to brushing his horse. His face had closed up into an unreadable rock, though, and Cheyenne felt remiss.

The silence that hung between them was pregnant with all that had transpired between them the night before.

"Were you at the meeting?" Cheyenne asked into the silence.

Duke shook his head and scoffed. "You would make a good scout, Miss Goodnight."

"They said nothing about having your help, though they did mention the sureness of the shots which felled the McLaury men. They were glad to see them gone."

"Tell me more about the McLaurys," Duke said, ignoring the compliment and trying not to steal too many glances at Cheyenne. Even in her flowing riding habit, he wanted her, but that want was bolstered by admiration. Strange that only a day of knowing someone would merit that.

"They lived in Missouri for a time," Cheyenne began, playing with several pieces of straw. Duke watched her begin to weave them in her fingers, turning the straw into something it wasn't before. Was it magic or simple dexterity? He wouldn't have been surprised by either.

"The family is large, as I told you," she continued. "They once lived in St. Louis but were run out of town quite quickly, from my understanding. Even for those who accepted their presence in Missouri, their tactics were...are...less than savory."

"Do tell," Duke said. The more information he had about the ruffians, the better.

"Ah, how do I put this delicately?" Cheyenne kept her weaving. What would she make with those nimble fingers of hers?

"I don't need delicate," Duke said.

"No," Cheyenne said with a sigh of remembrance for their kisses the night before. She could still feel the searing heat of his lips along her neck, his hands in her hair holding her head just so. "No, I don't suppose you do."

She didn't speak for several moments as she added more pieces of straw to the creation. The design began to take shape in her hands, a star or a sun or something of the like.

"They began capturing those who disagreed with them. They would fill them full of whiskey, would ply them with money sometimes too, I think. And then they would load up a wagon full of them and cross the border."

"All the way from St. Louis?"

"It is my understanding that they would spend weeks with

these individuals, keeping them full of spirits."

"And then?"

"They forced them to vote in elections with fraudulent, names, places of residence. Full of liquor and threats to their family, what other choice did they have? And when the authorities showed up, the McLaurys were nowhere to be found. Only poor sods sick on liquor having no idea where they were. Many of them died or never saw their families again. Sheriff Monroe has taken many of them in here, to begin new lives because many of them do not remember a time before they were taken, so much did the McLaurys poison them with drink and God knows what else."

Duke was quiet when she finished, and he gave his horse one last pat before he ushered her back to her stall. He would not be riding this moment. No, there was too much to think about.

"What has the town done about this? I saw your store of ammunitions. You would be a fool to think that the McLaurys don't suspect you will defend yourselves against them."

"That's just it," Cheyenne said, the light of defiance returning to her eyes. "We have thus far only allowed ourselves to just keep them from taking the town. Besides my own attempt the other night, we have not mounted an attack against them. It would be foolish of me to think that they will not do something after what I have done. Not that they will know it was me. But they will think it was the Devil or some such, I'm certain."

"Pity for them," Duke mumbled. He imagined men unaware of Cheyenne's power trying to take her away. It didn't end well for them in his imagination.

"And what about you and your people?" Cheyenne ventured.

She chanced a look around to make certain they were alone. "Are there other…marshals nearby?"

Duke looked like he still didn't want her knowing his true occupation. "My commander is posted up near Fort Riley. There will be other rangers, scouts, and marshals arriving over the next several weeks. Rumors of soldiers, too, but I wouldn't hold my breath."

"To help flush out this particular group of individuals?"

"Them and others. And I need to begin planning how to draw them away from town," Duke said to no one in particular.

"I can help you with that."

He turned to her, "You would only get hurt."

Cheyenne made a noise that Duke didn't have time to feel wounded by. "I know what a dangerous place I've come to, Duke Channing. The snares and rabbit holes of the prairie are known to me."

"Then you will know just how serious I am when I say that you must stay out of this."

Cheyenne got nose to nose with him and all he noticed was how wonderful she smelled. God, did she bathe daily? She smelled fresh and lovely, just like a lady from Boston should. Even in the night, she had smelled lovely, felt lovely against him.

"I will not stay out of my own business. You can either work with me or you can work at this on your own. Good luck killing scores of men without my knowledge and my…." she was at a loss for words for a moment. "For my skills," she finished finally, hot from having to defend herself. And Duke was so close, and he had quite the smirk on his face.

"Are you laughing at me?" she asked hotly. She had the most unladylike thought that she wanted to put a fist right into that slightly crooked but very handsome nose of his. Maybe it would straighten out him and his handsome appendage.

"I would never laugh at you, Cheyenne Goodnight. You are much too pretty and smart for that."

He hadn't stepped away from her. She could feel the heat of him still, just like at the dance, like when he had kissed her. It was as though lightning was caught between them. Well, he certainly made a good raincloud, she supposed.

She felt flustered, but she didn't want to step away. To step away would show him that he had won this...whatever it was.

A hand brushed her sleeve gently, so gently. It was a modest touch, after they had shared so much more the night before.

"Do you regret last night, Miss Cheyenne?"

Her eyes flashed. Good. He'd gotten more of that sweet anger out of her. It was amusing to rile her.

"No," she said flatly. If anyone were to come in, this would be the height of inappropriateness. Well, the night before had been worse, she mused, but this was nearly just as bad.

"Then show me."

"Excuse me?"

"Show me that it wasn't a mistake."

"I beg your pardon. I am not a circus animal to be ordered around at your whim. I enjoyed last night very much, thank you very much, but I don't feel that a stable is quite the place for..."

And with that, he claimed her lips for his own again. He'd never been one for stealing kisses. Stealing innocence, yes, but not stealing kisses.

But Cheyenne was different. Her kisses were different. He'd expected the kiss today to feel drole after their excitement under the stars, because how could it now? It was the way of things. But it wasn't. Her lips were softer today, even more willing to part for him. He had taken her by surprise the night before, but it seemed she was expecting this today.

Her lips parted eagerly for him, but her tongue tested the waters tentatively. She drew back once to laugh, and he ravished her neck. There, the skin was softer yet, and smelled of night flowers and roses. He nipped at the delicate skin there, relishing the way she sighed and arched into him. He curled an arm around her waist to keep her there, snug against him.

She'd never known this kind of want. The kind where she wanted to throw all caution to the wind. His kisses, his questions, his not-so-subtle needling at her had kindled something within her that took her breath away. And when he kissed her, she forgot to wonder about his supposed great love, so thoroughly did he steal all the thoughts from her head.

Chapter 11

"**I** want more of you," Duke said against her neck.

Cheyenne was dizzy from what his lips were doing to her sensitive skin, like when she had too much wine at dinner. Her neck and shoulders tingled even when his lips moved to her jaw, the side of her face.

His lips made her want to do reckless things, things which no lady should want to do.

But she wanted to.

And she knew how dangerous it was. She had heard rumors of it in Boston, had seen girls just out in society suddenly disappear, only to appear again walking with a baby in a pram in the park with a husband.

But here on the prairie, to be a rebel felt like the only way to be.

"Come upstairs with me," she whispered. "There are too many eyes here."

He watched her with eyes full of want for her.

They went into through the servants' door in the back of the building, and she pulled him by the hand as though she felt the same urgency that he did. There was an innocence about her that was not the innocence of others. She was innocent but aware of the repercussions. How much easier his life would've been if he'd had her kind of wisdom in his younger years.

In the kitchen, he pressed her against the wall next to the door and stole with his lips whatever she had opened her mouth to say. He felt the teenager again, insatiable, uncaring of whose eyes saw them. Was this simply the next part of his life, or did Miss Cheyenne Goodnight do something to him that no one else had?

She broke away with stars in her eyes. "Not here," she whispered, taking in the empty room. It was unusual that Cook wasn't there. She pulled him toward the stairs, then dropped his hand to hitch up her habit and ascend.

Up in the hall, Duke froze. It was as though a transformation had happened. He was suddenly in town, Boston, perhaps, anywhere more established. There was every sign of wealth here that one could fit into a space, and yet it was not gaudy or ostentatious. His own mother could not have done a better job of picking the finery to fit into the place.

"How long have you been here?" he asked suddenly.

"Two years." She took in the ornate doors, the plush rugs that ran down the hall. Ah, yes, he wouldn't have been suspecting this. She smiled. This was their oasis in the desert. She preferred to be out running on the prairie but having some comforts did help pass the time.

"How many servants do you have?"

She puzzled at the question. It wasn't one she expected from a rogue on the road. "We brought ten with us. I suspect we will hire more once we build a house. That is some time off, though. Why do you care?" she asked as she pulled him into a perfectly adorned sitting room. She locked the door behind them and pocketed the key.

He pulled her close against him, desire raging through him still. Here were more mysteries from Miss Cheyenne, more intrigue. He felt he could relax here in this airy, comfortable place. The brothels in the West left a lot to be desired, but this was no brothel.

In another moment, Cheyenne had forgotten about Duke's strange questions as his mouth assaulted her every inch of bare skin. Her neck, her wrists, that spot above her breasts which was flushed with pleasure now. She felt like she had when she'd had the punch at Lady Sierra's party in Boston. All dizzy with the sweetness of it.

He pressed her back against the pillows of a settee. Roving hands found her stockinged feet, slid from the top of her pretty foot all the way up to her knee. Her stomach churned with desire and nervousness. How would it feel to have him touch her? She had only ever imagined, had only ever seen the erotic images in the books which were passed around by the society in Boston.

He paused and caught her eyes with his. The eyes of a man consumed with desire, the eyes of a man who got what he wanted. And in the moment, she wanted it too.

"Yes!" she whispered on a sharp intake of breath, answering some question which he had not spoken aloud. While it should have unnerved him, it only served to make him want her more, now, and quickly.

His fingers kept snaking up her leg, feeling at the hollow behind her knee, teasing at her inner thigh, which she felt was damp with sweat.

His fingers slipped through her petticoats, and she felt the lightest touch over her most sensitive place. She gasped at the electricity that went through her.

"You are a rake," she said with a weak laugh. Her head spun with want, and she swore she heard the beat of a drum somewhere. No, the heartbeat of the prairie, which lived within her. Her head thrown back, she laughed again, this time to feel the pleasure of it vibrate through her as his touch between her legs seemed to.

His fingers grazed over her womanhood again. "Such an old-fashioned term. Are you certain you haven't been reading things young ladies ought not?"

She gripped the cushions so she wouldn't cry out. "I certainly—oh, my God!—have not. I couldn't possibly think you've done otherwise yourself."

Her desire was a palpable thing against his skin, and he could feel the heat of her all the way through him. She was flushed and beautiful, her perfect mouth an 'o' of pleasure.

Leaning down, he kissed her knee and sent her into shudders. It should have only been refreshing, but it tugged at his guilt to see her so overcome at his attentions. This was no woman pretending to feel pleasure so the man would feel he was getting what he wanted. This was a woman feeling pleasure from her skin that sizzled straight into her soul.

They both wanted this pleasure; that was plain to see. And feel. And when he slipped a finger inside her, she gripped the couch so hard it groaned in protest. His own desire strained against his pants, and it throbbed with each new sound he drew from Cheyenne.

"Duke!" she said on her next great exhale. It was hard to breathe with the molten pleasure she felt. She could feel how slick her thighs were with it. She had no time to be ashamed of it, for just then Duke slipped another finger inside her and she forget even her own name.

A primal rhythm beat between them, and Cheyenne lost herself in the drumbeat of the prairie within her. Duke gave and gave as she took. Took all the pleasure he could give to her. My God, how was it possible for a person to feel like they were floating like this?

And a crescendo was coming. She felt it rise within her, burning even hotter than the molten pleasure she felt. Where it should have burned her, it only served to fill her further, to open and fill places within her which she did not know were empty.

Flushed with desire, she shuddered with her release against his fingers, and it was like nothing she had ever felt before. She had touched herself before in the privacy of her room, but to share that with another person instead of just hearing about it? It was another thing entirely.

Her world became a blur of color and light and all she heard was Duke's quiet laugh as he slid his fingers from her. The molten pleasure cooled, but the memory of its warmth remained, filling the empty places within her still.

She opened her eyes to find Duke watching her. And as she did, he slid his fingers into his mouth and licked her essence from them. And it stirred something within her to watch something so intimate. Words of their fated union were on her tongue, ready to leap out.

And then he was offering to help her stand, to help her rearrange her skirts. Her legs were weak and wobbly, and she leaned on him for support. She looked in his eyes when she did, and he held her there for a long moment, each seeking something in the other's eyes.

She wanted to laugh, though. She wanted to talk about what had just transpired. Duke clearly did not. Well, that suited her fine. He was older than she, and more experienced, so he probably didn't want so young a woman yammering on about her first...experience. They would have time enough for that, she knew. She could wait.

There was a noise on the stairs and they both looked to the door. The moment gone, Cheyenne hurried him to the servants' stairs and bid him farewell. Silent still, he took her chin between his fingers and gave her that soul searing look again. He opened his mouth to speak, but at the sound of a door closing down the hall, he settled for crushing his lips to Cheyenne's, then quickly and silently heading down the stairs.

Cheyenne took her weak legs back to her room, where she sat in her chair by the fire and let her mind wander over the last hour, amazed and without words for once in her life.

She was just a diversion, Duke tried to tell himself as he slipped down the stairs. She was only a means to an end while he was here. Why that thought might make him feel guilty, he wasn't certain. He wouldn't have normally been above taking the young lady's virginity but seeing as she was a witch and her father was his best ally against the McLaurys, well...he would have to tread carefully there.

He was grateful for the company, but the itch to move on, to chase the outlaws grew stronger. He would need to tackle the McLaurys here, then get out of town. At least, that was what he kept telling himself as he slipped into the hotel and to his room, where he found himself remiss that he would soon be washing the exquisite scent of Cheyenne Goodnight from his hands.

Chapter 12

How did the world keep going as though nothing had happened? Duke had awakened something in her, something which called to her magic as much as it did to her as a woman. Was this love? Was this fate? Cheyenne, sitting at her lacquered table in front of a small mirror, brushed her hair while she daydreamed and mulled over all that had happened.

The day had been cloudy and mild, perhaps a sign of things to come. Autumn was still far off, but today she could almost believe the dog days of summer were over. Cheyenne had a lesson that evening, and though she had not seen Duke that day, it did not lessen the elation which had carried her through the night and that day.

When she arrived in the sitting room her grandmother was already waiting for her.

An almost cool breeze ruffled the lace curtains in her grandmother's sitting room (Oh, how she longed to be on that settee again in her own sitting room with Duke!), the room where she stored her magical wares.

Cheyenne remembered being young and sneaking into her grandmother's chambers in their house in Boston. Dozens of times, she opened the drawers of the large, charcoal colored cabinet that housed a hundred tiny drawers and hundreds more bits of stone and feather and crystals and rocks and many ground spices and things for which she had no name. Sometimes, she touched, sometimes she simply looked when her own magic warned her from touching or getting too close.

Looking back, her grandmother must have known that she was in there snooping around, but she never said anything. Perhaps because Cheyenne never harmed herself or made a mess of the stores, or perhaps because her grandmother wanted her to learn should she do something wrong. She had never asked, but she always remembered the awe she felt when she was within that room and with those magical items.

"One must hone their magic," Frances said, standing straighter than she usually did.

Cheyenne waited, rapt. She had long waited for the time when her grandmother would show her the extent of her powers, would give her more instruction than she was able to in Boston.

"How have you lived this long not able to stretch your magical legs?" Cheyenne asked. "I felt I was going mad in the city, unable to practice what I am."

Her grandmother laughed, her eyes not quite so milky today. Magic gave her Sight, allowed her to see better than even if her physical eyes worked as they used to. "Dear girl, I spent my summers in the country, traveled to places where magic is accepted. I had many opportunities to conjure, to practice. I was saddened to see that with the way the world turned, you did not have as much of a opportunity. We have done some of our own in the summer, but now, let us immerse ourselves in earnest. You have much to learn."

And learn she did. Cheyenne knew that she had only begun to touch the kind of power that she could have eventually.

As dusk faded and night came on, Frances guided her to the large windows, which Cheyenne thew open for her.

"It is a new moon. You know why this is important." It was a statement.

Cheyenne nodded.

"See the stars above?"

"Yes, of course."

"No, girl, do you *See* them? See them, name them, feel yourself among them. They are where we come from, where the magic lives. Breathe them in, feel yourself among them, feel them within you."

Cheyenne closed her eyes, took a deep breath and let it out. She cleared her mind. Then, she opened her eyes and looked to the heavens.

The sky was the deepest of blues before it would be black, and the stars shone out like diamonds. Even in the deepest part of the night, it seemed the sky on the prairie was not just black. No, it sported shades of purple and indigo and the deepest of blues too. It lived and breathed just as Cheyenne did. She pulled that thought, that feeling, into her, let it fill her.

Next to her, she knew her grandmother's eyes had grown clear as she, too, gazed upward. "We are thankful for the gift of this power upon us. We are grateful that our ancestors were chosen to bear this gift. This gift which we use for the good of man. This gift which we use naught for personal gain, but to help the world around us."

Cheyenne breathed deeply, slowly, feeling the well of that magic from the sky pour into her. It was clear and cold and shimmering as it filled her, made her feel as though she might burst with the power of it.

Her grandmother's voice became distant, as though it also came from the sky. "Draw them down to you. Draw the magic through you."

Cheyenne did, opening herself fully to the beauty of the sky above. She lifted her arms wide, so her arms formed a bowl shape, a shape which magic could pour straight into her.

And she felt something so big, so filled with the essence of life, that it drew tears to her eyes. And within it, what she had felt with Duke the day before, that golden shimmer which gave the clear, cold magic a warm, pulsing center. It gave the magic something she had never experienced before, something which made it feel dearer to her than it ever had before. And as she stood there with her grandmother, her soul bared to the universe, she felt her part in the universe crystallize, become certain. Though she could not put it into words yet, the great world above told her that she was on the right path.

Chapter 13

Duke walked into the sitting room as a great cascade of what looked like the very fabric of the sky poured down from the heavens and spilled into the two women standing at the window. Stars shimmered within the waterfall of space, a river that rushed with no sound except that of the wind.

The hair on Duke's arms stood on end as it sometimes did when lightning struck too near.

The animal in him said to run, but the man in him was fascinated, in awe. He had seen much on his travels in the West—ghosts, spirits, creatures which might either want to eat a man or steal his soul—but he had not seen anything as beautiful and terrifying as this. Those other creatures he could avoid, sidestep, or trick into letting him go along his way, but these were human women. Humans who looked as though they could command the stars and yet they chose to live in the prairie, in the middle of nowhere, where life was its hardest. They could have the world in their hand, and yet they chose not to.

The great waterfall trickled to a stop like water poured from a glass. A great hush came over the room, as though all sound had been taken out of it. Time slowed or stilled, the lights dimmed. And in another moment, all was normal again.

"How was the show, Mr. Channing?" the eldest Goodnight asked. Frances Goodnight, he had heard her called. Isaac's own mother.

"Oh!" Cheyenne said as she turned around, a look of...was it fear on her face? "I didn't know he was there."

"I did," her grandmother said, and Duke noticed that the woman's eyes were clear tonight. No trace of age showed within those emerald eyes which mirrored her granddaughter's own. She was seeing him. Seeing inside him, too, he felt, and wanted to close himself off from it.

"Cheyenne, see that this man gets some tea. I'm going to retire to my rooms for the time being." And with that, she was gone from the room.

Duke watched Cheyenne closely. She glowed with her recent exertions, and Duke found himself growing hard at the thought of how like their last meeting she looked. Hair tousled, skin flushed, eyes wide with excitement. A man would have to be ten years dead to not be wanting her again.

"She's very bossy," Cheyenne said, then rang for tea.

Duke stepped closer to the tempting morsel in from of him, and she backed up, as she had when they first met. He felt the thrill of the chase come upon him again. That Miss Goodnight had inspired that in him was an interesting puzzle. One he hoped to solve by getting her on the nearest soft surface again. "What were you frightened of when you saw me?"

Cheyenne put the side of a sofa between them. "Of you."

Duke stepped near again. "Me?"

"Of what you would think. You have seen me conjure, but you have not seen me like this."

Duke thought back to the spirits she brought forth to chase the ruffians. How seeing those men lifted from their saddles had instilled a great respect for her in him. "I believe I would witness this again overseeing those things you brought forth come for me."

Cheyenne smiled, her eyes snapping. "Oh, those. They would not hurt you. They only come for those who have malice in their hearts."

And what would he be when he left this place? The thought sizzled through him like coffee drunk too hot. He felt shaken suddenly, off-balance. That wasn't like him.

"Is something wrong?" she asked.

"Just wondering if there are others like you?" he said as he recovered himself. All would be well, even if—when—he left. He had and would continue to make it clear to Cheyenne that this was just a stop on the road, lest she get ideas about where their intimate relations might be going. She was a smart, progressive woman, though. She would be fine.

"That's a sore subject. I have asked my grandmother, and she hasn't given me an answer."

"Why not?"

"Because it is up to that witch to decide whether or not to tell. I don't see the harm in it one witch to another."

But Duke saw the problem in it. "I don't go around broadcasting that I'm a marshal. That's asking for trouble."

"I don't mean that. I mean...don't you tell other law enforcement who you are?"

"I don't. I operate outside of their bounds, even. And I move more easily through towns when my identity is unknown. Most only think me a sharpshooter looking for trouble. The government lets this rumor circulate. I get access to places I otherwise wouldn't. Places that lawbreakers and bail jumpers often congregate."

He watched Cheyenne absorb this information. As smart as she was, she was young still, and at least five years his junior, perhaps more.

When she finally looked back up at him, her green eyes sparked with mirth. It jogged his heart to see her turn those brilliant eyes on him, and he felt himself soften.

"Thank you," she said. "You've explained it much better than my grandmother did. I think she sometimes speaks in riddles so that I will quit pestering her for answers."

"You're welcome," he said with a short bow.

"Are you here to spy on me?" Cheyenne asked tartly.

Duke raised an eyebrow. Her shifting moods were adorable. "Your father called me up here."

"He said nothing to me."

"I imagine he doesn't tell you everything."

"I know next to nothing about you," Cheyenne said, agitated that she wasn't getting anywhere with Duke. It was as though he couldn't answer the simplest of questions about his self without turning the question back around into something that poked fun at her.

"It seems you know a great deal more about me than I you," he replied. For some reason, irking her amused him. And he wasn't so keen on answering her questions or telling her anything personal if he could help it. The less she knew, the better.

The tea arrived, and they sat quietly regarding each other while it was poured for them. Tea service. Something else Duke had missed sorely. He sipped his tea, savoring it as he watched the wheels turning in Miss Goodnight's head. He couldn't wait to hear what came out of her mouth next.

"Why did you kill those men in Laredo?" she asked. "I heard of it just two months ago, and the papers said you killed them without any cause and that you were on the run. And yet, here you are, saying you're here on assignment."

"Does that frighten you?" he asked into her silence.

He was rewarded with laughter in her sparkling eyes. "No, it does not frighten me, Duke Channing. I imagine it frightens some ladies. I imagine it entices others."

Duke got her implication, and he was surprised by it. He would have thought Miss Goodnight would show more decorum than that, and especially after their rendezvous. "I killed them because they were wanted by the United States government, and when they resisted arrest, they found out why I don't ask twice. They were the worst sort of men, and I didn't feel badly about it. Next question."

Cheyenne considered his words with an impassive face. "When did you last kill a man?"

"Two nights ago, with you."

Her aggravated sigh was adorable. "Before that."

"A week ago not far south of here."

"Why?"

"Gracious, woman, I don't have to answer to you." Duke found himself uneasy at this line of questioning. Where was she heading with this?

"Who do you answer to?"

Ah, there it was.

"God," he snarled, at the end of his patience for her endless questions. Why couldn't she just take herself and her endless questions somewhere else? "I will answer to God and God alone when I die. For now, I serve the United States government, my own conscience, and the western wind. Does that satisfy you?"

She appeared to mull over her response, but he could tell by the way her lips turned up into what could only be considered a devious smile that she was not at all satisfied. "I only seek to understand who you are and why you are in my town."

"Your town."

"It is as much mine as my father's."

"This dusty place hardly deserves the name."

And he knew he'd made a misstep when he saw the same green gleam in Cheyenne's eyes as he had the night before. That it was in a lit room made it all the more unnerving. "A fine thing to say for someone who lives in the dust."

She'd stung him with that one, but not so deeply it would scar. He'd chosen to live in the dust. He'd chosen his death out in the desert, on the prairie, somewhere out in the open where God would see him. Somewhere where his body would rot under the open sky, bones picked clean by vultures. It was what he deserved after he had let his own siblings have that fate themselves.

"You have me there," he finally said.

She was testing his patience, too. "I killed them because they had already murdered a group of women in a brothel. And then they crossed me when I attempted to take them in. Even less than you are crossing me at this very moment."

There was that green gleam again. "Oh, am I? I was unaware I was so nettlesome. Do tell me how I may behave."

"You are the most unladylike lady I have met."

"And that is such a bad thing? Did that not serve you well yesterday? Have I not been enough for you? Or is it that I am not pliant enough for you?" There was hurt in her voice, Duke noticed, but how it had gotten there and what, if anything, he could do to make it go away, he didn't know.

Duke wanted to shake her. When he said as much, she laughed the cackling laugh she had in the night under the open sky, but this time it was laced with a hurt he felt deep inside. "Shake me all you like, Duke Channing. And I shall reward you for your trouble."

Trouble indeed, he thought as he watched her flounce from the room, skirts disappearing into the hall.

Chapter 14

He'd been in this town less than a week and already he'd had a skirmish with the ruffians, kissed a smart-mouthed woman with a pretty face and fierce magic streak, and found himself in the Goodnights' lavish quarters for a second time. He hadn't had a streak of luck this good in, well, ever. He would need to step carefully. Luck this fair was bound to run out just as quickly as it found him. As a marshal, he knew how to be prepared for that eventuality.

And the more he looked at the rooms, the grand hall, did some calculations in his head, he realized that there was no mathematically possible way for these chambers to exist. There was too much space up here compared to the rest of the place he had seen. Was it magic or some kind of illusion?

Cheyenne had made herself scarce after their conversation. That was for the best, Duke thought. He didn't want to find out that night what the prairie looked like from the perspective of a rabbit.

Duke wondered what men's business Goodnight wanted, and he'd see whether the man knew what his daughter had been up to in the night. He harbored no shame for the kisses he'd shared with Cheyenne, for the pleasure he had given her, for that had been given as much as he'd taken. He'd hardly slept after for wondering what the rest of her felt like, what it would be like to have such a woman full of confidence in his bed.

Or hers.

A wicked grin pulled at his lips before he schooled his features when Isaac Goodnight entered and addressed him. They gave each other a hearty handshake.

"I wanted to thank you for your help these last days, and the night it began. Dead or alive, we've got two more of the McLaury boys than we had before, and a number more left without their horses and their supplies. The more we can siphon from them, the better off we shall be."

Duke took the seat offered him in the comfortable room. He noted that Miss Goodnight's name wasn't included in the thanks. Duke figured it would be tactful not to bring up that while he might've shot a few men, it'd only been because they'd been nearly stunned to death by the spirits Miss Goodnight had raised to help them. "I'm happy to have been here to help."

"It's not every day a marshal comes through. Especially one with a reputation such as yourself."

Duke still didn't like that his business was so known here. "I'm not accustomed to having my true purpose known."

"I come by it honestly," Goodnight said, settling into the couch with his tea, which a servant also poured for Duke. Duke eyed the extra cup at Goodnight's elbow. Ah, there was the tea that Cheyenne had abandoned in her haste to leave the room. He hoped Goodnight simply saw it as an oversight on the staff's part.

Duke took the offered tea and folded his milk in silently. Six o'clock to twelve o'clock, six o'clock to twelve o'clock. He felt Goodnight's eyes on him while he did it.

"Major Brogan Taylor has been nearby helping with the ruffian situation. He informed me that you might show up here."

"I hadn't told him I was coming."

"Even though he requested you do so? Seems you're here on assignment whether you like it or not."

Duke set his tea down. Whoever Isaac Goodnight was aside from the simple rumors Duke had heard, he clearly was in the pocket of the other authorities in the area.

"I understand you might be able to buy your good name with men in this area, but I'm not going to play these games with you."

Isaac Goodnight surprised him with a laugh, as he had when they first met. "I served with Brogan at the Battle of Palo Alto in '46. And sailed with him on a tea clipper to India. Just once, though," he said with another laugh. "Once is enough for that arduous journey."

Duke was reminded of his father's own adventures. That he kept to himself, though he had a feeling this Isaac Goodnight knew about his father's adventures because he'd been there as well.

"I must apologize, then. I'm grateful to have you in my corner."

Isaac dipped his head in response and sipped thoughtfully at his tea. "I understand you had some help with the matter the other night."

It didn't shock him that Isaac brought it up. It shocked him that Isaac was acting so nonchalant about his daughter wielding such tremendous power. This was where he would tread carefully, as carefully as watching another man shift his weight in such a way that told Duke he was going to reach for his gun. As carefully as he would trail the men near the Missouri border who were looking to sway free elections with fear and force.

"I'm not so certain my services were even required that night," Duke finally said.

Isaac surprised him again with a bark of laughter. "She would go charging in with her skirts racing to keep up, with nary a thought to whether she might need help."

Duke opened his mouth to reply, but Isaac beat him to it. "I realize it was her choice, but she is young yet and sometimes overconfident. I am worried for her, as fathers ought to be, but she needs a firm guiding hand to keep her from someday getting herself into a spot from which she may not get out of."

Duke didn't want to argue that a woman with powers such as hers could likely be as confident as she wanted all by themselves. He wondered what trouble other men tempted by her beauty had found. He imagined the whole of Boston teeming with rabbits and had to suppress another grin. Cheyenne was turning him right soft.

Isaac cleared his throat. "There is one more thing...."

"Anything," Duke said, at ease now that he felt confident his impeachment upon Cheyenne's honor was not public knowledge.

"With the McLaurys lying in wait—yes, they are," he said to Duke's attempt to interrupt. "It is how they work. Their continued presence is not good for town morale. I need to get back to Boston and recruit reinforcements who have experience with these kinds of ruffians. I should like for them to follow me from this place. Warren needs breathing room with the election nearing."

The scout in him was interested. And while he technically was on an official assignment at the moment—'remove the ruffians from the area' was vague but still an order—he wasn't going to pass up this opportunity. "Where do I fit in?"

Chapter 15

Isaac cleared his throat again. He was nervous, Duke saw, but he wasn't prepared for what the man said next.

"I know who you are, Duke Channing, son of Thomas Charles. I knew the man in Boston, saw him move his fur trade and his goods to the southwest and get himself settled there. I served with him as well as Brogan during Palo Alto. He rules the land. He has a son, as I recall, who ran away from home some years gone."

For once, Duke didn't know whether to challenge this man or hightail it out to the stables and saddle his horse. It occurred to him a moment later that neither was an option to him. He was stuck here on assignment. "Becoming a scout and a marshal is a mite different from running away. What do you want from me?"

"It's what you can do for me."

"And that is?"

"I need my daughter protected while I'm away."

Relief washed over him. Protect Cheyenne? Not that she needed it, but he could handle that responsibility. "There hardly seems a need to call my true name into this on account of something so easily done."

"You cannot stay here and protect her as a single man."

The silence between them drew out. Duke thought he heard Miss Goodnight tittering in her rooms down the hall. Was she hearing them and laughing at him now?

"So you're proposing I…what? Act as her guardian in your absence?" If it were that simple, why did it feel like there was more coming?

Isaac let out his breath in a long sigh. The man looked old, Duke realized, harried. "I propose nothing. You are to marry my daughter so I may conduct my dangerous business without need of worrying whether my daughter is taken care of."

The implication of the statement didn't occur to him immediately.

This Duke was not expecting. Before the anger hit him, he sat in stunned silence looking at the serious man before him.

"You're mad," Duke said, any thought of decorum gone out the window.

Isaac laughed, "On the contrary. I like to think I'm a man who knows an opportunity when he sees it."

"You don't know me," Duke said in disbelief. "I can walk out of here, and you wouldn't—won't—ever see me again."

"Not once your father knows you're here."

Duke heard the ringing in his ears before he realized that it was his anger. He hadn't spent years away from that godforsaken place in the desert just to have some stranger boot him back there. And now he had an impossible decision to make. Chains there or chains here.

"This is blackmail," he said, feeling like a kid being kicked into the dirt. "I'm not a child who needs a beating for running away from home."

"I am offering you an olive branch, young man."

"A whipping from an olive branch, more like," he replied vehemently. The aforementioned branch fueled his burning anger. He'd come here to escape and now? Now he was worse than trapped. If he ran, the federal government would bring down a heavy hammer on him for defecting—though the sting of even considering that dishonor stayed him. There had to be another way.

"Can't you bring her with you? She seems a...capable young woman."

The look on Isaac's face told him he wanted to know what Duke meant by 'capable,' but he didn't ask. Duke hoped they had spoken closely enough of Cheyenne's magic for the man to think that was all he meant. "You of all men should know why I won't be bringing her with me."

Duke desperately wanted to tell Mr. Isaac Goodnight that he knew good and well what could happen to a woman on the road, but the fact that Miss Cheyenne Goodnight was no ordinary woman seemed to negate that danger. Duke also wanted to tell Isaac that he knew the man also might not make it to his destination before the trouble caught up with him. But he didn't. Isaac already knew.

"I will appoint you my place *in absentia*. Legally speaking..."

And it dawned on Duke why that might be important. "Legally speaking, she can't run the town while you're gone."

Isaac sighed, somehow managing to make it sound exasperated and gentlemanly at the same time. "It's not that I don't think she's capable. She is. Perhaps even more so than I."

That Duke was surprised to hear, but he didn't say so. He hadn't thought Isaac Goodnight anything except capable. And strict to the letter of the law. As he was being here. That reputation had preceded him, as he'd heard most outlaws avoided his town as a rule. That's what made the McLaurys, and now the additions they'd had to their numbers, all the more concerning.

Perhaps Isaac was referring to his daughter's...other skills, but that wasn't something Duke was about to poke at either, insinuation that he knew or not.

"There are any number of eligible men around. Major Taylor, your deputies," Duke sputtered, hating that he couldn't find his footing here. "And the likelihood that your town collapses while you are away is...." But he couldn't finish. He couldn't say anymore because he knew that Isaac Goodnight was right. And that was a punch in the gut.

"I know who you are, Duke Channing. I know your father. Major Taylor has vouched for you as well already."

Duke banged a fist on the arm of his chair. "You simply cannot entrust me with this. My God, I could abscond into the West with her, and you'd never see her again. I could sell her to the first brothel I come across, I could..."

"But you won't," Isaac interrupted.

And that perhaps more than anything enraged him the most. That somehow this stranger knew him better than he claimed to know himself. He stood, wanting to feel powerful standing taller than the man sitting down and giving him fatherly look when that was the last thing he wanted.

But he didn't. He felt small and stuck and pinned in a way he hadn't his entire adult life. His adult life which he had spent running from feeling that very thing.

"How long do I have?"

"Three days."

Duke felt the anger freeze to steel within him. Fuck decorum. He turned on his heel and left the room.

Chapter 16

Cheyenne was fuming.

"I will not leave you unprotected while I am away. To have you with me would only encourage the McLaurys to follow and cause mischief."

"And you cannot say he is my...brother? My cousin? This is absurd!"

"There is no better protection than a husband, my dear. Your mother would agree if she were here. I must do things to the letter of the law. You must either understand that or, barring that, respect my decision."

Cheyenne thought about how Duke was connected to her, how their fates were intertwined. But she hadn't wanted it this way. She had thought she had some choice in how the plan went. But this? This would doom them for disaster from the beginning. How could anyone grow to love a person they were forced to wed, fate or no? And after their strange fight in the sitting room earlier, she felt even more at a loss. Did Duke Channing like her at all?

"But him!" she said aloud before she could stop herself.

Her father was surprised at her outburst. "You have an objection to this man?"

She bit her tongue. It was not like her to speak out of turn, to speak without thinking, to let her feelings loose into the wind.

Duke's comment about already having his great love stuck somewhere between her heart and her lips, lodged there to fester, to make her choke when she least expected it. How could this man be her own soul's mate if he had staked a claim on his one love already?

His searing kiss and roving hands had said otherwise, had kept her awake until dawn pressing her thighs together to ease the ache of want between them. But this wasn't the way it was supposed to be. 'Forced to marry' certainly didn't sound like 'meant to be.'

"I have hardly had a conversation with him!" She finally got out.

"And had I arranged for you to marry any number of the eligible suitors in Boston whom you liked far less, you would be miserable today. Is that not so?"

Cheyenne had nothing to say to that. Her mother's words echoed around in her head, butting against Duke's own words about already having his great love.

"If, and I say *if*," her father began quietly, the power in his voice stilling Cheyenne for the moment. "If Duke Channing and yourself find a gross incompatibility while I am away, we will annul the marriage upon my return. If," he said sternly.

"But we can't…"

"This is my town," her father said forcefully. "And we will do as we wish in it, on my word. But you cannot do that."

That brought up Cheyenne's ire faster than nearly anything. "But I can!"

Isaac Goodnight's mouth set into a firm line. "Not without

a man by your side. Not without that help. The West might be different, but I still must have you protected. I know you are more than capable, daughter, but I fear for your safety should you attempt this alone, when I am not here to be by your side. I cannot lose you, Cheyenne. I cannot lose you when I have already lost so much. Your mother…" he trailed off, the pain in his voice searing straight into Cheyenne's own heart.

This made Cheyenne fall silent. Yes, her father was right, as much as she hated to admit it. He did what he did out of love, even if she couldn't see the right in it at the moment.

"And after having heard tales of spirits who chased some of the McLaury men away, I know Mr. Channing must already know you a great deal better than any other man on this continent. Is that not so, daughter?"

There was a warning in his voice which she had heard a thousand times. *Do not share your gift with anyone. Do not let anyone see. Do not lose your head and conjure in anger.*

"He riled me. Besides, I could have dispatched him had he caused trouble. The prairie would not mind one more rabbit."

Isaac shook his head. "You know your mother would say it is not a performance. And my mother…."

"I was tired of hiding it."

Isaac's face grew stern. "That is a child's response. Try again."

Cheyenne fought the urge to stamp her foot. The time for that was over, she saw. If she was to be married, that meant she was a woman. She could act like one. She set her mouth in a firm line, forcing the biting words back down her throat.

"I felt him worthy of Seeing," she finally said, quietly. There, that was the honest answer.

Her father seemed to consider that, and he didn't press the

issue further. "I want you protected while I am away. This is an honest man."

"Honest?" she sputtered. "He says he's a marshal, but he's nothing more than a reckless rebel, an outlaw."

"Daughter." Isaac's strong tone silenced his daughter. "I know this man. His father. He is from good stock. I cannot take you with me."

"But isn't it far more dangerous here? Please, take me with you!"

"I expect them to follow me. I will not have you with me to slow me down." And to the heat that ignited in Cheyenne's eyes when he said this, he said, "I will reach Boston much faster alone and unfettered, and the town needs protection. *That* we will discuss before I leave. For now, there is to be no more discussion here."

Her father was right, and that was the end of it. She knew how stubborn she could be, but she had the good sense to know when she needed to keep her mouth shut and do as she was told. She *would* be better protected with a husband. And Mother wouldn't have led her astray. Surely this would all work out for the best.

I must trust them both, she thought with pain in her heart for her mother, and more pain in her heart that her father should have to make such a decision to ensure her safety. Surely good would come out of this.

Chapter 17

He rode hard for Junction City. Not because he needed it, but because it felt good to let his horse fly across the prairie, to feel the freedom the ride gave him. Alone on the prairie with no one in sight, he finally felt like himself, finally felt the tension of the last days melt away. His shoulders relaxed and he breathed deeply of the fresh air. It didn't matter the size of the town—it always smelt of shit and unwashed masses. Cheyenne's quarters had to be exempt from that, though, and the scent of her sweet perfume lingered on his clothes still.

He'd grown a soft spot for Warren. There were just few enough people that he didn't feel as caged in, but with Isaac Goodnight's proposal—no, his *demand*—he would be trapped in a place which could only grow larger.

Being around people too much did that to him. He didn't understand it, not when he'd been born and bred into a society that valued socializing so much. He was better with his hands, better with a horse, better with a gun than he'd ever been socializing. He could do it when he needed to, but goddamn it took everything out of him when he did.

His father had blessedly not forced him to socialize, not

that there was much in the desert territories, but it had always been a relief when everyone had left, and he'd been able to head out into the desert on his horse to be alone.

Alone was how he liked it, with the great outdoors.

He had to admit that it had gotten lonely in recent years. Not that he wanted a *person* to keep him company, but he wanted more than what he'd gotten in the brothels and saloons along the way. He wanted more than the stiff camaraderie of his fellow scouts and marshals and commanders. And he'd turned down his own position as commander for that very reason—he would have to talk to people too much.

He sighed and stiffened his spine in the saddle. He'd clearly already stayed in one place for too long.

Duke was still sighing when he traipsed into his field commander's office.

"Channing, please sit."

Duke did. Brogan Taylor's field office had improved since his last visit here. And Duke was glad to not have to report at Fort Riley down the road. Junction City was growing much more quickly than Warren. He wouldn't be surprised if the train made it here within ten years. Sooner, even.

"I'm shocked you didn't put up a fight when they told you to leave Texas. Even on an errant assignment."

Duke set his dusty hat on his knee. "Don't waste your breath; you knew I'd accept. I'm a U.S. Marshal. The States and their territories are my jurisdiction. I'm working for the same end you are, just by…alternative means. And I follow the trouble wherever it takes me. Lately, it's brought me here. Which I think you already knew."

Brogan wasn't impressed. "Full of hot air as always. What do you have to report?"

If Brogan hadn't been his superior, Duke would've led the conversation with Isaac Goodnight going behind his back. But with this being his acting commander in the field, he swallowed his pride, though it stuck somewhere between his heart and his belly and festered there. "That it seems there's more going on here than we suspected," Duke began, thinking of Cheyenne and her own knowledge of the enemy camped not far from the town in which she lived.

"What I have to report is probably the same reason you've got this place on the up and up." Duke gestured to the room around them. "You don't hang a portrait unless it's a long stay. A permanent one," he finished.

Brogan nodded, looked around the room. "It's looking that way. There's been more trouble in this area in the last two years than since there've been people out here. They've been saying there'll be war before long. Kidnapping, threatening, intimidating, and generally terrorizing isn't a far cry from killing. Atchison is likely to bring in as many men as he did last year, and I'm certain the South has a few more to donate to their cause. I fear we are at the prelude to a great struggle."

Duke absorbed the news with a sour feeling in his stomach. Scouting was one thing. Bringing in ruffians was one thing. Killing criminals was one thing. War was another entirely. "Seems they needed to come back this way to focus on the smaller towns, the ones more easily cut off from trade and supplies."

"And being near the border helps their cause," Brogan said as he looked at the map of the area on his desk.

Duke stared down at the map himself, saw the markers that numbered the men of the opposing party. "Why haven't you suggested we just ride in and take them?"

"They're backed by Atchison. One whiff of us mounting an attack on the McLaurys, and he'll send in two thousand men to obliterate us. No, we must be more strategic, I'm afraid."

"And, what, be ready for an attack from Atchison when we do pull the trigger?"

Brogan nodded, his mouth set in a grim line.

"There's something else," Duke ventured in the silence of mortal contemplation that followed.

"There always is," Brogan replied, lighting his pipe. "Let's have it."

"There's a...situation in Warren."

"I'm shocked."

"Isaac Goodnight is heading up to Boston for reinforcements. It leaves the town without its principal player."

"This I know. You're thinking about accompanying him?"

The man was a damn liar. Duke balled his fists, then relaxed them. "No. No, he'll do fine on his own. No, it's about something he's asked of me in his absence."

Brogan waited in silence. That the man knew what was coming infuriated him.

"He's asked me to wed his daughter. As a protective measure for the town. And you know of this."

Brogan, not one given to laughter, pulled hard on his pipe, exhaled, and settled further back in his chair. "Yes, and I know Goodnight. He's a fair man with a firm hand. He would not ask such a thing lightly."

"It seemed lightly enough when I was there," Duke replied darkly.

"Isn't she fair?"

What a question. Fair? If darkness were fair, he supposed. If the sultry night were fair for its hidden mysteries. If the prairie were fair for its splendor that not many could appreciate. Yes, she was fair. Fair and dark and everything that a man could want in a woman. She was unique, yes, as unique as each prairie sunrise and sunset.

Yes, she was fair. She had a smart mouth that tasted of ambrosia, a mouth that he was all too willing to silence with a kiss when she got too smart.

He felt for a moment that he couldn't speak. How was it that this woman could creep into his thoughts even when he didn't want her to? How she could wend her way into everything he did, and even when he was spitting angry at being blackmailed—forced!—into marrying her, she still found a way to soothe his temper with her memory.

"She is," Duke said. "A mite fairer than any woman I've had the pleasure of knowing." He kept her abilities to himself. Brogan might be as close as Duke had to a friend, but there was no knowing what kind of reaction witchcraft would bring.

He supposed it wasn't quite fair to call what she did witchcraft, though. Witchcraft was of the Devil, and Cheyenne certainly did not worship such a cause. And if the story she told were true, then it was simply how she was, how she had been born. And he wondered how many others like her were out there. And did she know any of them? If the gift traveled through the father's side, then perhaps it wasn't such a surprise that her grandmother was living on the prairie with the family.

Brogan tapped the bit of his pipe against his lips. "If war is on the horizon, we are in an excellent place to weather it. And with the fort being built, I can't imagine a more suitable place to put down roots. And if these McLaurys turn out to have Atchison's full support, we might be here a while anyway. We can't have them getting the word out that they can do things like this. It might give other groups ideas that we don't want to spread."

Duke nearly fell out of his chair with shock. Did his commander just suggest that he take Isaac Goodnight's proposal seriously? How could he have, and so nonchalantly?

"He…" Duke began, then stopped. He didn't want to sound like a simpering child. "Goodnight threatened…actions… against me should I not comply with his wishes."

And then Brogan did laugh. A great belly laugh that came out of nowhere. Duke sat, stunned, unable to say anything else as he watched his commander grow red in the face with laughter.

When Brogan finally composed himself, he said. "I never thought I'd live to see the day. A U.S. Marshal—and Mr. Duke Channing at that—afraid of a woman."

Duke balled his hands into fists, squeezed them until his knuckles turned white. "You think what he's doing is fair?"

"Fair? It's an alliance that would unquestionably profit all parties. Isaac Goodnight has money and people and supplies and munitions enough to supply all of Fort Riley. And the man loves the prairie. He loves this great country and what it could be. I see no better alliance for you than this. And if she is as fair as you say, which must be quite fair, as you have left of many details that you normally do not—then I think, yes, you should snatch her up and be done with it."

Duke sat with his shock, trying to process it, to see it as Brogan did. "Are you married?" he asked carefully.

"I am," his commander said with an arched eyebrow. "She lives with her family while I travel until we find a permanent place. I believe this to be it."

Brogan couldn't have been much older than he. "I have never been party to something so absurd."

"This is going to be your home base. Our priority is the border ruffians. Atchison led over 5,000 men here last year to vote in the elections. We've significantly curtailed that number this year, thanks in part to scouts and marshals like yourself, but I tell you, I won't be having it any longer. We need to strike these men in force, or we'll lose the town, the elections, and our lives."

"I don't like staying put," Duke said.

"Chasing ruffians between here and the border would be too suffocating for you? Or would you rather go back down to Texas, where I hear a man can disappear into the desert and never be seen again?"

Duke wisely kept his mouth shut.

"I've an aim to promote you, Duke Channing, with leave from your formal commander in Washington. Taking a wife is a wise move. Building a home in the area or at Fort Riley is a wise idea. You are an intelligent man. Now, let's get down to some business here. We've a small contingency coming in from Texas to help us, and we need to organize our next move."

Duke settled in to talk with anxiety still gnawing at his gut. This hadn't at all gone the way he wanted it to. Getting out of this arrangement was getting trickier by the second.

Chapter 18

There was no trace of the passion they had shared when she saw him next. Cheyenne had ridden out to one of the nearby hills where a limestone outcropping offered one a place to view the country below in all its splendor. Below, she could see the town and the prairie rushing out beyond it into the setting sun. The sun hurt her eyes, even though it blazed a muted red and orange as it set through the haze of smoke that lingered in the air. The native peoples were burning a great area of grazing land with help from a recent lightning strike, and the smoky air had given way to spectacular sunsets the last few days.

She shouldn't have been surprised that Duke had followed her there, but it was that he had done it without her knowledge that raised her rancor. She hadn't heard a sound from him, hadn't so much as sensed that there was someone following her, even with her gift guiding her innately.

"You must have your own kind of magic, Duke Channing, to be able to follow someone on horseback and not have them know."

"I'm a marshal, a ranger," he said. "This is what I do."

Cheyenne turned from the setting sun to roll her eyes at

him. "I try to pay you a compliment, and I see what I'm met with."

She watched as Duke's forearms flexed. He was angry. She still found it attractive. "You think I need your compliments?"

Cheyenne felt the need to argue back with him rise in her. And then dissipate. She felt oddly cold for the heat of the evening, the still-warm sun on her skin. She had turned even more deeply golden here in the Kansas Territory sun, had cast aside the notion that she must stay indoors or under parasols at every moment. Here she felt free.

Until Duke. Until this. Until the idea of finding the man she was fated to be with had turned confusing and troubling.

"I'm certain this was your idea of a joke," Duke sneered at her when she didn't answer his prodding.

"Then it is a trick played upon myself as well," Cheyenne said hotly. She trembled with the questions burning inside her. *Who are you? Where have you come from? Are you the man I am fated to be with? If you are, then why do you say you have your great love already?*

Duke had no fair words for her truth, and the curses which crossed his lips, though not directed at her, hurt her more than simply stating that he did not care for her company. And when he turned to her, she knew not whether to run from him or to him, so conflicted did she feel.

"You could have the lot of us enchanted." He gripped her by the arms, aware just a second too late of the fire that snapped in Cheyenne's eyes

Cheyenne set her own hands on Duke's forearms and dug her nails in just hard enough to drive her points home. As her fingers set on his skin, he felt little shocks go through him. "Enchant the lot of you so I could be in more dire straits than

I was in before? Enchant the lot of you so I could send my only family away from my person? Enchant the lot of you for what *good*, pray tell?"

Duke shook her gently, but some of the hardness had gone out of his eyes. She relaxed into his grip, letting him hold her as a willing captive. Just as, she supposed, her father had known the measure of this man, so she knew, too, that he would never harm her purposefully. He might have a great love somewhere already, but he had not yet run from this place. He was here, following her, despite what his words might say. But would that be enough?

They stood there in the half embrace for a long minute.

"What is it that you fear so?" Cheyenne demanded. Before a shadow passed over his eyes, she saw something there that he wished to say but would not. Duke pulled away and hid his face from her. Their connection broke.

"Tell me," she pressed. "This life is hard enough. No one said that you had to go at it alone."

"You would not wish for me to lay upon you the things I have seen and done to survive in this world, Miss Cheyenne," Duke said quietly, his back still to her.

"Then tell me the good things you love in this world," she said, pushing back against the uncomfortable feeling the request invoked. "You have left behind another woman for me. Or have at least left her behind."

At that, Duke snapped to attention, eyes finding Cheyenne's. "Who told you that?"

"You did. Your great love."

Duke's eyes roved over the prairie that swelled and undulated to the setting sun. Thin wisps of smoke from chimneys were visible to the north. Someone would be cooking dinner, snug in their home. It would be sweltering, to be sure, as would be the fires on the prairie some miles distant. He'd ridden out to check on them, though he knew he need not. The natives knew their land as they did the backs of their hands. They knew its rhythms, its moods, its fickleness.

He stole a glance back at Cheyenne, who had resumed watching the sun set herself.

"I want you to open your heart to me," she said. "Speak to me, at least, so I may learn more of your character."

"That is easier said than done. I am a bad man, Cheyenne. There is no one here to tell you that I have no heart to give."

"Because it is already taken by another woman."

He didn't answer.

For the first time in her life, Cheyenne felt uncertain. How could their love be fated when his heart belonged to another?

Duke sighed, his own feelings warring with the logic Brogan had spoken to him earlier in the day. "I said I would protect you. I don't intend on letting you get hurt in your father's absence."

"And then you'll leave once he returns," she retorted.

"I want nothing more than to be gone from this place. I'm a man of my word, though. Don't you understand that?"

His words hit her squarely in the chest. The man might not have the magical power that she did, but he had a power with his words, with his body, with his might. And he had used that against her in this moment.

"I understand," she said quietly, even though, in her heart, she couldn't bear the thought.

Chapter 19

L eft alone on the bluff, Duke could see the entirety of the valley below him, and the great prairie and its swells and curves that ran on to the horizon. He had traveled over much of the Kansas Territory, south into Texas, and into the great desert where his parents had settled. And this was the place he always enjoyed resting his eyes on the horizon the most. The sunsets and sunrises here could not be beat. Perhaps that was one thing he could look forward to now that he was to be chained to this place. Temporarily, at least.

He frowned as his thoughts inevitably spiraled toward Cheyenne and his current predicament.

The society his family had kept had been their own. And the women he'd had along the trail were either destitute from being abandoned on the trail or their husbands perishing in some violent manner. But Cheyenne was a world above any of that. His parents would have thought her a suitable match. She would have been perfect, right down to her shiny shoes which she deigned to get dusty. And so, she pulled on boots in their stead and set them right in the dust, ready to work with the man beside her.

He couldn't parse it.

He hadn't been in the place he had been born for nearly twenty years. He'd seen no reason to go back there. He's made certain, of course, during the Mexican skirmish, that his family was well out of harm's way. But to go back there? He would have to be a desperate man indeed to do that.

He had been twelve when his world shattered. He had been playing outside and lost track of time, lost track of where he was. He hadn't heard the rumble of the storm coming, hadn't realized that the rain a mile away was already beginning to flood the arroyo which he and his siblings played in. It was dry, dusty, hot. He had been warned to pay attention to these signs, but he did not heed them on this day.

They were all out looking for him, because of course James and Mary had been outside with him, under his charge. And he'd heard them shouting for him far off, but they were children, busy with their games, busy in their own world, and they shouted for him every day.

He'd been poking at something in the dry creek bed. It had looked like the skeleton of a monster, something so large and ferocious that he couldn't believe it was real. Its teeth were nearly as long as his arm. Most of the long-dead thing was buried in the creek bed, and he felt compelled to keep digging it up. He had to know what it looked like, to see how big it was, this fantastic creature that rains long past had dredged up from the arroyo. It looked like it must have been a dragon, but if only he could get to where its wings were.

Digging with a stick was going to take him all day.

The sound of distant thunder didn't get his attention. James and Mary were a ways off, digging in their own holes, chasing birds and ground squirrels who got too curious.

By the time he realized what the rushing sound was which was growing louder by the breath, it was already too late.

And when the wall of water came rocketing around the bend, all he could do was gape at it. It rushed as red as blood, as red as when the Nile ran with blood in the Bible. He had heard that story in a Sunday sermon, and all he could think as the water rushed toward them was that it was blood. Deep, dark blood. That the end of the world was upon him. Never in his life had he felt such terror again, even when faced with the business end of a rifle. Even when he'd rushed straight at enemy forces, certain he'd die, he hadn't felt the fear he did that day.

And so he stood there, dumb and frozen in fear as he watched the very earth itself roar toward him. It was blood and then it was the monster he had been poking at, roaring down the creek, its great gaping maw ready to devour him.

There was another sound, too. Hoofbeats on soft dirt. And then, voices. Mother. Father. Lizzy, his mother's maid, and the family's governess.

In another breath, his mother rushed into the water to grab the children she would never see again. Lizzy scrambled in with her, skirts catching on the rocks and brush. His father rushed in and grabbed him as he stood there staring, mouth agape. The water hit them like a fist. Duke and his father were knocked sideways just as the elder Channing was wrapping his arms around his son.

Duke didn't know which way was up, and as he gasped for air, all he breathed in was water. Water which had left him dizzy with its force. Time ceased to exist underwater. It roared and pounded relentlessly, tearing at his clothes, trying to tear him from his father's grip.

And then he and his father were both scrabbling for dry land, clawing and grasping their way to safety, his father pushing him ahead by the seat of his trousers, pushing his son to safety first. And as he lay there struggling to pull in air and breathing in dirt, all he could hear were his mother's screams that never seemed to end.

Fever took him for days afterward.

When he woke, his first shaky steps were to a carriage to carry them to his brother and sister's funeral. In his stupor, he hadn't known. Three fingers on one hand were broken from how hard his father held onto him on the floor. He had black bruises on his arms. When he had asked who the funeral was for, terrified of the answer because his brother and sister were not there by his side, his mother had set her mouth in a grim line and pulled Duke into a fierce embrace. His father began to weep.

Duke, still in the throes of whatever illness had come upon him from the waters of the raging arroyo, had looked from his father to the caskets and back again and fainted.

It took him another year before he was able to walk unassisted. And in that time, he hadn't spoken. He couldn't. Because what would he say? There was no apology great enough for the burden he now carried on his shoulders. He had been charged with protecting his siblings, and he had failed. He had failed and there was nothing he could do to fix it.

And what had he done after that? Run off and become a U.S. Marshal after years of just trying to survive the west. He became a marshal to get into the thick of it in the most godforsaken parts of the country, to uphold justice and the law, even when he had to take the law into his own hands.

His own guns. Frequently. No one wanted to rot in a jail in the West. They would rather take their chances in a shootout. But woe to them if they picked a battle with Duke Channing.

So, tell his father, would he? Duke barked out a laugh. Isaac Goodnight's threat wasn't empty, and Duke had initially written it off as a childish one, but the more he thought about it, the less he liked the idea. He hadn't been home in two decades, and though Goodnight's statement told him that at least his father was alive and well, even thinking about that closed chapter of his life brought up things which he would rather not think about. Ever again.

Even if this was all a sham, it was a far cry better than getting shot in some godforsaken town when his luck ran out. Someday it would. He was a mortal man, and death came for them all eventually. But here he could protect Cheyenne as he hadn't been able to his own family, and perhaps he could glean some happiness from that. And if not happiness, then rest and recovery for whatever the West could cook up for him next. And when Isaac Goodnight returned and these ruffians were taken care of, Duke would go on his way. Let Major Taylor or his formal commanders in Washington give him other places to go. He wouldn't be tied to one place.

He trotted his horse in a large circle around the McLaurys camp, which had grown significantly in size over the last week. In all fairness, they shouldn't be calling them the McLaurys any longer, but what to call them in that stead, he didn't know. Giving them a name would give them power, and he wasn't aiming to do that.

They could see him from that far away, but in the late evening after their supper, they weren't keen on chasing a single rider down. He would report all this to Brogan tomorrow. Brogan who had told him to go along with this terrible idea.

He would atone, and then he would leave. He wouldn't pretend that he didn't find Cheyenne Goodnight fascinating. He'd bet all he owned that he was the only man on the continent courting a witch.

Who was betrothed to a witch.

Soured by the thought, he turned his horse and spurred him toward town. Like it all or not, he wasn't going to show up to his own wedding looking like a tramp. He had work to do.

Chapter 20

Duke was readying himself in his room when he saw something appear in the corner of his eye, near the fireplace. Shirtless, as he had been in the middle of pressing the garment he lacked, he whipped his spare firearm from its hiding spot just under the edge of his bed and turned toward the intruder, prepared to fire.

The figure ghosted from view, then reappeared. He lowered his weapon. Cheyenne's grandmother stood at his hearth. Seeing as how his door was still shut and locked, she must have magicked herself there or some such.

He hastily grabbed for his shirt and pulled it on to cover himself. "Christ! Witches," he mumbled under his breath.

"That we are, Duke Channing." Frances Goodnight seemed unperturbed by bother having a firearm pointed at her and Duke's state of undress.

His heart still threatening to crawl out his throat, Duke buttoned his shirt as quickly as he could and tried to recover his sense of decorum. "To what do I owe the pleasure of your... appearance?"

"I appreciate your acceptance of my arrival."

"I am unaware of any other way than acceptance."

"Then you are a rare find, Mr. Channing."

Duke said nothing. Frances didn't either, and Duke couldn't leave the silence be.

"To what do I owe the pleasure of your company?" Duke asked again, all earnest politeness. Magic or no, Frances Goodnight didn't seem like a woman he wanted to cross.

"You are a man of the law," the old woman said. "And are the law, which is governed only by your moral compass. The law does not bind you here, even for your betrothal to my granddaughter. And so you feel no remorse in leaving. Not yet, anyway."

Duke felt a prickle down his spine at her words. She had struck the closest to home of anyone. Had she a window right into his thoughts, she might not have gotten much closer. But she was wrong about the last part. He didn't and wouldn't feel remorseful. There was no place for remorse in the West. A mistake like that could kill a man in an instant.

"Do you read thoughts, Mrs. Goodnight?"

The laugh that came out of the woman sounded eerily like Cheyenne's. And was so out of character for the regal woman who rested a bejeweled hand on top of her cane which looked like it could inflict considerable damage when wielded properly. And he had no doubt that the woman could wield it if necessary, no matter her advanced age. The Goodnight family was impressive, that Duke would admit freely.

"Quite fortunately, I do not. Can you imagine the hubbub that would cause? My own thoughts torment me, but that of others? I shouldn't be able to get any sleep," she said with a sly wink to him.

Duke kept his mouth shut. He knew better than to overstep his bounds when in the presence of a woman of stately bearing such as this.

"No, Duke Channing, I do not read thoughts. But I am quite skilled at reading people. My granddaughter is not half bad at it herself, but it is a skill that takes a lifetime at which to become accomplished. You must read many a person on your travels as a marshal in these parts."

How they had all found out his occupation without his once opening his mouth was a mystery. And one that no one else, to his knowledge, had discovered in his nigh fifteen years at the occupation. "That I do."

"Then you also know that my Cheyenne is genuine. You know that she is smart as a whip and faster still than one with both her wit and her tongue."

Duke said nothing.

"But what you may not be able to see is her tender heart. She is young still, and still as yet unaware of the way men work. She might have flirted and spoken sweetly in Boston, but for all her more mature ways, she is still ignorant yet. Do you see this?"

"I have known the woman less than a fortnight. But I have been on the receiving end of much of her wit, as you call it."

Frances' face was carefully blank. That, Duke knew, was also practiced. "Then let my words be a warning to you. And a warning to you should you not heed them."

"I have told Miss Cheyenne my intentions are not to stay," Duke said hotly, feeling very much put over the fire by this woman. "She knows I am not the marrying type, nor do I intend to lead her on into places which I cannot go."

"Into love, you mean," the old woman said.

Duke, even for his anger, didn't speak. He hadn't been chastised in many years, and to be scolded by a woman of her stature was humbling and infuriating at once. He had a great amount of respect for this woman's wisdom and her words, but they weren't the words he wanted or needed at this juncture.

His face must have said as much because Frances gave him a gentle smile, then turned and went to the fire. Her fine silk dress rustled as she did so, and Duke noted that even for her apparent blindness, she knew just how close the fire was, and stayed just far enough away that her dress would not catch the flame. He suspected that even without her sight, she knew a great deal more than anyone else in this household.

"Go on your way, Duke Channing, the sharpshooting Marshal. Your bride waits for you. You'll find your own way yet."

"And if I've found my way already?"

She smiled but kept her face turned to the fire. "Ah, the ignorance of youth. You must forgive me. I should not tease you when you are in such a state. Go about your business, then. But have a care for Miss Cheyenne."

"I would not hurt her intentionally."

Frances rested a hand on the mantle, the smile fading from her lips. "Hold your tongue, Mr. Channing, before it wags away without you. I'll not abide by untruths here, not when I know otherwise."

Duke, his mouth set in a hard line, was about to find a less polite retort when Frances Goodnight left the way she came—fading from view until he was alone in the room again.

He didn't need to take advice from dour old ladies, but even for that rebellious thought, he picked up his coat and stalked out of the room. The altar awaited him.

Chapter 21

Cheyenne was all nerves on the morning when she was to be wed to Duke Channing. She wanted to wear her red dress, but that color sometimes caused a commotion in such a small place as Warren was. Navy blue might be more suited. She still couldn't decide. She needed her mother here to help her. The thought brought tears pricking to her eyes.

She turned toward the fire. "Grandmama?"

"What, child?"

"How old were you when you were wed?"

Her grandmother laughed and walked slowly over to where Cheyenne was looking over her wardrobe trying to decide which dress of her best would be suited for her wedding. Her stomach dropped. Her wedding!

"Fifteen, dear girl. Much younger than you are now."

Cheyenne didn't roll her eyes, but she wanted to. She knew she was too old for those kinds of behaviors in front of her grandmother. She'd been rapped on the knees enough with that cane enough, but she did allow herself a sigh.

"And were you nervous? I don't mean about the bedroom part," she said frankly. "I am worried about the after. The...

homemaking."

"Ah, my dear. Come, take my arm and we'll walk the hall."

Cheyenne reached for her morning coat and did as she was instructed. The pair walked out into the quiet hall.

"What do you think of Duke Channing?" her grandmother asked.

"I think he is boar-headed and arrogant, but handsome and smart."

"And do you trust him?"

"Yes," Cheyenne said without hesitation. "I do not think he trusts himself, but what he tells me is what he believes is true. I do not think he wishes to deceive me. Or deceive me with the intention of…spoiling me," she finished carefully. The memory of his hands on her, of his lips and his strong form, welled up within her, with the passion and the darkness and how the power she had felt moving between them.

"And if he chooses to leave when your father returns?"

Cheyenne's stomach flopped. That was what she worried about the most.

"Mother said this was the man I am fated to wed."

"Did she say you were fated to wed him or fated to love him?"

Cheyenne stopped at the window at the far end of the hall where there was a velvet cushion on a seat before the window. It was there that her grandmother released her arm.

"Think on it, my dear. I am going to have a bit of a lie down while Anna and the rest finish readying you. But think carefully with your mind, not your heart. While they may want the same things, our heart can cloud our judgment. It is what gets us hurt more often than not." And her grandmother swished slowly and gracefully back down the hall while

Cheyenne stood before the window. She sat and looked out through the portion with clear panes while the stained glass above it threw blues and purples and reds down the wall and to the floor. Outside, the prairie was waving gently in the breeze.

"A man will come in from the West for you," Cheyenne repeated as she had so often throughout her life. "He will be tall and strong and steel-eyed, and his heart will be full of rebellion."

And she saw Duke in her mind's eye,

And then Cheyenne saw the truth in the words. "She said he would come for me," she whispered. "But she did not say he would stay."

And she sank down into the window seat and wept.

Chapter 22

She fingered the lace at her cuff, mulling over and over the events of the last days. Rumors in town of her hastily arranged marriage did not bother her. Let them think she was with child or whatever excitement they conjured for themselves. She had larger concerns. She had had her cry at the window and dried her eyes. She had chosen her navy blue dress because she had an inkling Duke would like the color.

Mother hadn't said that he would stay, but she hadn't said that Cheyenne couldn't convince him to stay. If he was still in town, that was.

Duke hadn't shown his face for the last day, and Cheyenne thought that certainly he had abandoned her just before they came to the altar together. Not that she blamed him. He was and always would be a rebel at heart and even breathless kisses with a witch were no match for his wandering spirit. Were no match for whatever woman held his heart.

Her stomach was tied up in knots, and she paced restlessly through her rooms. The gown had been her own from Boston, updated by Anna after poring over *Godey's* and *Graham's* most recent fashion plates and some scrambling to find enough ribbons and appropriate fabrics.

It wouldn't matter, she told herself. He would not show.

But he would show. He must! She felt that she would know had he truly left. She tried to convince herself.

It wasn't until she heard the sound of his footsteps that she could finally sigh in relief.

When he strode through the doors, he was a man changed.

Where he had gotten his fine clothes and had his hair tamed, she did not know. She nearly didn't recognize the man whose cold steel eyes were now penetrating her very soul. He'd shaved the traveling stubble from his face, and she saw clearly the fine structure of his face, marred only by his slightly off-center nose, surely from being broken in some fight or another.

Scrubbed clean and clothed in finery, Mr. Channing was even more the picture of a gentleman than he was the night of the dance. Her father's knowledge of his parentage had set her at ease before, but now her nerves were set aflame. Who was the man, truly? And why had he agreed to such an absurd demand?

He might have looked away then to shake hands with her father, but she couldn't tear her eyes from him. She knew that form, had felt it pressed against her in passion just days before. She had felt the bunching muscles of his back, his arms, his chest. She'd felt the calluses of his hands sliding up her arms, drawing shivers with every inch he touched her. Had felt them on her legs, touching her in places she wanted to allow no other.

Thinking about what he had done to earn his body set her insides aflame as much as touching it had done. She had stolen kisses as much as decorum allowed in Boston, but it was nothing compared to Duke. Standing there in the church trembling in passion for the man down the aisle from her, she felt she might burst into flames right there in the church.

And she wondered. She wondered if now, as man and wife, he would wish to feel her again, or if the bonds of matrimony would cool his desire once and for all.

For all her confident words, she felt the flush crawl up her face, her ears. His hard eyes flickered to her once more, then away.

Once next to her, she felt the wall between them. Aside from the one soul-piercing look when he had arrived, he hadn't so much as spared her another glance.

She worried through the ceremony, speaking the words she was asked. Once her father returned, would Duke take his leave? Would he treat her with respect when her father wasn't here?

And another thought, one which she couldn't help but give power to: Would he ever kiss her again like he had the first time?

She stumbled through her vows, still trembling. Trembling with fear, desire, anticipation.

Duke was sure, proper with his words. He was as steady with his vows as he was with a gun.

"You may kiss the bride."

"Cheyenne?" Duke's voice pulled her back to attention, snapped her eyes to his. Her stomach fluttered. She felt she could lose herself in those eyes. They saw everything.

See me, she thought. *Please, see* me *as I truly am. See us for what it could be.*

If he had heard her, he didn't say, but he was gentler than he'd ever been with her, taking her hands in his and drawing her near. Her heart hammered in her throat, feeling every moment of anticipation welling up within her.

When he kissed her, she expected a chaste embrace to match his coldness toward her, but as soon as his lips were on hers, she felt the power rush between them again. It felt like the night in the clearing again, the intensity wrapping itself so tightly around her she thought she might choke.

And so he lingered on her lips perhaps longer than was appropriate as their mouths remembered what they had nearly forgotten in their memories in the days since. He took her chin with his thumb and index finger and tilted her head back so he could have a deeper drink from her lips, and her heart did a slow, unsteady turn at the motion. This didn't feel like the kiss from a man who would disappear into the shadows when the first opportunity presented itself.

When they finally pulled away, Duke's hard eyes had been softened at the corners. They lingered on her as his lips had, searching for something in her face.

The pastor chuckled and said something about their being blessed with many children, and Duke's eyes hardened again, and he turned away from her.

Chapter 23

Cheyenne had never been afraid of the dark or of being alone, but she felt it intensely now. Frustrated by that feeling of weakness, she gritted her teeth and set about her evening ablutions. That done, she sought out Anna, but no one stirred in the hall. It was too late. Had Anna expected Duke to undress her? Now that she was married, Cheyenne didn't know what was proper or expected any longer. Her mother was not here to tell her, and she would die before she asked her grandmother.

With Anna likely asleep, Cheyenne was tasked with undressing herself by herself. It was late, she was tired and had a headache.

The ties of the corset she was able to somewhat manage by twisting her body while she looked in the mirror. She could step out of her pantalettes and her hoop, which she hung over her dressing table chair. But once she tried to remove her overdress, she found she was stuck. Not to worry, she would just wiggle out the other way. But the dress wouldn't budge. Not one to give up easily, she tried to hitch the dress over a chair and have it help pull the offending garment from her. Then, the corset slid partway off, and then her arms were jammed in the air. She tried the chair again.

But her dress didn't move. She was stuck. How on earth did Anna manage this with her every night and make it seem so easy?

She huffed out a huge breath and tried to wriggle herself free once more. Something must've gotten off-kilter because she was suddenly being stabbed by something. And oh, my, that hurt! What was that?

Not a minute after she'd cried out, the door to the bedchamber burst open. She turned toward the sound.

From what she could see through the gauzy layers of fabric, Duke was frozen in the entry to her rooms, assessing the situation. He was dusty again, but he didn't seem remiss at the sight of her own untidy rooms. He studied her and the pickle she was in. Where had he been? He probably thought she was already abed—coward.

"Oooh! Oof!" It looked like he was trying to hide a smile when she bumped into the privacy screen she should have been disrobing behind.

"Are you alright?" his cautious voice asked.

Cheyenne froze with her arms stuck awkwardly in front of her. This was just perfect. What a time for Anna to be unavailable.

If she didn't ask for help, it might be some time before she could get her own self undressed and out of duress. And images of being stuck that way all night long didn't comfort her either.

"I find myself stuck," she finally said.

Duke was silent, his face carefully blank now. Smart of him.

"Will you help me?"

There was a note of panic in her voice that didn't make him

feel better. Had he come upon his woman at a brothel in such a state, he might've helped her quickly remedy the situation, but with Cheyenne? He felt like he was watching a horse with its leg caught in wire. Why it would actually pain him in such a way when the situation should have been comical or nothing at all, he did not know. And not knowing was an easy slip into anger. Perhaps she had orchestrated this to get his attention? No matter that he was already coming upstairs to see what she was up to. Even that he had wanted to come see her irked him. Why couldn't he stay away from her?

"You think I don't understand how girls like you are?"

And now he was interrogating her while she was stuck. How ungentlemanly. "If you think I'm fast and loose, you've come to the wrong place. I might enjoy what we've been doing together, but don't mistake my eagerness with you for eagerness with others."

She stood there in her half undressed state staring at him while he stared back at her, though she had to bend at an awkward angle to look at him through the top of her gown. "This is ridiculous. I need help."

"Can you not, ah, charm yourself out of this?"

Her laughter was muffled by the acres of fabric. The sound of it touched him unexpectedly. He wondered what else could make her laugh, could rile her humor instead of her stubbornness.

"No," she laughed. "No, I cannot. I rue the day that I was not given simple magic with which to reheat my tea, lace my own boots, or charm myself out of clothing predicaments. I may summon the otherworldly, but I will always be bound to the hearth to heat my tea."

He sighed. That was sense he couldn't argue with. He

approached her warily, though, unsure where to start.

"Where do I begin?" he asked, as though he were being asked to perform surgery.

She might've shrugged. As it was, the towering pile of fabric and lace only briefly moved up and then back down. "Anywhere. I believe some of the buttons have become caught and the corset needs to be loosened considerably."

"Where is your girl to do this for you?"

"Asleep, as I would like to be. I thought I needn't wake her for such a simple task, then I thought perhaps she had done it on purpose."

"On purpose? Does she pull tricks on you so often? I have heard of staff fired for less than that." And on that note, Duke snapped his mouth shut. Best not give away too much of what he knew of finer living. He would prefer to keep the rebel cowboy act up. Forever, if he could manage it. There were some things that Cheyenne Goodnight never needed to know.

There was a shuffling and shimmying within the many layers of fabric, and even in her state, she was stunning, her pretty stockinged feet and ankles now revealed from under her dress.

"Certainly not," Cheyenne replied hotly. "Anna is a gem. I meant only that…well, that it was my wedding night. I didn't know if a husband was meant to do…this," she finished very quietly.

They stood there in the stillness those words created. Then, gingerly, Duke began to shift and pull the layers wrapped around Cheyenne. How had she managed to get herself this trapped? Carefully, he freed buttons caught on lace, and corset strings somehow wrapped about fabric. He felt her shivering under his hands, and the more he uncovered of her, the more he felt himself drawn to her yet again. Again and again and again.

Cheyenne's skin was afire as he went about his task with sure and gentle hands. The man could've been a surgeon his hands were so steady. To be so sure a shot, she reasoned, one must have steady hands.

Each ghost of a touch reminded her of how fiery their passion for each other could be. She wanted that again, dammit, wanted to feel him touch her that way now that he was her husband. Or had that taken the game from it for him? She wanted to ask, but she didn't know how.

As he peeled back another layer of fabric, their eyes met, steel to fire, and she felt the pull of his gaze deep in her belly, in the place between her legs which ached for him now. She thought of his hands on her breasts, his fingers sliding inside her, and her knees grew weak with want.

"Your eyes are haunting," he said.

"Yours reveal far too little," she replied, but still she was captivated by them. Did the man ever let his guard down?

"I would be dead now without my guard up at all times."

The magic she had felt at his touch waned, the passion began to cool. "Is everything about life and death for you? Where is the middle ground? Where is living?"

He scoffed as he gently unlaced her corset to free her further. The feel of her clothing under his fingers took him back to their time in the sitting room, the feel of her thighs slick with her own desire against his skin. He grew hard thinking about it. He could have her, he knew, but he had grown wary of her. It was after their kiss in the church, a kiss which was not the chaste one he had been prepared to give her. She was just too damn bewitching. He was an animal, after all, perhaps he sensed that her…skills…were a threat. She might've joked about turning him into a rabbit, and he might've pushed her initially, but he didn't really want to find out if she could. He could admit that he was frightened of her, in a way. It was a healthy respect for a creature who was dangerous, who could harm him should she wish it. It was why men avoided rattlesnakes and scorpions in the desert, why reaching one's hand under a rock without looking first was a sure way to a quick death. He had no intention of touching this woman again without first looking and regarding very carefully.

"Living is life and death," he said. He was rewarded with a huff from her. "You disagree?"

She stilled when his fingers brushed her skin again. He must be able to feel the passion he ignited in her. "No, but you don't have to make it sound so dramatic. I understand you're a scout, a marshal, but you chose that life. There are far more dangerous occupations."

"Than tracking and killing people?"

"You're doing it again!" Cheyenne huffed. "Dramatic!" she said as Duke was finally able to pull the offending garment fully from her. With it came her shift.

And then she was naked in front of him. Her entire body tingled with his touch still. Even though he'd kept his fingers mostly away from her, she could feel him all over her skin. Those calloused fingertips which made gooseflesh fly all over her in an instant. Those fingertips which must burn for what of her. They must. For how could he not feel the way she did?

His gaze was doing the same thing now. She could feel his hands all over her. Could feel his fingers inside her again. She quaked with the memory of it, nearly brought to the pinnacle of pleasure simply from his eyes on her, appraising her nude form.

She was stunning. Her golden skin which would never be the creamy milk that so many men thought they desired. The wild hair and even wilder eyes which both pleaded and commanded, which would have and must have caused an uproar in polite society. Those men knew nothing. They knew nothing of beauty.

Her hair was a wild thing after her fight with the garment, all frazzled dark curls cascading over her shoulders and over her breasts. He longed to dive his hands into it as he had done in the days past. But now? Now he was chained to her in this place until her father returned. That was no way to kindle passion. She didn't know that he could give her nothing but dust and a broken heart. He would spare her that pain.

He reached for her, then drew away.

Cheyenne looked like she had been shot. In an instant, her eyes shot sparks at him, and she reached for her dressing gown, which she wrestled on with her back turned to him. If he didn't like the sight of her, he could just say so. He didn't have to stand there raking his eyes over here just to decide that he didn't want what he saw any longer.

"I'll sleep elsewhere tonight," Duke said coolly.

"I'll not have you sleeping on your feet or the floor on my account. Besides, shouldn't we be sharing a bed? You are my husband," she said just as coolly. Two could play at this game.

"I thought you couldn't stand me."

"That's you. I'm perfectly able to sleep next to a person."

Silence.

"Will you leave when my father returns?" she asked, more for her own selfish wishes than to hear the answer she knew he would give.

"Why should I do otherwise?" Duke asked, as though his leaving were a matter of fact.

The absolute certainty of it hurt her. It surely was only because he didn't know her. She could—would!—turn this around. She would find a way.

"So, what is it?" she asked, trying to temper the coolness in her voice. She had to regain control over her emotions if she wanted to win his affections. "What is it that drags you away from here? Or who?"

"You wouldn't understand." And he wouldn't let her goad him into either a shouting match or telling her the truth.

"If there is another woman, you have only to tell me. I want nothing to do with competing affections. I would rather marry Sheriff Monroe than stand between you and your great love. Leave if you must. I can throw myself at a man and beg to be his wife. I would do that to sever you from this place if it pains you to be here."

That idea irked Duke in a way he didn't like. He didn't particularly *want* to let Cheyenne go be with anyone else even if that's what was good for her. That absurdity was not lost on him, but the truth of it only served to rile him further. "Don't be foolish," he said. "What's done is done."

What was he doing? She had just given him permission to leave, and he hadn't taken it. Had she truly enchanted him, and was just testing her powers now? But no.

"You act as though my very presence pains you," Cheyenne said. "And yet when I tell you I will find my way if you were to leave, you refuse. I know not what to make of it."

Duke clenched his fists and turned away from her. "I will sleep in the sitting room."

And then he quietly let himself into the adjoining room,

leaving Cheyenne to tuck herself into bed for what she knew would be a restless night. Duke Channing was a puzzle with pieces that didn't fit together.

Cheyenne pulled herself in a ball under her cold covers and squeezed her eyes shut. *Oh, Mother, if this is what you meant, I wish you would have told me. This is no life to lead. But if there is any saving this, please, please lend me your strength.*

Chapter 24

Heartache was her new and constant companion each morning when she opened her eyes. She wished for a word that would convey the confusion she felt with Duke and the worry she felt at her father leaving, but it escaped her.

Her days together with Duke swam behind her eyes constantly. She pored over the memories, seeking the answers to the questions she didn't even know. Did he or didn't he care? It seemed that there were moments that he did, that the passion she felt was reciprocated. It was certainly reciprocated in the bedroom...or the prairie grasses, as they were wont to do.

But did he care?

She analyzed every second, going over it all again and again, and all it left her with was no answers and a headache. And still Duke slept in the room adjoining her. He was a perfect gentleman when they were forced to be together, but she didn't miss that he avoided touching her skin. Any small brush from her gave him a start. Not knowing what to do about it, she tried to keep her distance. She didn't want to frighten him, to force him to be near her, but he appeared at her side nonetheless, choosing to be there while upset that he was there at all. If her father noticed, he said nothing.

The morning before her father left, she went into her clearing and put together a small charm that he could carry with him. She had made them for them both before they'd come here. In Boston, she had stolen away into the wooded section of the park they lived near and did what she could with what little the city green space had to offer. Here in the wild of the West, she had everything she needed. This time felt different, though. This time felt much more dire and much less like an adventure.

"This is a charm to protect you," she said quietly later that morning, pressing the leather bag into her father's hand.

"You are exactly like your mother, you know," Isaac said as he tucked the gift into one of the saddlebags. "Always giving, always thinking of others."

Cheyenne laughed through her tears, "You have mistaken me for someone else. I am selfish yet."

Isaac smoothed his daughter's hair as he had done each day since she was a baby, and Cheyenne closed her eyes and remembered every single one of those moments. She would cherish this one most of all.

She could feel Duke's eyes on them as he watched from a few paces off. Her heart did its slow turn as it did when she caught him watching her. She looked away until her father moved to shake hands with Duke.

"My daughter has you to thank for her protection while I am away," Isaac said pointedly.

Duke wisely kept his mouth shut about Cheyenne being able to care for her own self quite sufficiently. He bowed low to Isaac Goodnight. "She is under my protection until your safe return."

Goodnight gave Duke a glance at that, perhaps sensing the meaning behind those words. Duke stared back, almost wishing the man would challenge him there. But no, he would not kill an honorable man in a gunfight. Not unless he shot first.

And then her father left. He rode away on his horse packed up with goods enough to reach Kansas City. He would ride hard on the trail, taking whatever back trails he could and riding the main thoroughfares when there was traffic to help hide him. She watched his horse disappear over a hill, helpless to his plight. She wished for some comfort, but none came.

Her lips still burned from the kisses Duke had given her at the wedding—if one could even call it that. But he had kept his distance since then, and she didn't' know if he would simply leave now that his promise was fulfilled, and her father was gone from sight.

He watched her from a few paces off, his stance that of the gunfighter she knew him to be. Arms crossed over his chest, legs spread. He looked relaxed, but to Cheyenne, who had studied the wolf and the coyote and the other animals which had stalked them on their way here, she knew that he was poised for battle. Poised for attack. His job as a marshal had been crafted just for him, Cheyenne thought. He was a man born to do what he did—take out the troublemakers, make them pay for their transgressions against the country by any means necessary, all while being accountable to himself and only himself. And holding onto whatever great love he held somewhere in his bitter heart.

"Duke," she said, not knowing what to say next. What was

their plan? What would they do if the McLaurys mounted their attack before her father came back with reinforcement? What if they followed him on the trail and killed him?

"Duke?" She said again, a hot panic clawing at her throat as she thought more of the dangers of her father leaving the relative safety of Warren.

"My cars are working fine," he replied, not moving from his spot. He was brooding, she saw, and the dark shadows which passed over his handsome face made her want to make him tell her what troubled him so.

"What do we do now? I'm worried that if my fa—"

"We go about our ways," he said. And then to the look of surprise on her face, he said, "I will not stray far, *wife.* Worry not." And then he turned around and walked away.

Cheyenne, not wanting to stick around for a crowd, fled inside and up to her rooms.

She hadn't expected to miss her father so instantly and so intensely. And she refused to entertain any notion that he might not return. He would get help, and he would return. That was that. And if Duke left when he returned, Cheyenne would go back to the way things were before Duke.

Alone in her rooms, she didn't know what to do. Where had Duke gone? Would he be back? Could she even trust that he would be back? Could she keep her worry in check?

She knew what fate was, and now she knew what lust felt like, but what about love? She had concentrated so hard on her mother's first and last words to her, believing that things would fall into place immediately, that she hadn't given any thought to the notion that fate, perhaps, didn't mean love. The thought turned her stomach sour. She'd built up a fantasy in her head with love at first sight followed by everlasting love.

And what was that built upon? Clouds in the sky, apparently. Sand, washed away by the sea. Ice, melted into water, then nothing.

And for the first time in her life, she regretted that she remembered every moment of her waking life.

She fell into a fitful sleep on the rug by the hearth, her only pillow her tears and her wounded vanity. What had she thought? That her beauty and body alone would keep Duke Channing interested? That he would want to stay to keep stoking at the passion they had between them? Or would he take a sampling of her and then leave? She should have turned him into a rabbit when she first saw him. She should have turned the dreamwalkers on him when she had them take the McLaurys.

But, no. That wasn't Cheyenne Goodnight's way.

In her fitful sleep, she dreamed. In her dreams, Duke was touching her, kissing her, devouring her. His lips seared the delicate skin of her neck, burned over her shoulders while his hands gripped her arms so hard it hurt. Her sleeping mind showed her what it would feel like for his mouth to taste her everywhere, to taste her in the most delicate of places. Oh, she had seen the erotic drawings, had imagined more than enough, but in her dreams, it felt so much more real.

She woke with a gasp, then covered her mouth with her hand.

But there was no one else in the room to hear her.

Angry at her disappointment, she stood and stole out into the dark in her nightdress. Danger be damned, she would find herself again in the night, under those brilliant stars. The night which woke the magic in her. The night which refilled her very soul. There, she could speak with her Creator. There, she would repair her broken heart.

Chapter 25

He didn't expect to find her out under the moonlight again, but then again, he realized how much he had to learn about this woman who was now his wife. He had met her in moonlight once; he should have expected it again.

Wife. What a word. It twisted like a knife in his guts.

He kicked at a rock in the road, then cursed his action. He'd gotten careless during his scouting, making too much noise, not paying as close of attention to his surroundings as he should have.

He was forgetting his mission, forgetting himself, in this drama with Cheyenne. He should be patrolling the area more thoroughly, should have already come up with most of a plan. The longer he—and Brogan—let these ruffians settle in, the harder it would be to remove them.

Duke watched her from a distance in her clearing. She must've known he was there, for she stopped her dancing and sat in the grasses, her back to him. In her white nightgown, she was like a ghost. A shiver hit him. He had seen his share of ghosts on the trail—every man did—but that she might be an apparition struck him. Perhaps this entire town was only a mirage. He'd seen enough of those in the deserts of the southwest. Hot and thirsty days as a boy playing in the dust and sand, one saw things. Ghosts, spirits, demons, whatever one wanted to call them. He knew better than to disrespect them. Let them be, they'll let you be. He wasn't afraid of spirits, but he did have a mighty respect for them.

But he wasn't letting Cheyenne Goodnight be. Cheyenne Channing. He winced.

He didn't want to admit that he was afraid to touch her again. Whatever she had done to him, it had seared him to his very soul, had nearly cloven him asunder. And whatever that was, he had to get away from it quickly.

He walked closer to her, drawn to her fire. Part of him sounded an alarm, a warning before he was burned beyond saving.

When he was near, she turned and faced him. Her hair was down, and the long, curling locks stood out starkly against the pure white of her nightgown. He knew what it felt like to touch those locks, and though his mind told him to run, another part of him wanted his hands in her hair again.

"You find me again in moonlight, Mr. Channing."

"I would have thought you would drop the formality by now. You did earlier today."

"I would if I knew better the person to whom I am wed. I'm shocked that you even care," Cheyenne said bitterly.

"I said I would protect you. I don't intend on letting you get hurt in your father's absence."

"This town is much more mine than it is yours," she retorted.

"I am here on assignment," he hissed in return. God, the woman knew how to crawl right under his skin. "I am here to remove the ruffians from this area. By any means necessary.

By chaining myself to Isaac Goodnight's daughter if I must. And I did."

Cheyenne didn't lash back at the barb, though it stung her hard enough. "What a coincidence. I am here to bring peace as well," she said.

Duke laughed. "You? You mean your father and the arsenal he has at his disposal?"

When Cheyenne looked at him with surprise and heat in her eyes, he continued. "Don't think I missed those crates we walked by the first night I was here. I know those manufacturers. They make fine gunpowder, fine arms."

"And now that my father is gone for the moment, I will work in his stead."

"You might have your...skills," Duke said, "but do you have the training to organize the town in such a fashion? And what makes you think they will listen to you?" And he recalled what her father had said of his daughter, the faith he had in her. The trust. That was something he did not abide by, Duke knew. Trusting no one had kept him alive until now. He didn't need to start before he left again.

"I can make them listen," she said, her eyes glowing green.

"Somehow, that does not seem the manner in which you would convince them."

Her eyes dimmed, and the ghost of a smile tugged at her lips. "You're right. I wouldn't. Knowing that I could terrifies me enough, but using my power for personal gain like that...I can only imagine the repercussions I would face. I can only show them my passion for this town, share my father's strategies, and hope that they feel the same."

"You would sacrifice yourself for this town," Duke said. "Those men are not men who listen to reason."

"I can pick up a gun, then. I am not shy."

No, Cheyenne was certainly not that.

Chapter 26

Though his words stung, Cheyenne didn't want to deny that she enjoyed this banter with Duke. He challenged her in many good ways, but most of the wrong ones too. But if she wanted him to share more of himself, shouldn't she share herself, too? Anxiety squeezed her stomach at the thought.

Cheyenne sat in the grass and patted the ground beside her, feeling nervous. "Come. Sit."

Duke hesitated, and as he stood above her, half blocking the stars from view, Cheyenne felt the power of him, the maleness which he exuded just by existing. She reached out to gently touch his leg. This time, he did not flinch.

"Sit with me."

With a grunt, he finally did, leaning back on his elbows next to her.

"Can I tell you about my magic?"

Duke's eyes found hers, and the starlight reflected there made his steel eyes seem to glow. "What about it?"

"Where it came from."

Duke looked up to the stars, "I like a good story."

"It isn't just a good story. It tells how I came to be."

He looked back at her, and Cheyenne could have sworn there was a smile on his face. "Is it not still a story even if it is true?"

She mulled over that, pulling her dressing gown closer around herself. She didn't want to let Duke see her now. Where she had not felt modesty before, she felt it now after his eyes looked through her.

"We came from the stars."

"That makes no sense."

"Will you let me tell my tale?"

He said nothing.

She looked back up at the sky, letting the glittering mass above her soothe her aching heart. She let the sight of the twinkling firmament fill her up. It was more than any man could do for her; she was convinced of that now. Duke could do more…if he let himself.

"Long ago. So long ago, they did not write down what was done because they had no writing, my people lived far north of here. Once, long ago, a great land bridge connected this continent and the next."

Duke 'humphed' at that.

"My people were a small group then. Maybe seventy-five of them. Perhaps a few more. But that winter was harsh, and the bridge offered little more than whipping winds and wide-open plains.

"But the stars were brilliant.

"When food became scarce, my people cried out to the stars to help them.

"They could go no further. They had reached a wall of ice, a glacier that blocked either exit from the bridge. They could not go back the way they came, and they could not go forward.

With their bellies empty and their hearts desperate, they cried out. They cried out for help. They cried out with all the passion for life that their bodies had left. They sang to the stars for mercy. They sang to the wind, to the great grassy plains which they had traveled over. They sang for the dreams of their children, whom they had traveled this far with so they might find a better home for them.

"And something—someone—heard them. There was an answering call from the stars above. The night shook with the vibration of it. And the people cowered, thinking that the end had come for them.

"But it hadn't.

"The stars above granted the men among them the ability to shift, to become the wolves which lived in this grassy tundra. They were able to run further, faster, to find prey which as humans they could not. This they brought back to the women, who had received their own gifts of survival from the sky. From the stars, they received magic, magic which was borne of necessity. Magic which allowed them to protect the pack, to protect them from the elements, to protect them from the predators which followed. And the men were able to take those predators down, so they could feed their families.

"And the stars gave them a path through the glacier. It was slow going, and it was a hard path, but on the other side was a wide new world. A world of temperate forests, a world of wide-open grasslands as the glaciers receded. They did not all survive the passage, but those who did prospered in this new land."

Cheyenne waited for Duke to make a smart retort, but he didn't. He sat, rapt, now watching her as she told the story.

"They passed down their gifts and abilities. Though only

women received the magic and the men the wolf shifting, the women only passed the gift on through their sons, whose abilities became latent when there was no longer a need for their shifting."

"That means this gift was passed onto you from your father. Yet he is not a wolf?" Had he heard this story from anyone else, he wouldn't have believed it. But from Cheyenne, after seeing her magic, he had to admit that anything was possible now.

"He is not because the gift came to me. I have heard there are other families out there, from the wolf side, who bore great packs of wolves from the original line. But the magic only passes from mother to son to daughter. I will bear a son who possesses no magic, nor any wolfishness. He will, in turn, bear a daughter who knows magic."

Duke flinched at the mention of a child. Cheyenne quickly tried to cover. "I meant only if I have a child. Should I bear one, it will be a son."

"Sounds like your destiny is written in stone."

"In the stars, yes."

Duke felt suddenly angry at her tale. How was he supposed to believe in destiny and fate when his siblings had been taken from him at such a young age? When if he'd made a different decision, he would have an entirely different life? His decision had taken his siblings from him. And yet here lived Cheyenne, so certain that her destiny was written in stone that she did not question it. She believed unquestionably. It was maddening.

"I don't think there's any place for me in all this anyway. You ought to stick to your own kind if this is the kind of life you want."

Cheyenne laughed. Shocked, Duke turned to look at her.

It hadn't been a laugh of humor, though. No, this had been a cold laugh. "You are so always on the lookout for death that you have no intention of ever living, do you?"

"When you live a life as I've lived, you learn that there is no such thing as happy endings."

"Or any sort of happiness?"

He said nothing.

"You've found no happiness here?"

"Nothing that I'm sure is lasting."

He could see her arched eyebrows even in the dark. "It's as though with every movement of your mouth you wish to insult me. When you are not claiming my lips with a kiss. Do you detest me or not?"

He didn't answer her.

Fickle, she wanted to call him, but it wasn't that. He was scared, perhaps, insecure.

"What in life thrills you?" she asked.

He looked up at the stars, then at her. "You do."

The answer was honest, and it seared right through her, sent little shocks down her spine. "Because I am a woman or because I could kill you or turn you into a helpless creature?" she asked, trying to keep her tone light while her heart was trying to leap through her chest in anticipation.

"Both."

She didn't have an answer for that. "You are a complicated creature, Mr. Channing."

And so was she, she knew. Complicated, but sure. And why had she been sure? Because her mother had told her all those years ago that a man would come into her life? How could she be so certain that it was Duke Channing? It felt right, yes, but what if fated love still took work—from both parties?

She let out a long sigh and tipped her chin up to the stars. She longed to have them speak to her the way they must have spoken to her ancestors, to give her answers, to give her hope, to help her figure out the muddle she had gotten herself into with Duke Channing. She didn't know what to feel when every other word out of his mouth was to insult her, in between kissing her senseless and doing a number of other things to her which left her breathless *and* senseless.

"What do you want out of life, Duke?"

"To live."

"You are insufferable. You know you're living right now, right? You know that you are living every moment you draw breath?"

"And what do you want that you do not already have?" Duke shot back. "I could leave here, and you would remain happily in your town living your life as you had before me."

"I long to have your hands on me," she said, though the words strained from her mouth. "I have dreamt of you these nights. I cannot get you from my head. I want...I want you, Duke."

He stared at her with those unreadable eyes, eyes which she knew were capable of incredible fire, which surely could be filled with warmth if he let them.

Duke reached for her then and encircled her small wrist with his large fingers. He pulled her gently to him, so close that she could smell the remnants of the day on him: sunshine, dust, the prairie, man.

He bent his head to capture her lips in his, to nibble and suck on her bottom lip, sending tantalizing shocks through her system. His artful mouth knew somehow just what rhythm to find, to meet her slow passion with a slowness of his own.

Cheyenne gave into it, desperate to feel his hands on her, desperate to have him near her. If only he could read her passion, could feel what she could be for him in her kiss. If only, if only, if only. She thought it so hard that tears came to her eyes even as want for him coursed through her.

And when he pushed off her dressing gown and threaded his hands under her nightdress, she raised her arms up to the sky so that her skin might feel the night air, might feel him more closely against her.

Chapter 27

He lay her down in the tall grasses on her nightdress. The night and the soil still held the heat of the day. The grass rustled as they settled into it together. And Duke felt drunk on Cheyenne's presence.

Away from her, he could tell himself that this was a terrible idea, that he was as bad for her as she was for him. But when he was around her, it was as though the entire world fell away from them. All that mattered was the passion she ignited in him, that roared into being simply by the turn of her wrist or the fall of a wayward curl.

Cheyenne made noises of haste as she helped him with his own clothes. His shirt, his trousers. And when she beheld him, she reached for his manhood, grasped his hardness gently in her hand.

At his gasp, Cheyenne began to stroke him slowly, maddeningly slowly. But he didn't want to tell her to move faster—her hand felt too good, too damn *right*. She explored him with curious hands, sliding up and down his shaft and hitting spots which he'd never known could be so sensitive. Until now. Until Cheyenne.

But he wouldn't have his release until he'd felt every inch of her body. He took her hands and pressed her back onto the ground and began his own exploration.

Her silken skin was like butter under his hot hands and melted just as fast. She arched up underneath him, bending when he pushed, moving with him wherever he wanted. And he was drunk on the power he felt over her. If she had enchanted him, if she had trapped him in a dream, he almost didn't wish to wake. And when she was naked before him like this, he didn't care how quickly she could bewitch him. He just had to have her, as though he might die if he didn't.

His best horse was a wild colt he'd broken with turns of gentleness and a firm hand. Cheyenne might not be tamed, but she answered his firmness with pliancy, answered the demands of his hands with great sighs of pleasure. He had the feeling that even for her boastful words, she had not experienced like this before. Even for the confidence and surety of her person, she became a student under the tutelage of his hands.

In the moonlight, she moved with him, soft hands touching the tensed muscles across his chest and abdomen. Slow and methodic, then, upon being seized with pleasure, she set her nails into him, marking him.

And for the first time in his life, Duke cried out in passion, lost within the haze of lust and want that surrounded both of them.

Duke knew a few things now. West was where the sun set. Storms rolled in from the south. The stars were a man's truest guide, and moonlight became her.

The heat of the summer night glistened all over her. Pearlescent moonlight highlighted the golden dips and swells of her body which heaved with want with each breath.

Even for a witch, she couldn't have conjured the heat he felt between them. Even the sweat he licked from the underside of her breast was hot. Her breath came in ragged gasps, and she whispered his name like a chant, hands roaming his body with the open curiosity of the inexperienced who have wanted for too long.

And if she wished to torture him with words from her smart mouth, he would return the favor with his hands.

Gently he cupped the mound between her legs, feeling the soft hair there, feeling how ready she was for him. She gripped his arms so tightly, he thought he might see crescent moons from her nails the next day. He didn't mind. Not now when he held dominion over her, when he held her release cupped in his hand.

She mewled when he slid two fingers into the wetness between her legs. It took no longer than a handful of seconds before she was shuddering with release beneath him and around his fingers.

Her emerald eyes saw only him, and they shone in the starlight.

"Take me, take me," she begged, her hands grasping at his muscled forearms which were slick with sweat. Even that touch made him want her more.

"I'm a bad man, Cheyenne," he said, though the threat felt empty.

Her eyes glittered, "You are a man who made choices as we have all made choices. You are my man."

Duke plunged into her. She cried out and arched against him.

He expected it to feel the same. He expected to seek his release immediately and be done with this coupling until he wanted again.

But nothing with this woman was what he expected.

He fit perfectly within her, and she squeezed his cock with each roll of her hips. Waves of pleasure carried him away, wave after wave of it which was her slickness and her thighs pressed hard against him and her hands holding him down to the earth.

She wrapped her legs around him as he quickened the pace. Something within him said he had to have her then, that he couldn't be entwined with her closely enough. Beneath him, her eyes were closed, her head thrown back in ecstasy, those dark locks spread against the night prairie.

And in the moment of his release, when he cried out with her, she opened her eyes and looked right into his heart. Her brilliant emerald eyes that knew that all would be right in the universe, eyes which trusted in the very things which he did not. Eyes that captured his heart in that very instant, eyes that told him he would never be his own man again. Not now that he was hers and she his.

And he knew he would never be the same again.

Chapter 28

Something had changed in Duke. They fell into a sort of rhythm sharing space with each other, sharing Cheyenne's bed and every dark and secluded corner. Each couldn't keep their hands off the other.

But Cheyenne didn't speak of love and fate, and Duke didn't speak of leaving. The unanswered questions between them grew. Each could feel it, but each kept their secrets to themselves.

One morning Cheyenne walked into town to see what was new in the Leonards' shop, but once she heard the gossip going around, she turned around and went right back up to her living quarters.

When she walked in, Duke was hard at work in a chair by the heart in the sitting room, cleaning his firearms. She watched him quietly, catching him in an oddly vulnerable moment while he did something that he so obviously loved.

"I suppose if I suggested that you let the staff clean your pieces, you would decline," Cheyenne said softly.

Duke turned to look at her. "You think right," he said.

Oh, how handsome he was, Cheyenne thought. His white shirt was half unbuttoned, long sleeves pushed up to his elbows while he was hard at work. His hair was still mussed from their lovemaking that morning. And, perhaps the most charming, his stockinged feet, free of his boots, being toasted by the fire even though the day promised to be hot.

Cheyenne gave the man in front of the fire a brilliant smile. "I need to meet with the sheriff. I'd like your help."

Duke set down the firearm he had been cleaning. "Of course. What is it that you need?"

"I heard today that a great tree had been dragged across the road at the entrance to town. They must've needed at least a pair of strong horses to do it as quickly as they did. And the young deputy who would usually be patrolling that area—Ingraham, you know—they haven't heard from him in several days."

"He didn't tell you or the sheriff he was going somewhere?"

She shook her head.

Duke had wondered if all the McLaurys would begin to see if they could poke holes in the town once they realized Isaac Goodnight was gone. But whether they knew or not, this was only the beginning.

"After we speak with the sheriff, I need to go scout," Duke said as he shoved his feet into his boots and began to lace them. "I must know for myself if there is a change in the ruffian camp, or if they have added to their numbers."

"I'm going with you," Cheyenne said, then knelt to help him finish lacing up his boots.

"Like hell you are. And get up, you shouldn't be down there lacing my boots. It's not right."

Cheyenne kept at his boots, tying them so they weren't too tight but not too loose. "I'm going with you."

"You aren't a scout," Duke said, softer this time. "Thank you.

My back aches something terrible today. That helps me."

She could feel him watching her there, kneeling at his feet. He had squeezed her heart with his thanks, though her intention had only been to help him, not to make him thank her.

"Tell me what I need to do then," she said as she straightened one trouser leg down over a boot.

"You must be quiet."

"I can be silent."

Duke looked her up and down. "You must not be seen. And in those clothes, you'd be spotted in a moment."

Cheyenne looked down at her red skirts, then up at Duke. "I would wear my riding habit, which is brown silk."

"And still cumbersome, I imagine? And flashy?"

Cheyenne thought over her wardrobe. She did have a few pieces from when they were traveling, so as not to look like an easy target on the road. "I have simple prairie dresses."

"That would be better, though this isn't up for discussion as you aren't coming with me."

"How do you know so much about women's fashion?" And as soon as she said it, she realized that a man like him, on the road for so long, would be intimately familiar with women's fashions. She felt herself blush before she could stop it, a feeling she was not used to in the slightest.

Duke's smile didn't help, his lips curving into a devious grin that had her rapt. He had been so attentive in the week since their coupling under the full moon. He reached down and took her chin between his thumb and forefinger. The look he was giving her was positively wolfish.

"I can find a pair of my father's trousers. A shirt. I would blend in better that way," she sputtered.

141

"You aren't coming with me," Duke said as he stood and offered her a hand.

"Try to stop me," Cheyenne said as he helped her stand.

Duke bit back another retort. He didn't doubt that she would follow him, whether he said she could or not. He gritted his teeth. Isaac Goodnight had known exactly what he was doing conning Duke into this. Watch his daughter? It would be all he could do to stop her from running herself right off a cliff, magic or no.

"Fine. But there are rules."

"I can handle that."

Duke sighed, but he couldn't keep a smile from his face. Isaac Goodnight was a goddamn devious genius. "I am going to help you out of these clothes, and then you must find something else to wear. We're leaving in an hour."

Chapter 29

When he saw her next, she was a woman transformed. In the men's trousers, her legs sheathed in fabric, she was unbelievably arousing. She'd found suspenders to go with her outfit, complete with a tawny shirt that would hide her well in the prairie scrub. Her hair was still piled on top of her head, though, one wild curl trying to escape at her forehead.

Unable to stop himself, Duke reached out and touched the curl, then slid a hand to the back of her neck and drew her near. There was a wariness in her eyes. He didn't blame her.

He leaned in close and felt her hot breath sigh along his jaw. Though she wore a man's clothes, she smelled just like the wild prairie flower she was underneath her disguise.

Duke ran his hands down her arms, then over her hips which were suddenly much more easily felt in these clothes. Even though he had just had her, he wanted her again already as he explored her body in these new clothes.

"You would stir the blood of dead man, Cheyenne."

She smiled wanly at him. "Even in these clothes?"

"Especially in those clothes. Fine work. You'll hide well in the prairie brush."

"What now?"

"Now we plan."

And they did. They would take a little-used animal trail that Cheyenne knew about from her own rovings which would lead them to the far end of the McLaurys' last camp. If they were there, they would hang about to see how many of them were still around. If they weren't there, they would track them to their next destination.

"They used to get supplies in Leadville," Cheyenne said, "but we convinced them to quit serving them. Why are you staring at me?"

"That outfit. It's absurdly...provocative. Where would they go now?"

"Junction City, perhaps."

Duke finally asked the question which had been bothering him. "What about your magic?"

"What about it?"

"How could we use that to help us? I don't know what all your skills are. What all you can do."

"You've seen me conjure spirits. I can call upon any number of those. I can bring on fog. I can conjure fire. Many of the skills are those which aided the hunters in ancient times. Not all of them are useful today."

"Can you fly?"

Cheyenne cast her eyes to the ground.

"What? Can you or not?"

"Some of my ancestors were able to."

"But you cannot."

"No...not yet." But she didn't want to tell him that she needed a mate for that, that when they wed, she expected her powers to grow a hundred-fold. But they didn't. They had remained the same after their wedding day. It had created a hard knot in her stomach which followed her everywhere. She didn't know if it meant that Duke was not her true match, even for the surety she had felt that he was.

Duke sent a strange look her way, then cleared his throat. "What else can you do?"

"I can bring wind, can turn a man into any number of animals. Only one at once, though, and it takes a tremendous amount of my energy. If I do that too much, I am useless for a time."

Duke nodded, "Yes, you'd want to conserve your energy."

As they continued to plan, she felt Duke relax in her presence. She found she liked this planning, this crafting a plan, a strategy. It was like preparing for a hunt, she realized, like her ancestors would have done, but different, modern. She was using her powers as they had been intended, and it felt better than she could have ever known.

The thrill of the plan, the hunt, the chase coursed through her. Sometimes, she longed to know what it would be like to become a wolf as her male ancestors did, to feel the wind of the night through her fur. She was grateful for her magic, but still, she wondered.

At dusk, after they had spoken to the sheriff, they stole through town on silent feet.

Chapter 30

It wasn't until they were well out of town that Duke pinpointed something that was bothering him. He couldn't hear Cheyenne walking in the prairie grasses at all. Somewhat incensed that she was quieter than he when this was his profession, he said something.

"It is magic," she said simply. "I can silence you further."

"As a rabbit?"

He could feel Cheyenne's smile in the dark, and she laughed a quiet, throaty laugh that hit him right in his chest, then traveled further down to between his legs. "You would be quieter that way, yes. But I mean your footsteps as a man. I can make you silent like me."

"I'll allow it," he said reluctantly, "though I wish you would have told me you could do this when we were planning."

Cheyenne muttered quietly under her breath in what Duke thought was her reply until the wind around them stirred unnaturally. A curious sensation passed over his feet and legs. When it had passed and the wind died, he cautiously stepped onto a stick in the brush near him. It made no sound when it snapped under his foot. Feeling strangely giddy, he full-on jumped into the brush. Not a sound. He felt as he had as a boy, full of wonder for the world.

"Don't test it," Cheyenne admonished as she giggled. "Magic is an honorable venture, and only those who trust it may use it. We are hunters seeking prey; we need to be silent."

Duke stopped, endeared by her sincerity. "It really worked."

"Of course it did. Come, it won't last all night, though."

At the first camp, there was no sign of anyone. Duke dug through the ashes in a campfire and found them only warm when he stuck his hand all the way into their depths.

He took his hand from the ashes and looked over at Cheyenne. Her faintly glowing green eyes watched him in the darkness. Rather than be unnerved, he welcomed her night vision. It would give them a leg up on the McLaurys at night and keep them safe from snares, traps, and other more natural nightly foes. "They have been gone from here for nearly a day. No more."

"They would head south."

"Toward town?"

"Toward the river. Toward Junction City. But they would pass by us to do so, to see if anyone was paying attention."

"That's likely when they kidnapped Ingraham—if they took him and he's alive. They circle back around like vultures."

"I imagine so, yes."

"I must go to my commander and tell him all of this as soon as it's light."

"Let us find Ingraham first. I want to know if he is alive. I don't want my father to return and think I have let the town go the ruffians."

"That might give the army more incentive to move in," Duke mused. "If we had proof that he was alive and they had captured him. We need to report any actions such as this. Build a case against them."

"You think he's alive?"

"I can almost guarantee it. The McLaurys want men to vote for them. They only kill when threatened."

They moved on, making good time in the darkness. Not half a mile from town, Cheyenne pulled on Duke's sleeve. "Look, there." She pointed off to the east. "Can you see it?"

Duke squinted into the darkness, but he saw what she meant. A tiny pinprick of orange within a copse of trees.

In silence, they moved through the grasses across the prairie. Duke stole glances at Cheyenne, but she was focused and silent, moving with intent. He admired her ability to focus on their task without prattering on. Come to think of it, he didn't think she ever prattered on about anything. He admired that about her, he found. He had always inevitably grown tired of the women in brothels who nattered on endlessly about the mundane. They were concerned about their hair and their attire and whether they had a new fan or the latest fashion. Cheyenne didn't seem to care. And Cheyenne said what she wanted to say, and succinctly at that, and that was all.

When they reached the camp, Duke heard more voices than he wanted to hear.

"Goddamnit," he growled.

Cheyenne threw him a questioning glance but didn't speak.

He pitched his voice low and bade her stop before they drew nearer. "There are too many of them. This does not bode well."

"Can you get him? Can you save Ingraham?"

Duke calculated in the dark. "I would like to try. I don't think they would give him up even if we had come in the day with a contingency from the army. They would only deny Ingraham's presence."

"I have my wolves," Cheyenne said.

"Only if things go awry," Duke said. "We are too outnumbered to start a fight with them. I can slip in for Ingraham and get back out without being noticed. But if there is a skirmish, please do…what you can."

In silence, they drew nearer to the camp, staying outside the light of the fires that had been lit. Cheyenne saw many faces she recognized from her two years in Warren, but there were many strange ones as well. And many more than she had expected.

Over across the camp, they saw a sagging figure tied to a tree. Ingraham. Cheyenne pointed in the direction of the form and Duke nodded. He saw, too.

"I am ready to summon the wolves if we need them," Cheyenne said.

Duke hesitated, finally asking the question he had been wondering. "Are they real?"

"No," she said. "We have not seen real wolves from my family tree for many hundreds of years now. These are simply their spirits."

"When they are distracted, I'll grab Ingraham. You must stay here undercover. They cannot see you."

"They will not see me," Cheyenne said. "I am the wind to them. They will not grasp me."

Duke hesitated, though. Suppose something should happen to Cheyenne? A strange knot formed in his stomach, and he reached for her in the dark. She let him pull her into his arms, let him pull her into a deep, lingering kiss, let his hands feel her through the strange clothing she wore. Pressed against him, she could feel his excitement for her, could feel the hardness of him between them. And in the desperation of his kiss, she wanted to feel that he kissed her in love.

When he pulled away, she looked up at him expectantly, but he did not say anything. But he touched her cheek gently with one rough hand, a hand that was hot and knew just how to touch her. With another soft touch at her jaw, he disappeared into the night. Cheyenne, full of questions and more hope than she could handle, leaned down to once again become part of the earth, to be ready to summon the things which the earth would give her.

Chapter 31

His footsteps were still silent as he traipsed around the camp. Duke chanced a look behind himself. He left no footprints even. A prickly chill washed over him which he tried to shake. Cheyenne would not do anything that would hurt him.

Near the center of the outer camp, Duke saw a dark form tied to a tree that had been stripped of its branches. It was a convenient place to tie those they captured, Duke thought darkly.

As he crept closer to the man, whom he recognized as he got closer, Duke felt eyes on him. Friend or foe, he was not certain. He needed to act quickly. He softly prodded the slumped figure and knelt to begin working at untying the man.

When Ingraham woke and saw him, his eyes grew wide. Duke made a gesture of silence.

The man next to Ingraham opened his eyes, and in a flash, Duke was grappling with him as the man called out. Once. Long and loud.

Duke took the man's bedroll and pressed it over his face while he sat on the man's chest. This was not a glorious death, nor was it one he would be proud of later. But to escape with his life and the deputy's? He did what he must.

The noise was enough that other men stirred. Duke looked at Ingraham, knowing that he was losing time for both of them to escape unharmed.

The sound of a hammer being cocked—a Navy, like his own—had him hitting the dirt as the shot rang out.

No time now.

Chaos ensued.

Duke stripped off his hat, grabbed the bedroll from the man he'd just killed, and wrapped himself in it. It was dark, so most all the men wouldn't know yet what had triggered the alarm. The next seconds were critical, and he hadn't survived war in the southwest just to get killed by a bunch of untrained ruffians.

Over the din, a howl arose from the darkness. It was the most unearthly sound Duke had ever heard. Even the wolves of the desert southwest hadn't howled so chillingly.

And then men were screaming.

At the far side of the camp, he saw one of the wolves, though it moved gracefully and didn't seem to ever touch the ground.

Another wolf slid by near him, lifting its head for a long moment to study him. Duke could not suppress a shudder at the beautiful creature. It did not seem quite real, as though it were made of smoke and ash instead of blood and bone and fur. Its eyes and the tips of its fur glowed a preternatural purple, and it studied Duke far longer than he liked. But whatever the animal saw in Duke, he did not see him as an enemy. He slid on through the camp and into the chaos.

Shots rang out from everywhere at once. Everyone would look like the enemy, Duke knew. He'd been awoken in the night during an ambush before and knew that initial panic could grab hold of a man if he wasn't trained for it. For weeks on end, his commanders had woken him from a dead sleep in the night to have him fire his gun at a target until he could do it without missing.

Duke slid through the dirt to reach for Ingraham, but the man's head flopped loosely against his shoulder. Blood spilled onto the ground around him. He felt around on the man's blood slick neck for a pulse and found a faint one, growing fainter still by the moment.

"Goddamnit!" Duke cursed for the second time.

The spirit wolves raced by them, snapping at the scrambling McLaurys.

Duke didn't want to holler for Cheyenne, but he didn't know if she possessed any kind of healing powers. What kind of witch would she be if she couldn't heal people? Isn't that what a lot of them did? With no frame of reference, he felt stuck. But he had to choose.

"I'm sorry," he whispered as he released the ties which bound Ingraham but left the man there. His wounds were too grievous. He wouldn't make it even if Duke had been able to get in and out silently.

A woman's scream split the night.

Pure terror ran through Duke. It was the sound his mother had made that day twenty years ago, a sound which was seared into his body forever.

The scream pierced the darkness and momentarily silenced everything else going on in the camp. Men's shouts died in their mouths, scuffling stilled.

The wolves stopped in their tracks and looked toward the west, surely where their mistress was being accosted at that very moment. The two near him growled, hackles raised, and ran off toward the sound of the scream. Duke took off a moment later. The remaining wolves ran with him, forming a protective shell around him.

Sick panic ran him straight through him, and for a moment, he was a child again, half-drowned and scrabbling for dry land while his mother screamed and screamed and screamed. He ran faster, pushing men and horses out of the way as the wolves snapped at anyone who dared get nearer to him.

When he came upon the scene, two of them had her arms and her eyes blazed with unearthly green fire. Duke could feel something coming, something that roared like a freight train, something that felt like a tornado, but she didn't need to destroy the countryside to rid herself of the men holding her.

Duke drew his guns and steadied his breath. The world around him fell away. Even the chaos quieted as he focused on the men holding his wife. *His* wife. *His* woman. He had made a vow to Isaac Goodnight, and he'd made a vow before God.

In the stillness that surrounded him, he aimed his guns. In another hair's breadth of time, he fired both of them together.

The explosion of the shots stilled everything except the wolves. In another instant the men standing on either side of her were hit between the eyes. They fell backward into the dirt, dead. The roaring sound stopped, and Cheyenne stood trying to draw breath.

Duke ran to her, feeling her over for wounds, keeping his touch as gentle as he would with a new foal.

"He hit me here," she gasped, setting a hand over her middle.

Duke could feel no blood, no ghastly wound. And yet his

heart still raced with fear for her. "He knocked the breath from you. Come," Duke said gently. "We have to leave this place."

"But Ingraham!"

"He's dead. They killed him," Duke said as he pulled her out into the darkness of the night prairie. They had to get to cover before they were captured themselves. What a goddamn disaster!

Chapter 32

She'd never felt pain like that before. It radiated from her chest and through to her back. She couldn't pull in a full breath.

Duke dragged her through the hazy predawn light and to a dugout nearby. It wasn't the safest place, but Duke wanted to make sure she wasn't maimed too terribly before they took the long way back to town. The wolves came loping back toward them one by one, tongues lolling.

"I should never have allowed you to come," Duke said as he pushed aside the scrubby bushes which had grown up around the dugout. The shelter was primitive, but it was shelter.

Cheyenne drew in shallow breaths, feeling that at any moment, she might faint. No, faintness was ladies pretending. This was a struggle to keep conscious, to keep awake.

Once inside, Duke lay her carefully down, gentler with her than he ever had been. He unbuttoned the man's shirt she wore slowly, and despite the pain, she felt desire for him. Perhaps it was the near-death experience and burst of energy that coursed through her body now, but she wanted the man who looked like he'd seen a ghost.

She tried to crane her neck to see her chest. And there,

between her breasts was a bruise the size of a man's fist. Its purple feathers spread to the sides of her breasts and down halfway to her navel. Duke placed a warm hand very gently over the bruise. "You will need to put cool water on this. Ice, when we get back into town. You will be sore for weeks."

Cheyenne took a shallow breath and slid his hand from the bruise to her left breast. "Touch me. Please."

"You're hurt."

"I know what I am. And I want you." She moved his hand over her breast, her nipple hardening under the touch.

"You are mad," he said in a rough voice, now tracing his fingers so gently around the puckered flesh of her breast.

She reached up and squeezed his arms, felt the heat of him through his sweat-soaked shirt. "Then fall into it with me."

"We have to leave."

"Take me first," she begged.

He couldn't tell her no.

Slowly, carefully, Duke undressed her from her strange clothes. It felt almost erotic that she wore no underthings beneath the man's shirt and trousers. Duke sucked in a breath when he slid the pants down and discovered this.

His eyes found hers, "You ran off into the wilderness with naught but a man's shirt and trousers." His voice held a kind of awe that she didn't know how to interpret.

"And suspenders," she said with a smile that turned into a grimace when she tried to laugh.

She reached to undress him, but he beat her to it, slowly shedding his clothes to reveal the muscle beneath. Muscle corded at his neck and in his arms as he reached overhead to finish removing his shirt. Dirt and sweat mingled on his skin. She reached for him, touched the firm muscle of his abdomen, counting the ripples of muscle there, then trailing her fingers upward to softly rake her nails over his chest. His sensitive skin there stiffened to attention, and he let out a little sigh of pleasure. She so loved finding the spots which made him sigh.

Duke returned the favor with his calloused hands, sliding his hands over her breasts, then dragging his fingertips in maddening circles around first one nipple, then the next.

The feeling of wanting to slip into unconsciousness faded the more aroused she became. Somewhere beyond her desire, she wondered why, why that might be.

He helped her stand and drew her naked body against his. Even for the passion in his kiss, he was gentle.

And then he turned her away from him so her backside was flush against his hips. She could feel the hard length of his arousal against her leg.

He pressed her back gently forward until she had to brace her hands and arms against the wall of the dugout, leaving her backside exposed to him.

Clever fingers found her lips and slid them apart, feeling the wetness there which would soon drip down her thighs. He parted her legs a little further, and then he eased up against her entrance with his hard length.

She gasped, "Yes!" and pushed back, wanting to take more of him.

He backed up slightly, laughing quietly. "You want all of this?"

"You're teasing me," she gasped as he slid just inside her again.

And suddenly, he thrust all the way into her, all the way to the hilt, and she cried out. He was quick to reach up and clasp a hand over her mouth.

"Shhhh," he whispered. "You must be quiet."

Oh, Lord, how can I be when he's doing this to me? His hand over her mouth only made her want him more, made her want to scream for the passion she felt building inside her. Passion. And love. Love for him, love for what he did to her. It filled her as much as he did in that moment.

"Now, please, now," she begged.

And so, he did. Taking her slowly, achingly slowly, his hands gripping her hips. He thrust slowly in, all the way, then all the way back to the tip. Again and again and again, never slower, never speeding up. It was all Cheyenne could do to stop herself from screaming with the pleasure of it.

"Oh, Duke! I'm…" And she shuddered around him as her arousal peaked, her muscles squeezing him tightly as she rocked against him through her orgasm.

And it felt like it should be impossible, but immediatcly after, it felt like she would crest against, that she was simply riding wave after wave of cresting pleasure. She felt golden, liminal, weightless. Her pain had disappeared into the haze of want for Duke, for the man who felt so right against her. Inside her.

And as he pressed into her while she was pressed against the wall of a dugout in the early morning light which finally shed light into where they were, she realized why she felt better, why all she felt now was the physical pain of the bruise and not the feeling that she had used so much power to bring the wolves. She drew her power from him. He was her strength and her rock.

Flushed with desire and full of him, Cheyenne cried out softly at her release. Her legs shook as her insides clenched him tightly, and he moaned with her.

"Cheyenne," he said softly. "Cheyenne." And with another moan, he filled her. She felt him twitch inside her with each thrust, felt him spill from her and drip down her thighs, mingling with her own arousal there.

Duke pulled himself from her slowly, and she moaned anew, her sensitive parts quivering with half-want.

He turned her gently and gathered her against his chest. She went quietly, wondering at this new Duke who had a tender spot for her within the heat and the passion. She didn't want the moment to end, so she didn't say anything.

"Did I hurt you?" he finally murmured against her hair.

She had forgotten about the bruise entirely. She took a tentative breath and winced. "No. I forgot entirely that I was injured. You have a way of making me forget what's going on around me."

He laughed quietly, and the sound rumbled through him and against her.

As the first rays of the sun peeked above the horizon, Duke released her and handed her her clothes. He turned his back while she dressed, which she found both endearing and silly at the same time. But she still said nothing. Duke wouldn't look her in the eyes. Could it be that he felt the same thing she was feeling inside? That he, too, felt the shift that happened between them overnight?

"Duke," she said, venturing to speak though her heart began hammering in her chest.

"We need to get back to town," he said from the entrance to the dugout. "And I need to get to Brogan. The McLaurys aren't going to stand for this."

"I'll come with you."

Duke finally turned to face her, his eyes hot with anger that

Cheyenne wasn't expecting. Feeling so vulnerable, Cheyenne took a step back, his glare hitting her right in her heart.

"No, you'll stay in town. It's my fault that you're hurt."

"Duke, I could fall from my horse tomorrow and break my neck simply riding through town, I…"

"Enough." He cut her off. His eyes looked sorrowful and angry now, they looked like they had tears in them, but when Cheyenne stepped toward him, he took a step back. It was like they had reversed positions. "You'll stay in town, under a watch. I'll have Brogan send two or three of his people to guard you."

"Duke, I'm quite capable of—"

"I said enough," he said, loud enough to silence her. "Come. We're going back to town."

Cheyenne straightened her suspenders and followed him quietly, her heart hurting, wondering how they had gone from such earth-shattering passion to something that left her queasy inside.

Chapter 33

Duke tried every trick he knew to not think about the pain in Cheyenne's eyes. And the searing scream that sounded just like his mother haunted him through the next days. He wasn't good for Cheyenne, and nothing good would come of his staying here. Her injuries had fully shown themselves by the next day, and though she tried, she could not rise from bed. He had seen men with far worse injuries heal and move on just fine, but seeing Cheyenne hurt like that...it did something to him.

He would die a young man doing what he did. He knew and accepted that. But he wasn't going to let Cheyenne be around to see that, nor would he let her get hurt again on his account. It would be far too easy for her to get killed just being with him. He had never felt the kind of passion he had with her and was beginning to think that he never would again. And it would be better for him to have had it and know she was still alive than to be the cause of her death and have to live with *that* for the rest of his own life.

He had never been afraid of death. After he'd lost his siblings, it was as though no risk was too great. Death did not scare him. But the terrifying pain his brother and sister must have felt, the terrible pain he had begun to inflict on

Cheyenne just by being around her, well, that scared him.

He took a deep breath and focused on the ride, pushing his horse toward their destination. Brogan would give him an assignment, something tangible, and Duke and Cheyenne would go their separate ways once her father returned home.

Brogan was deep in pondering over maps when Duke walked into his office.

"I heard there was a skirmish last night," Brogan said without looking up.

Duke didn't shy away from the statement. "There was."

"Quite a lot of ruffians were killed. Quite a few more than I suspect one man could handle on his own."

"I didn't earn the title of the best sharp-shooter in the West for nothing," Duke said. But still, his heart beat faster. He remembered the wolves, remembered how they moved through the camp, killing with strong, efficient jaws. Had anyone seen Cheyenne conjure? Surely she had hidden and had only been found accidentally.

"It seems something got to them after you were there. Did you hear anything last night? Wolves? Coyotes?"

"I was dead to the world once I was back in town."

Brogan hemmed at that. "Well, it was either the biggest coyotes I ever saw or a pack of wolves. But they killed the weak ones and must've chased down some others. We need to keep an eye out for them, too. We don't need to worry about another enemy. The McLaurys are enough."

Duke looked at the markings on the map, memorizing the positions of the camps that Brogan had found. "Drawing them away might be a better bet. The largest of the camps."

"They want easy targets, and they're not organized. They want to stay put."

"Split them up, then. If we go at them at once, Atchison is bound to send his men immediately. Fifty, one hundred, we can handle. Two thousand we cannot."

"If we kill them all outright, there will be no one to ride to Atchison."

"We don't have the manpower for that."

"And the Fort refuses to send soldiers?"

"They have been chewing on that for months now. I'm not holding my breath."

Duke gathered his thoughts. Something needed to be done soon, before Atchison decided his own men were needed here.

"I'm concerned they're getting used to violence. They were not shy about killing Warren's deputy once they knew w…I… was in their camp." Duke kept his posture relaxed but cursed himself for the slip.

Brogan didn't seem to notice. "These men are not organized like Atchison's men were. I get more of a sense of…insanity from them. Chaos. I think they may follow a single man on horseback the way they followed Goodnight for a time. It would buy the town more time to strengthen its fortifications. And hope that Goodnight returns soon."

"Any word from him?"

"No. He should have returned by now."

Duke didn't like the feeling of fear that sentence sent through him.

"The Fort claims to have scouts telling them that the McLaurys are ready to strike any day now," Brogan continued.

Duke felt fear spear him again, hot and fast. "But they cannot."

Brogan looked at him incredulously. "They aren't planning their raids around your timetable, marshal."

Duke wanted to plant a fist in his superior's face. "I am aware of this. But with Goodnight gone and the head of our… forces, for lack of a better word, absent, they are exploiting our weakness."

"Smart of them," Brogan said.

Duke curled his hands into fists. "Then we plan around that. If they wish to strike, then we must be ready. What have you truly heard of reinforcements? What has the fort been 'chewing on,' as you call it?"

Brogan glanced toward his door, then lowered his voice. "I have heard tell they won't be sending any."

"What?" Duke growled.

"They are willing to let the situation go."

Duke felt the surprise thrill through him. "They would let the town be taken?"

"I'm only repeating gossip at the fort. It could be they send them still but want the McLaurys to think they aren't. But I've not got a good feeling about it."

"Without Goodnight, then, the town is doomed."

"I know," Brogan said, his mouth a hard line. He loved this part of the country, and he was willing to lay his life down, but not needlessly. The fort had extra men. There must be some way he could convince them to send a small contingency.

"Can *you* spare men?" Duke asked.

It was a time before Brogan replied. "That would be in direct defiance of my orders."

"I'm tired of orders and rules," Duke said.

"Always the marshal," Brogan replied, which got a wry smile from Duke.

"What did you get into all this for?" Brogan asked.

"Keeping men accountable," Duke said. "That's the short

answer." And always in the back of his mind was the rushing torrent of water which should have taken him, too. His family should have been childless after that day, but here he was, a ghost, still roaming the prairie.

"I'll see what I can do," Brogan said. "There may be some strategy which only requires the fort send a handful of men. New recruits who need practice. Something of the sort."

"Thank you," Duke said. "Write me in town when you figure something out."

Duke thought about Cheyenne and her wolves on the ride back to town. How the creatures had looked at him, looked *inside* him. They had seen parts of him that even he didn't want to think about. How they looked more real than he felt most days. They had a purpose, given to them by Cheyenne or whatever higher power she looked to. And what was his purpose besides keeping men accountable? What could there be in this world that might give him back the meaning that had been ripped from him all those years ago?

Chapter 34

"Anna, I…" Cheyenne began while Anna was dressing her the next day. She sucked in a breath when she turned her head too quickly, and the pain from her injury struck her.

"Yes, ma'am?"

"Never mind," she said with a smile at Anna in the mirror. "I'd just like my hair arranged with a braid at the side today."

"Of course."

Cheyenne debated the best way to say what was on her mind. She had no real friends here in town yet. There were other affluent families in town, but none had young daughters her age. The Monroes were with child, but none of the affluent had brought their of-age daughters as her father had. The lack of prospects here on the prairie had much to do with that. And while that stock would be much easier to converse with than the ladies of the town, she still hadn't felt a kindred spirit with any other young lady her age. Only Anna and two of the other servants who accompanied them had any inclination that Cheyenne possessed abilities beyond the reach of other mortals, but they had been chosen carefully by her father, and both of her parents before that.

After she was dressed fully for the first time since the incident, she walked slowly down the hall to the sitting room where she knew she'd find her grandmother.

"Grandmother?"

The woman turned toward the sound of Cheyenne's voice, her milky green eyes crinkling at the corners. She patted the sofa beside her. "Please, come sit, child."

Cheyenne sat on the floor at her feet, her skirts pooling around her.

"Grandmother, I wonder about Duke."

"What do you wonder?"

"You have the same magic running through your veins. Did you know you were destined for grandfather when you met him?"

Her grandmother leaned on her cane and appeared to think over the question. The woman had a regal bearing, was used to the luxuries of town, and Cheyenne had been surprised when she had wanted to come out to the Kansas Territory with them.

The woman sat with a straight back, her deep blue velvet dress draped artfully over her knees and to the ground. Ornate gold designs scrolled over her dark hickory cane. Though she could not see with her eyes, she could still navigate with her magical sight, a skill that Cheyenne herself had not yet honed.

"I knew before I met him. My great-grandmother—if you can imagine how things were in her time—told me I would meet a man with kind eyes who would step on my toes when we danced. In a time when such things were more important, I thought that any gentleman wouldn't do such a thing.

"Until I met your grandfather." There was a smile in her

voice, and Cheyenne felt one pulling at her lips too. She leaned her arms on the sofa and set her head on her arms, looking up at her grandmother.

"He trod on my toes until they were numb, and I begged him to stop so we could have some punch and rest my poor trodden digits." Her laugh was that of a much younger woman as she remembered.

"And he knew about your magic?"

"He did."

Cheyenne thought on that. Of course, they had to find a man with whom they could trust their secret. It was why finding their fated match was so important. If they told the wrong person, it would mean certain disaster for the entire family.

"What did you do with your magic when you were my age? You hardly speak of it except to be certain I am keeping my abilities secret. I must know. I am old enough now."

"You are old enough to hear more, yes."

Cheyenne waited with held breath. She had heard some stories from her father, but seldom did her grandmother part her lips to tell a tale. She was stalwart, hardy, and stoic.

"I loved your grandfather. I knew that if he did not take to my magic, there would be a way to either make him forget or make him disappear. Those were strange times, though, times more accepting than today, I am afraid. In the cities, at least.

"But we went to the country house—Harlington Hall, which you have spent much of your own time at—and I went for a walk with him.

"We walked until dusk, and on our way back, we were come upon by a bear. Without a pistol or anything to defend

169

ourselves, we would have been mauled or worse in a normal circumstance. But I conjured a pack of wolves to chase him off."

Cheyenne shivered and wondered what her grandmother's wolves were like, if they were the same as her own. Her own were such fierce, beautiful creatures, who only half existed on this earth. The McLaurys had felt her fury through the wolves the night she and Duke had tried to save Ingraham, and the animals had been as terrifyingly awesome as she could have imagined. They had protected her and Duke in their time of need, accepting that both of them were worthy of guarding. She had not yet told her grandmother of that night, but her grandmother had a way of knowing. She probably already knew.

"What did grandfather do?"

Her grandmother smiled down at her. "Of all things, he went down on one knee and proposed marriage to me the instant we were safe. I bade him wait until we were returned to the house, to make it proper and public. But so great was his thankfulness that we were safe that he did not question what I had done."

Her gaze turned more serious. "Child, we are fated to be with men who accept our gifts. It is the way it has always been. God and our ancestors would not play such a trick on us."

"But what if Duke does not love me?" Cheyenne ventured, breathing life to her deepest fear.

Her grandmother's eyes become clear for a moment. "Then he is a fool for running from what is meant, from what is good for him. Men have been known to do that."

"And what if he runs from me? I should not want to chase him."

Her grandmother scoffed quietly. "Dear child. No, you will certainly not chase him. Besides unladylike, it would do nothing but make a man run further. No," she continued. "Do not chase him. If he runs, he will return to you. It is fated."

Cheyenne bit her lip at the sharp comeback that bubbled up inside her. Duke Channing was no normal man. If Duke Channing ran, Cheyenne knew he would not return.

Chapter 35

Another week went by, and the gnawing feeling that something had upset the balance between town and the ruffian forces plagued Cheyenne. After Duke's outburst after their misadventure to recover the poor deputy, he had been quiet but attentive to her. He went and spoke with the sheriff about Ingraham's death, and to have it on record that the McLaurys were resorting to violence. He was so busy with the happenings in town that Cheyenne hoped he would forget that he wanted to leave. Hoped, with doubt in her heart.

Exactly a fortnight from their sneaking into the camp, Cheyenne was walking to post a letter to Boston when she saw several dusty figures walking in her direction on the boarded walk. She remembered their clothing meant to conceal them on the prairie, the unique buckles they sported on their belts, the disheveled, dusty faces which had been so close to hers that night before Duke had felled them. She dipped her head, but it was too late.

When one caught her eye, he leaned in to say something to the other. And when the other looked at her, they hastened their steps toward her.

Heart pounding, Cheyenne slipped into the door she was walking by and shut it behind her.

When her eyes adjusted to the dim light, she realized what dim, candlelit, smoke-filled room she had tumbled into in the middle of the day. The few "patrons" sipped claret at tables covered in dark cloths lit with a handful of candles

"Mistress Channing!" a voice said. Cheyenne opened her eyes to see Sweet Jenny, owner of the town's only brothel. Oh, what a door she had chosen!

Cheyenne did not have time to be choosy about her current circumstances. "Jenny, you must hide me."

Jenny's eyes narrowed in concern. "Is that new husband of yours treating you poorly, ma'am?"

"No, oh, no! The McLaurys," Cheyenne said breathlessly, hearing boots on the walk outside the door. "They have spotted me on the walk. I need a place to hide!"

"Maura!" Jenny called, and a young lady dressed in naught but her corset and bloomers hurried from a door covered by thick burgundy curtains. "Take Miz Channing to the Red Room. And lock the door," she said quietly.

Maura, with her wealth of dark, curled hair piled up on top of her head and crowned with the gaudiest comb Cheyenne had ever seen, took her arm. Her kind eyes looked Cheyenne up and down, "Come, my lady. Up here."

As they hurried up a set of stairs which were covered in a soft rug, Cheyenne tried not to trip on the many hanging curtains in the dark.

The environ would need to be plush, Cheyenne realized as she began to hear what was going on up the stairs. The noise made within these walls would go nowhere with as many curtains and tapestries were hung here. Had her father known this establishment existed? He would have, she realized, for he would have to renew their permit to be here. How much she had to learn about running a town in his absence!

Maura ushered her quickly into a room at the end of the hall, pulled the door shut, and locked it behind her.

Where would she go from here? Cheyenne roamed around the room, looking for a suitable place to hide. Every nook and cranny was stuffed with velvet pillows, embroidered pillows, silk pillows, silk tapestries, and mountains of blankets in every shade of red imaginable. Cheyenne clashed with it horribly in her navy day dress. It would take days to see everything. And it smelled like stale perfume that must be refreshed every time someone used the room, for there was a pretty powder table in one corner with two dozen bottles of perfume arranged just so on its glass top.

Then there was a sound at the window, and then it began to open. Slowly. Quietly. Cursing, Cheyenne dropped to the floor on one side of the bed. Surely the McLaury men wouldn't be trying to come in the window. How would they even know which room she was in?

Whoever it was, she wasn't going to be caught hiding under the bed just to be pulled out from under it defenseless. Cheyenne grabbed a lamp, fully prepared to throw it. She would not use magic unless her life was threatened, she repeated to herself over and over.

And then Duke Channing slipped into the window. He had a gun in one hand and had arrived without his hat. He must've been in a hurry. Cheyenne heaved a great sigh of relief, though his presence filled her with questions.

"How did you get up here? How did you know I was in trouble?"

The smile he gave her was darkly mischievous. "Would a marshal give away his secrets?"

"Did you fly?" she asked tartly.

Duke held a hand out for her. "That's your job, madam. Now, can we leave?"

"What? Through the window?"

"I thought your sense of adventure rivaled mine."

Cheyenne couldn't back down now. "But my skirts! They won't fit."

"Yes, they are more cumbersome than a man's trousers, that's for certain. Disrobe, then," he said, the dark, mischievous look not leaving his face.

"It's the middle of the day!"

"Disrobing in the middle of the day is improper? You have not been shy about it before."

"Certainly it is! Though a rebel such as yourself wouldn't understand that."

Duke felt the statement a jab, though why should Cheyenne think any differently? She had no clue about his parentage, and it appeared her father had hidden that from her as well.

"Disrobe and steal out the window with me or face these men head-on. Have you a gun stowed in those skirts somewhere?"

"Certainly not!"

"I never thought you to be so…prudish, my dear. And look at the fine establishment we find ourselves in. Would you shame them for their occupations in order to save your own life?"

Cheyenne sputtered. "That has nothing to do with it!"

"Then you must make a choice, my dear. I hear footsteps on the stairs."

"How can you hear anything in this hushed place?" Cheyenne hissed. "You must have the hearing of a cat."

Duke grinned. "There are certain skills that make a marshal better, yes. Come. We need to go."

Between the two of them, they divested Cheyenne of her skirt, hoops, and petticoats in record time. And like the night he'd helped her out of her clothing predicament, Cheyenne felt her desire for him grow with every brush of his hands over her skin.

Duke stood back and looked at her. "You'll fit through the window now."

Cheyenne looked down at herself. "This is ridiculous," she grumbled under her breath.

"And saving your life," Duke reminded her.

Cheyenne pressed her lips together to keep unladylike words from falling out.

Duke slipped out onto the roof, then helped Cheyenne and her ankle-length lace and ribbon-covered pantalettes out after. And her trim little waist hugged by her corset left nearly nothing to the imagination.

Cheyenne turned a sharp eye on him when she felt his gaze roaming over her. "It's nothing you haven't seen before."

"It's a mite more tantalizing than your men's trousers even. Tell me, how's the breeze?"

"Oh!" Cheyenne tucked the pantalettes closer around her legs to hide the open center. "If someone were to look up here, they would see that which only you are meant to see."

"We're on the roof of a brothel. They shouldn't think it strange at all."

Cheyenne huffed and turned her red face away from Duke. He thought he heard her murmur something untoward about his manhood, which only made his grin wider.

There was a cleverly placed ladder at the back of the building, though Duke had to help Cheyenne lower herself down to it. To her credit, she didn't simper or whine as he did so, though he could see the fear on her face. She did what no other woman he had known could do. On a daily basis. And she looked attractive doing it.

That was part of the problem, he thought as he followed her down the ladder. At the bottom, he tipped the ladder down to the ground should the McLaury men feel the need to go out the window themselves. There was no other woman like her. Well, perhaps there was one on another continent, but he liked this continent. And he liked this woman, try as he had to not. It wasn't just her irresistibly kissable everything, it was everything about her.

And that was a problem.

He shrugged out of his coat and threw it over Cheyenne's shoulders once they were away from the brothel and in a secluded alleyway.

"You meant to give me your coat the entire time?" Cheyenne asked.

Duke gave her the dark smile again. "Just thought of it," he said.

She muttered something under her breath again that sounded peculiarly like 'turn you into a rabbit.' Duke couldn't suppress a grin.

Chapter 36

Duke took her by the shoulders, and Cheyenne saw the serious look in his eyes. "Go home. Have Anna get you in another dress. I'm going back in while they're still in there. Do not leave your rooms until I'm back. Do you understand?"

Cheyenne wanted to argue, to tell him that she was perfectly able to take care of herself, but he looked so serious. "Yes," she said softly. "I will."

As he slipped back around the side of the brothel, gun at the ready, Cheyenne took one last look at his retreating figure, then hurried back toward her home. A moment later, a pair of gunshots rang out, followed by screams and a loud scuffle.

Cheyenne ran for home as quickly as she could, her stomach clenched hard in fear.

After she had put on another dress (and answered Anna's silent questions as to why she had come home in such a state), she waited at the hall door anxiously.

Duke returned a half-hour later, swagger in his step and a sparkle in his eye. Cheyenne released the breath she had been holding with worry.

"We have apprehended the two men who followed you,"

Duke said as he wiped sweat and dust from his brow (and something that curiously looked like blood). "I spoke with the sheriff when we locked them up—one with a bullet in his leg and the other with a face smashed up for his trouble. They'll hold them as long as they are able."

"And I have left my fine dress in the room of a brothel," Cheyenne said, unsure whether it was appropriate for her to want to laugh at such an absurd situation.

"Just think," Duke said, "they will put it to good use if you leave it for them."

Cheyenne shook her head as she laughed before she sobered. "They have never come into the town like this. Even with the McLaurys as one arm of a larger operation, I hadn't thought they would be so bold as to walk into town and attempt to take me in broad daylight."

"I am aware of their larger operation. And it shows how courageous they have grown, and their knowledge that your father is absent. That is grave indeed."

Her tart responses still caught him off guard. But if she had been submissive, quiet? No, he would not find her half as fascinating.

"I just don't understand how you expected to take them on all by yourself when you arrived."

"When I left for this area, my sources told me there was a group of brothers interfering with the free elections in the area. Kidnapping locals, blackmailing them into voting for their candidate. A group of no more than ten or a dozen."

"Well, there must be seven score or more now."

He resisted the urge to tell her that he was also aware of this. "I solicited help from a superior in the region for more men to help me."

"Who? Someone at the fort?"

"You certainly want to know more than you should care to know about. But yes, Major Taylor spoke to his superior and those he knows at the fort."

Cheyenne wished she had known all of this. Perhaps then this or other things could have been prevented. "I appreciate that you're summoning reinforcements while my father gathers his, but I, too, need to know the goings on if I am to help."

"Then tell me what we must do," he replied. Let her have her moment if she wanted it.

"Well, we do not have the numbers to crush the entire body. Frankly, I'm not certain we have the numbers to crush even the arm. Not by ourselves, anyway," she said quickly to his raised eyebrow.

"But," she continued, "I think with the numbers I have behind me, and if you are able to speak with your superior and find a way to garner his help, we might be able to beat them back."

"You would let them see you conjure?" Duke asked, surprised.

"No, no," she replied vehemently, feeling sick to her stomach at just the thought of it. "I would have to be elsewhere. Picking up stragglers or on the other side of the fighting from you entirely."

"That does not sit well with me," Duke said quietly.

"Pardon me?"

There would not be another night like the one with her wolves. They would ride together or she would not ride at all. "I would not have you unprotected on the frontlines of battle. You have already been hurt and now nearly kidnapped."

Cheyenne waved her hand as though to dismiss the words. "But here I am. I know the risks of living in this part of the world, Duke. I know there is a daily risk to my life here. But I would have my wolves with me then. They will protect me. I'll have charms and warding as well. I know my craft. I would not make such a suggestion if I felt I did not have a greater chance at success than I did at failure. There are many steps I can take beforehand to ensure a greater degree of safety. For both of us."

"But there is a chance of failure. You didn't have those things with you today. They caught you unprepared."

"And I could be thrown from my horse tomorrow. I might die of a toothache a year from now. What difference would it make?"

Duke ground his teeth. What difference *would* it make? It wasn't as though he were planning to stay here. Cheyenne's father would return, and this would become naught but a memory of a stop along the way. So why did that thought not sit well within him? Why did nothing with Cheyenne turn out as he anticipated it to?

"You are headstrong," he finally got out.

She barked her laugh which he had come to expect. "Aye, and do I pull at the bit, too? Am I a horse to be trained, then, Mr. Channing?"

"You are my wife. One nearly has whiplash from your changing moods."

She laughed again. Poor Duke Channing was far too fun to tease. "You seem the one with the changing moods, my dear. One moment you cannot take your hands from me, and the next it seems you are running for the door. So, which is it?"

Chapter 37

I t wasn't two days before more trouble came to town.

"They've captured another, Duke," Cheyenne said, bursting into the room, breathless. She finally opted for a more prairie-appropriate dress, though she was loathe to leave her silks put away. But she moved better in these clothes, even if they weren't trousers.

"It sounds like you ran all the way here to tell me."

"I did. It's Carter Vogt. The elder. He doesn't see well, and I'm worried what they'll do to him."

She could have sworn she saw Duke frown, but then his face was as impassive and impossible to read as it always was. "They won't likely kill him, so long as we don't try what we did last time. They need him to vote. Do you know what elections are coming up in nearby towns?"

She wracked her brain. She'd heard someone down in the taproom talking about… "Oh! Yes, in Junction City in two days."

The way Duke looked at her, she felt like he was taking on all her panic, her anxiety about the situation. She tried to calm herself. "I'm sure it's not as bad as I'm making it sound."

Duke looked grim. "Oh, I'm sure it's actually much worse.

There are likely others missing whom we haven't heard about." He stood and adjusted his gun on his hip, the two in his chest holster.

Panic grabbed Cheyenne by the throat. "There are? This is my town. I have to keep everyone safe."

Duke stood in front of her and set his hands gently on her arms. "You cannot keep everyone safe all the time. That is impossible. What you can do is make them aware of the present dangers. Go ring for some tea while I speak with the sheriff. I understand you need to show your strength, but will you let me help you with this?"

Cheyenne nodded.

"Good," Duke said. He kissed her gently for good measure. "I'll go see what they know. I'll be back."

But on his way to the sheriff's office, they found him before he could even reach them.

"Mr. Channing?"

Duke turned to see who had addressed him as though he were his father. He'd ridden how far to get away from the reach of that name? And how many years had he simply been nameless as he passed through town and trail as he helped keep the peace? And now here someone was addressing him in the manner he swore he'd never take possession of.

But it was one of Isaac Goodnight's deputies, Walker something or other. He thought again of the offer Goodnight had made before he left. He scoffed. Not in a million years.

Ah, yes, Scott. Walker Scott. "Yes, Mr. Scott?"

"Uh, we did a perimeter around the town. You know, as you said. And we found something."

"Something?"

"You'd better come to the stable."

James Monroe, one of the undersheriffs, came with them. He made Duke nervous in the way many lawmen who were out in the West under the guise of doing good did. That guise could hide all manner of immorality. He made a note to ask Cheyenne about him, as well as Isaac Goodnight when he returned.

At the doors to the stable, Duke knew he wouldn't be asking Isaac Goodnight anytime soon. Tethered outside a stall was Isaac's horse. Or what could have been his horse. The animal was covered in dried mud and all manner of prairie flora. It would take ages to clean the creature. It bore no saddle, and by the way the mud was caked all over it, it hadn't been wearing one for some time. It did still have its bridle and, curiously, a leather satchel around its neck.

Duke stood, stunned. Never one to be lost for words, for once, he had no response to the sight before him.

"We was riding north of town. You know where the big limestone field meets the forest? The big elms? Ole boy here comes crashing out of the trees, wild and foaming. I never seen a horse looking so wild. Took us a good hour of chase to catch him, even though it seemed he wanted catching."

"He's split a hoof," Duke noticed and cringed. The animal still looked wild-eyed and shied from him when he approached, then turned back to the bucket of grain he'd been given.

"Yeah, crashing over that limestone. Surprised he didn't break his leg over it."

Duke imagined what might make a horse spook like that. Or how a man would have to be riding for his horse to go wild. Nothing good.

"And he had no rider."

"Nah. Threw his saddle sometime. Had his bridle and this bag around his neck." He tossed the leather satchel to Duke.

Duke stared at the leather bag in his hand. He'd watched Cheyenne hand her father the small bag before his departure. He opened it. Whatever charm she had put inside was gone, but there was enough dust in the bag to know that the bag must have been flapping on the horse's neck for some time.

"Did you look around the area where you found him?"

"Oh, yeah. Poked around. Nothin' to see."

Duke looked to undersheriff Monroe, who removed his hat to run a hand through his black hair. "Scoured the area as good as we could considering the McLaurys and Indians about." And he spat off to his side.

Duke doubted they'd run into trouble like that out the way they'd come from. He would need to check that area for himself, though finding and reporting the body of Isaac Goodnight wasn't something he was looking forward to. And if Monroe thought he'd find trouble from the Indians in this region, he didn't know much.

So much for Cheyenne's charm protecting her father on his journey. Unless whatever had pursued him was stronger than the charm she'd made. Duke shivered, not cold in the slightest. While he'd known there were things along the trail that he couldn't explain with logic, facing them head-on was another matter altogether. He'd skirted all manner of things he knew not to tangle with.

He slid the bag into his pocket.

He felt worse about this than he could have imagined. And he told himself that it was simply because he didn't want to see another town fall to men who wanted to lie and cheat their way into not making Kansas a free state.

And he was going to keep telling himself that. He squashed down the feelings which lurked within that thought. He wasn't getting attached to this place, and he sure as hell wasn't getting attached to Cheyenne. Yes, he admired her. Yes, she was a singular woman. Yes, he was enjoying his time with her. But damned if he would let this place keep him rooted. He wasn't good for her or this town, and it would only be a matter of time that his sins caught up to him and caught her up in them too.

Duke cursed. Isaac Goodnight was dead. Taken on the trail by the McLaurys or something more sinister on his way back to Warren. And what then? They would come into town and take it. Take Cheyenne.

"You'll not speak of this to anyone," he said sternly to anyone listening. "Chey—my wife does not need this burden placed upon her at just this moment. Let us scour the prairie longer before coming to a conclusion."

Scott Walker and the other deputies nodded solemnly.

"Would you like for us to take another turn around the area, see what we might find?" William asked, voice smooth as silk. Duke found he didn't trust the man himself, but if Isaac Goodnight had, then he would need to do so for now at least. At least until they confirmed the worst.

"Look for vultures, birds circling. Otherwise, it's best we keep our eyes set on the McLaurys. It's possible this is a diversion."

The McLaurys were squeezing the town. That he knew. Wearing them down. He needed to get Brogan to act soon, before they organized more than they already had.

But if he could draw them away from the town himself...

A plan began to form in his head. If somehow he could draw

even two score of them away from the town, even briefly, Cheyenne might have a chance to save herself.

He had to leave. That was a given. With the right tactics, perhaps he could make the McLaurys follow him. Brogan didn't know the lengths these men would go to make Warren their own, to make all of the Kansas Territory their own. If he could draw them away from town, hunt them down one by one or draw them away long enough for Brogan to bring reinforcements or for Goodnight's reinforcements to arrive if he had sent them, then maybe he had a chance. He couldn't risk Cheyenne again, no matter her powers.

Chapter 38

The days which followed, the riding back and forth to Brogan's encampment and Fort Riley, the groveling and pleading that did not suit him, hollowed him out. He had begged for aid even if it was only new recruits, and though they had laughed at his request, they had granted it.

Duke intended to ride into the McLaury camp and goad them into following him. Not how he would have chosen to save Cheyenne and leave town, but he'd seen smarter men follow a lesser threat. And since he was known within their ranks already, he didn't think it would take much for a sizable group to take up after him.

So, he would find a way to poke the McLaury hive in two days' time, and ride toward the rocky outcroppings south of town. Fort Riley had promised they would wait with a contingent there. If Duke could funnel the group which followed him through the outcroppings there, the new recruits would follow and pick the men off who quit the chase.

And so long as the fort kept their word, he could be ushered out of town and assure Cheyenne's safety. With the McLaury forces split so, the town could handle whatever would be left of them. Cheyenne could lead the charge even if her father never returned. Isaac Goodnight had thought her capable, and Duke knew that she was. She would find a way to thrive in the role, gain the respect of the town, make them listen to her. Duke had to believe that she could or he was in danger of staying, of never leaving this place which he had somehow come to admire as did Cheyenne.

Cheyenne could take care of the rest with the help of the town. He had to trust that. She had her wolves, her spirits, the creatures which she could conjure. Between them and a hundred strong men in the town, they would crush the remaining McLaury men and their followers. She would be feared and respected, a woman of the prairie whom none would want to tangle with.

He walked up the stairs with resolve. He would leave, she would find another more worthy of her time and attention, and he would go back to scrubbing his corner of the earth of these people who wanted so badly to hold their lives in higher regard than others.

This was the hardest thing he would ever do.

It surprised him that it was difficult. It never had been before, but that was before Cheyenne. It was before the woman who made him think differently about the world. He'd wanted so badly for there to be a place in his heart for her, but there just simply wasn't one. He was married to his cause, and she would be better off without him. The only solace he could leave her with was not telling her of her father's demise. Let her find out after this had passed, after the McLaurys were gone, and her world had settled somewhat. So much bad news at once might kill her, no matter how strong a woman she was.

He found her in her sitting room, her pretty feet bare and

warming by the fire. It twisted the knife in his gut. He had to do this now or he never would.

"I must quit this place."

The confusion in her eyes was followed by a little smile. "When will you return?"

"I won't be."

Silence lapsed between them.

"So, this is it." She folded her hands in her lap, very proper, but he could see her shaking from where he stood in the doorway. She wore her cotton print, the one with the little red flowers all over it. He'd said he thought it delightful before, hadn't he? And here she was wearing it for him again when decorum would have told her not to wear the same dress twice. The knife in his heart slid deeper. He wished she would get angry, raise her voice, threaten to turn him into a prairie critter—something.

"It is."

"I'm sorry that I was not enough for you. I hope you are happier with the love who waits for you."

Duke winced. She had asked him many times about his great love, and he had never told her. He never could bring himself to say the words which had slipped from his tongue so easily before. Because now that he had met Cheyenne, those walls he'd put up with those words were crumbling down to the ground.

"I cannot sit still in town. The prairie, the desert, the wild places, they all call to me."

"They call to me, too," Cheyenne said softly, her voice full of raw emotion.

He hated what he was doing to her. Hated it. But it would mean she would live. He could give her that, at least.

"You cannot come with me. I desire the open prairie all to myself. Prairie and hills and mountains as far as the eye can see. My horse steady under me."

Duke saw Cheyenne finally make sense of the puzzle he had never answered. Hurt and pain and anger filled her beautiful eyes. "Is the West your great love, then?"

"She is."

"Greater than your love for me?"

He didn't reply. She could see some emotion running across his face, and she longed to know what he was thinking. They had come so far in the last weeks. But with the always present threat looming behind him, Duke had begun to grow restless.

"It is greater than everything. If I loved you, it would be greater than that, yes," Duke said, but he was unable to look Cheyenne in the eye when he said it.

And once the words were out of his mouth, Cheyenne felt the pain of it throughout her. And so deeply that even she did not have a retort for his comment. She could not express how deeply he hurt her in that moment. Even casting a spell in spite escaped her, so did his words steal her breath and her thoughts.

And her heart.

The silence between them grew longer and longer, and suddenly the sunset did not seem so bright that evening.

"You are a wicked man, Duke Channing."

"I have never promised otherwise."

And he hadn't, she realized. He had never promised her forever. He had never promised her that he would stay. He had said the words in front of the priest to satisfy her father. And now? Now he had what he wanted from her, and now he would go.

When she turned to look at him, the doorway was empty.

She couldn't say how much it hurt to know that. Hot tears threatened the corners of her eyes and she turned abruptly away from him. She closed her eyes, breathed in the scents of the prairie, let her beautiful moments with Duke flash behind her eyes. These were the things that she would cherish.

And when her father returned?

He would hunt Duke down. He would find the man who ran out of his promise, and he would kill him. She saw the thing with such clarity that it nearly stole her breath.

Cheyenne fought back the storm of tears as she raced to the stable, saddled her own horse, flew into the saddle, riding habit be damned. She spurred her horse as fast as she could, vision burring as the tears flowed.

Stoic. That's what she wanted to be, not the breast-heaving sobs that she was forced to ride farther out onto the prairie to have. She and her horse were out of breath under the open sky in the middle of the prairie, not a soul in sight, not a house or smoke from a fire visible anywhere around them.

She cursed at the sun and hurled great fireballs into the sky, throwing her anger and hurt into conjuring. Her horse danced under her, shy of the fire and of the screaming woman atop his back. She howled until she was hoarse, fueled by every hope within her which had now been crushed.

When she was spent, she sat there on her horse and tried to regain her breath. She felt hollowed out from the inside, but she could feel the hurt rising again already. How could a person feel this much in so short a time? Had she truly let herself feel so deeply for him that she was beside herself in grief?

And her mother had been wrong. She'd had the perfect life

with her father. She had certainly died too young, but their happiness in Cheyenne's first few moments shone through to Cheyenne even until that day. Her father loved her mother, and her mother loved her father. And both so deeply that it had left a permanent mark upon Cheyenne's own soul.

"Why?" She screamed into the sky. "Why did you show me the possibility of everything when I have nothing? When everything was ripped from me before it even bloomed! Why did I love you? Why?"

She dropped her face into her hands and wept bitterly.

Chapter 39

He shouldn't have stayed that final night. He should have left after he'd spoken to her the first time because with every moment that passed, he was in danger of staying, and that meant that the town was in danger, too. Cheyenne was in danger. But he would lure the McLaurys out at dawn, which meant he needed to be fresh if he meant to put Cheyenne out of harm's way.

But the way she moved, the way she looked at him even though her eyes were swollen and red from tears he did not see shed, he still wanted her. He craved her the way he craved water after a long day riding. And goddamnit, he couldn't keep himself from her.

He danced around her that evening, feeling her eyes on him with every movement. And yet she said nothing.

Witch or no, she was too good for him.

But when they met in the doorway of her bedchamber, when she blocked the way with her body and he tried to back out away from her, she launched herself at him.

She pressed her hot body against his and kissed him, a kiss filled with desperation. Every second of it screamed for him not to go. Her lips, the sinuous curves of her body which he had memorized over the last weeks, the way she arched into him as the kiss deepened.

He pulled away.

Bad man or no, he wouldn't do this to Miss Cheyenne Goodnight.

Because that's what she would become again once he left. She would find herself a man who would stick around, a man who could provide a safe home for her.

And with the McLaurys threatening Cheyenne, he had to leave. There was no choice. If he stayed, they would attack the town just the way they had attacked Isaac Goodnight on the trail. The only thing he regretted was that he would not be present when Cheyenne learned the news.

"I'm a bad man, Cheyenne," he said, his words a hollow echo.

"A coyote caught in a snare will do anything to escape," Cheyenne replied, her eyes dry and hard. "Even if it means gnawing off his own leg."

Duke couldn't tell her how apt her comparison was. "I'm running from my sins, Cheyenne. They've caught up to me now."

He knew she wouldn't simper and beg him to stay. No, that wasn't her way.

"You made a promise to me," she finally said. Her hands were clenched at her sides, and he could see the barely contained fury in her. He was surprised that objects hadn't started flying yet. But she knew, too, that he would see it was all a bluff on her part. She would never hurt him, but he could hurt her. Would hurt her in another moment.

"I made false vows to you, Cheyenne. I'm a bad man. I can't change who I am."

"You could if you tried."

"I can't."

"You mean you won't." He caught a glimpse of tears before she turned her back on him. "Curse you, Duke Channing. And damn you for ever making me think you loved me."

Duke's eyes were hard. "I am already a cursed man, Cheyenne. You cannot curse me more and hurt me any deeper than I already am marked." For that was the truth. And it was his burden to bear.

"I could turn you into a rabbit," she said with none of the seductiveness the statement had carried before. It somehow pained him more than her curse.

"You won't," he said softly.

Her shoulders tensed. "I wish I could," she said, then left the room in a flurry of skirts.

Chapter 40

He didn't sleep that night, and he wished he were sleeping out on the prairie or in bed with Cheyenne, but there he was, stuck on the couch in the sitting room in a purgatory of his own making. Both for what he had done to Cheyenne and what he was about to do on the prairie for God to see.

He felt the wild brewing in him, a feeling that was building to a crescendo. He felt like he had to get out of town or his flesh would burst into flame. The more he pushed aside the thoughts which he refused to acknowledge, the greater the feeling the leave prodded at him.

He looked in on Cheyenne before he left the Goodnight quarters for good. She was curled in on herself on his side of the bed, her fist pressed against her mouth as though she had recently been crying. Something stung at Duke's eyes, and he backed out of the room, wishing he hadn't looked in on her at all.

He pushed his horse too hard in the predawn light. And when they were near the camp, the lookouts sounded the alarms, though he was just one man. When a man sprang out of the brush, his horse startled but kept going, but when a second set of men hidden in the prairie scrub launched up, covered in prairie camouflage, his mount spooked and shied, eyes rolling around and showing the whites. Duke wrestled to control him as they rode into the edges of the camp. Most of the men were still sleeping, either in tents or on bedrolls out under the stars near their fires. Some were up early, stoking the fires, starting water to boil for coffee and tea.

And he was there to spoil all of that.

His horse was foaming at the mouth, eyes wild when they rode into the camp proper. His mount trampled through two campfires before the full alarm was raised. Red hot coals scattered everywhere, kettles boiling over the fire were cast to the ground, their contents hissing and spitting and burning any who were too near.

It took but ten more seconds for the fire to take. The prairie had been so dry these last weeks. Not a drop of rain and windy, hot days had taken the wet from anything.

Duke believed in a fair fight, that he would not shoot unless shot at first, but this was Cheyenne and her town he meant to save. *Her town.*

As the fire licked at every dry thing around it, as its light spread and illuminated the chaos, he drew his guns, took a deep breath, and fired.

Chapter 41

I n the early hours when light was just seeping back into the landscape, Cheyenne rose from bed as though called to the window. She must have been, for there she saw Duke galloping past on his horse. The sight confused her tired mind. Why should Duke be galloping away from town making so much of a racket? Would he not want to steal away quietly?

But not far behind him was a group of men on horseback. Fear gripped her and woke her faster than winter cold water in her washbasin. It wasn't simply a few men on horseback chasing him, it was two score or more. Were they descending upon the town, and Duke was leaving before they were all massacred? Was he leaving her to be taken by them too?

She scrabbled to grab her rifle and pistols, though she had her magic, too. She could shoot at least a few of them out the window before they could take the building. And God help them if they made it into her chamber.

But as she watched, on the verge of sounding the alarm, the McLaury men swerved wide of the town and followed the dusty trail kicked up by Duke's horse.

More men joined the group behind Duke, swelling into an

impossible size. Why would so many of them follow a single man out into the open country?

Fear of another kind welled up within her. As hurt as she was by him, she did not wish him grave harm. But what could she do?

She would let the magic decide. As her grandmother had taught her, if she simply opened herself to it, she could funnel the magic through herself, and let the universe shape the power which came to her. She threw open the window, gripped the frame to steady herself.

And so, she conjured. Drawing the energy from the deep well of sadness within her, she conjured. She called upon the ancestors whom she felt with every breath she drew and asked them to help her with this casting. She felt them behind her, giving her their own power. But even for that minute of conjuring, she wasn't released from the deep hurt which ballooned inside her. The joy she normally felt with her power was not there. And that hurt just as much as Duke's betrayal. And still, she called upon the power, drawing more and more, seeking that feeling of joy she always felt with it.

The power that filled her in those moments was immeasurable. She had never felt such a rush of magic within her. Her hair and skirts rustled in the power, as though it created a wind around her. But this was not the wind she had felt before. No, this held a snap and bite to it. It carried with it the hurt which had speared her heart.

And as she called upon her ancestors and those who would come after her, the power reached a crescendo, went to a place where she could nearly not control it. Spirits swirled around her, white and grey and black, pulled from the deep well inside her.

"I bade thee—rise up! Ride with this man! Follow him as long as need be, then return to me!"

The words came unbidden, sparked from somewhere within her, some long memory long before she was born. And then she pushed the great well of it out onto the prairie, out over the heads of the McLaurys and to Duke.

She saw Duke and his horse startle as figures on horseback began to join him as though from out of the prairie. They were ghostly at first, obscured by his dust, then they began to take shape, grow more solid. They were past and present and future, as she could see from her vantage point at the second-story window. They rode horses of chestnut and bay and roan and palomino and sleek black beauties with feathers around their hooves. With manes and tails flying, they ran.

Helping him or hurting him, she did not know. She did not know if she wanted him to come back or keep riding once the men following him quit.

They rode so quickly that they were in danger of riding out of sight in just another few moments. The McLaurys should be slowing, changing course, breaking apart and circling back to their encampment.

But the McLaurys did not slow. They did not turn when they saw the group which had joined with Duke and his mount. They simply rode on after them, their bloodlust apparent. Several fired shots at the still far-off riders.

And then they passed out of sight, with only a large cloud of dust settling in their wake to show that they had been there at all.

Cheyenne sank down to the floor in horror and exhaustion. Had she had given him a death sentence? Had her impulsive attempt to help him turned against her? Or had she meant to do that? Had her magic felt her pain and her hurt and attracted the McLaurys to Duke like a moth to the flame?

Horror turned to anger when she looked at the side table where Duke's pieces had sat for the last season. A single pistol lay there, one of his treasured firearms.

Why would he leave it unless he expected to die out on the prairie?

A hollowness filled her more with each breath that passed. Every second of it was seared into her memory. Every searing kiss. Every glance, every touch. She could still feel him touching her, how his rough hands made her skin tingle with his own power. How filled she had felt with her love for him.

With a cry, she stood and grabbed a vase and flung it into the fireplace. She relished the sound of it exploding against the bricks.

Chest heaving, she balled her fists in her nightdress so she wouldn't throw another breakable. Distant footsteps interrupted the silence. Someone would have heard the noise. Anna or Jonathan. Others, many others, would have seen and heard the McLaurys riding past town. But not her father. And not Duke, for he rode before them, ran before them.

She clenched her fists, wanting to grab another vase and listen to it explode.

She was alone, but she wasn't powerless. She would show them all what she could do.

Chapter 42

The McLaury boys followed him like a dog on a rabbit. Cheyenne had not made him take the form of a rabbit, but he felt as one, and as frightened. The ghoulish party which rode with him was both a boon and a curse, and as soon as the men who followed him discovered they followed but one man, he would not last long. He'd scouted before with a team of men, but being alone with scores of men on his tail, well, it wasn't going to end well for him.

A boon and a curse. He had seen her at the window, could feel the fury and the sadness radiating from her even as he rode out onto the open prairie. And what rode beside him contained that anger and that sadness. He felt the rush of power that she had sent out toward him, and in a second of pure terror, he hadn't known whether he would live to see the next moments. But then the other riders had appeared, beside him, around him, galloping with him. The noise had been greater than any calvary he had ever ridden with.

And even as he told himself that this was for her, that this was protecting her, he couldn't squash the terror he felt with each great stride of his horse away from her. His chest hurt, squeezing his heart in a tightness that he knew was his own doing. He didn't want to listen to his heart screaming at him to turn back, to go back to her. He couldn't listen to it. It hurt too much.

When he rushed through the funnel of craggy rocks where he had been told help would be waiting, nothing happened. He craned his neck to look up at the rocks above him as he rode with his ghost party of pounding hooves. No one was in sight.

Anger punched him in the gut.

He was alone. Well, as alone as a man with a hundred ghosts riding with him could be.

There was nothing left to do but to run.

Muttering a prayer to himself, he spurred his horse harder, the scent of smoke close on his heels.

Chapter 43

Cheyenne didn't know what to do in the aftermath of Duke leaving, and apparently taking a horde of the McLaurys with him. The fire hadn't made it to the town proper, but some of the homes being built and several outbuildings were lost to flames. No one had died, thank goodness, but there was one hell of a mess to clean up.

At least the McLaurys' camp had been burned out and the ruffians scattered to the wind. The few that came running into town, their asses on fire, were apprehended by the sheriff and his deputies.

After that, there was no word or sighting of the McLaurys for weeks. There was no word from her father. While he should have been back by then, she knew that the time for worry had not yet begun. Anything could have waylaid him. But he would return with men enough behind him to help them secure the safety of their town and put the criminals where they belonged.

Scouts reported that there was only a contingency of men left behind at the McLaury camp enough to keep their personal affects guarded. Since that meant that the rest of them would return, Cheyenne could set up her own scouts and guards in the meantime.

She had thought about setting up a sentry before, but since she had summoned the wolves on that night with Duke, she felt more confident in her powers. But how long could the wolves stay in this plane? Would it take more of her power for them to stay? Would it drain her? However, it was worth a try.

The edge of town at dusk was a lonely place to be, and Cheyenne felt the loneliness of it acutely. It pulled on her heart, pulled it in a million directions at once. But when the lump formed in her throat and tears welled in her eyes, she wiped at her eyes angrily. Duke didn't deserve any of her tears. She had work to do here.

Drawing on the vastness of the night around her, she called upon the wolves, could feel them distantly within her, around her. They weren't as near to the surface as they were last time, but she called to them just the same, whispering the words that had brought them forth before. She lifted her arms into the air, pulling in the night closer around her, wrapping herself in it.

And nothing happened.

Confused, Cheyenne knelt in the soft dust of the road, still warm from the sun that day. Focusing all her might on the wolves, she pressed her hands into the earth and called to them again. Perhaps it was that she had not called upon the earth from whence they came.

Nothing.

Fear slithered into the confusion, a pinprick, a snake among the grasses.

Where had her power gone? Desperate, Cheyenne tried to summon her strength. She pressed her hands to the ground again but felt nothing.

Shaking now and with dread filling her belly, she stood and tried to summon a flame, the simplest magic she knew. She held her breath.

Not even a spark came to her fingertips.

Cold fear ran through her. Colder even than the day Duke had gone, and she had sent the ghostly riders with him out of sight beyond the horizon.

She had never been without her magic. From the day she was born, she had felt the pull and tug of it within her, could feel the endless cool well of it just waiting for her to dip her hands in.

Had she used her power since Duke had gone? She wracked her brain. Surely she had used it for something. But no, no she hadn't, not since she had conjured the ghostly riders to usher him out of town. She had been exhausted after that conjuring but sleep and a meal had left her feeling more or less herself afterward.

She looked around. The sun had fully set, but the stars and moon were behind clouds this night. The darkness which came on was inky and she couldn't see through it.

She couldn't see through it.

Terrified, she touched her face with her fingers, closed her eyes and massaged them gently, hoping she was simply tired, that her tears had somehow blurred or affected her vision. But when she opened her eyes again, nothing had changed. Her night vision had nearly gone, too.

Panic crept up her spine and into her shoulders, which tensed with the realization that she was alone in the darkness, unprotected, vulnerable. She had no way of defending herself. She didn't even have a stick. She was alone on the prairie in the night in her day dress. She shivered even for the lingering warmth of the day. The air felt like it had something sinister in it. And with no way to defend herself, she wouldn't see it coming, nor could she stop it.

A wayward buffalo, a coyote hungry and out of options, something conjured by the darkness to eat her up. For somewhere out there, she knew there must be dark magic. As surely as she knew that the magic she used was for goodness, there was its twin out there used only for darkness and evil.

The McLaury gang was evil but thank God they did not have dark magic to use against Warren.

She raced home. Tall grasses tripped her up, and she fell twice slipping over limestone pieces sticking out of the ground where she left the road. She had begun to think she was hearing voices whispering behind her by the time she saw the lights of town.

She was winded, her breath hitching when she reached the back steps. The bones of her corset dug into her sides. Great God, why hadn't she gone out in the trousers getup again? Her breath still coming in halting gasps, she ascended the stairs with a greater feeling of dread each moment.

Anna saw her at the top of the stairs, and a hand flew to her mouth. Cheyenne put a finger to her lips. "Please," she whispered hoarsely. "Wake no one. Just bring me a basin of hot water. Hurry, please."

"Yes, ma'am," Anna said, curtsied, and ran off down the hall, silent in her slippers.

Back in her rooms, disheveled and frightened, Cheyenne hastily took her hair down with shaking hands, trying to make sense of what had transpired. Her grandmother was already asleep, and she didn't want to wake her. She had never said anything about this either. Nothing to indicate that one day one's powers could simply be gone.

She lit candles with hands that would not stop trembling. Memories of her childhood and teenage years tumbled through her head. Memories of magic. Moving the toy sailboat in the river on a windless day, feeling the power course through her when she was but ten years old. Shaking the trees to make them release their fruit at Harlington Hall when she was thirteen, much to her father's delight. In the privacy of their home, he had so enjoyed her magic, had encouraged her to experiment with it and learn it.

But now?

The darkness crept in around her, and she wished desperately for a fire, for more light to chase away this darkness which was consuming her from without and within. She untied her dress and twisted her arms behind her in vain trying to remove both articles from herself. How did Anna make this look so easy? The memory of Duke helping her from her dress, how he had touched her, seared through her memory. She stopped her frantic movements. Anna would be there with hot water soon, and she could help Cheyenne then.

Had her mother said anything about this? She sifted through her thoughts frantically. But her mother only had said those few words before she passed, and only the feeling of deep love and comfort beyond that.

All she could think was that she hadn't done magic since Duke had gone. Her mind fixated on it. Was he the cause of this sudden deficit? But how could that be?

Suddenly angry, Cheyenne balled her hands into fists. Staring intently at the fireplace, she concentrated all of her being on the wood there. Anna should have already been by to light it since darkness had already fallen. Cheyenne trembled with the exertion, every muscle in her body shaking and screaming in agony. Still, she pushed, tears of pain flowing down her face.

Finally, a spark. And then there was a great *woosh*, and the fire roared to life and licked at the wood waiting in the hearth. Overcome with exhaustion, Cheyenne dropped to her hands and knees, shaken and out of breath. As she knelt there trembling, trying to catch her breath, she tried in vain to understand it. Why would she lose her power now, now when she was only just somewhere where she could be herself?

Angry, desperate tears fell from her eyes. She shook with emotion. She pounded the floor with her fists and tried to summon the fire again, but felt nothing, even through her anger.

Anna brought in the hot water and helped her undress. When Cheyenne was clean and warm and wrapped in her nightdress, she dismissed Anna and sat in her chair by the fire.

She would be able to do nothing if she kept having these tantrums, these moments of weakness and abjection. Though she feared, she still had her head. She had her father's munitions, and she had her brain. If her father didn't return home before the rebels mounted an assault on the town, she would need to be ready. Without or without him. With or without her magic. And still, fear twisted within her like a snake in the grass, waiting to strike.

Chapter 44

When it became clear the men following him weren't going to give up, he knew he needed to come up with a plan. Quickly. He wasn't going to waste energy trying to simply outrun them. Outsmarting or outmaneuvering, them, though…that he could do.

Even when they rode through hills and rocky outcroppings with good cover, he knew he could not stop. There were too many men following him, and he didn't know if his ghostly convoy could shoot to kill or if they were simply the only cover he had.

When night fell on the first day, the spirits riding with him formed a circle around him as he began to make his camp. Too keyed up to sleep, he sat and watched the fire from his enemy's camp in the distance. When dawn was the faintest hint of red on the horizon, he saddled his horse and took off again. Exhaustion clouded his thoughts.

The convoy of spirits rode with him.

When they neared Wichita, he steered clear of the town. Suppose those who rode with him would come into town? How would they be welcomed? Feeling alone, for the men who rode with him did not speak, he skirted the town and kept to the open prairie.

The second and third nights, he let himself sleep, feeling a modicum of confidence that his fellow travelers would keep him safe. The men who followed kept their distance. For now.

On the fourth day, as night closed in on him at the Oklahoma border, there was a great groaning in the sky followed by a rush of wind, though the day had been clear and hot. Around him, the ghastly figures began to disappear into a twister that formed around them.

The whole of it rushed at him like a cyclone and before he could steer his white-eyed mount away from it, it barreled into them. It felt like he'd been hit with a tumbleweed sailing through the air—enough to jostle him in the saddle but not enough to unseat him. And then it felt like the air sank into him, like he'd swallowed a great gulp of air while eating. And then it was gone, settling inside him somewhere. Unnerved, he rode on, but felt as though he was now somehow in possession of a magic that was not his own. But he could not stop. He spurred his horse a mite faster, praying the beast would last.

He heard the faint cry of *"Sorcerer!"* behind him. Oh, if they only knew.

His heart dropped when a large part of the group split off and headed west. Now that he was alone, they would likely try to come around and upon him in the night or hole up and wait for him to run himself ragged into their rested and waiting forces. A single man was much easier to hunt down.

He knew what they were doing. Duke was as valuable a player as Isaac Goodnight at this point. If they could capture him, they would be able to take control of the town, and they would hold on tight. They would use his release as a means to sway the elections. Every man would need to vote their way and Duke would be released. It was a bold move so close to the fort and soldier support, but if they were swift about it, Brogan wouldn't know until it was too late. Cheyenne wouldn't know until they brought his traitorous ass back to town, where they would wrest control from her by any means necessary.

But he hoped Brogan would know before then. Especially once Duke didn't return to report after he'd set their camp aflame and basically stuck a stick in the eye of the bear.

That night when he made camp, he sat and watched the pinpoint of fire that was the other men's camp until his eyes watered. He could last about three days without sleep if he got no catnaps between now and then. He could almost ride across Oklahoma in three days if his horse could withstand the strain. If he hadn't shaken his enemy by then, he would head into the next waystation or town he saw and hope to pick them off as they came into town. It was the only advantage he had for being the prey they were herding and wearing down.

But they wouldn't take Duke Channing.

They must've been mad, to follow a man like that. A dog, a coyote, a lion from the prairie, they all would have given up by now. But these men were hyenas. There was a madness in their pursuit.

During the fifth night, deep in red dirt Indian territory, he slipped through the darkness and into the enemy camp. He counted a dozen men still following him.

Moving slowly and silently, he slit the throat of one who slept just far enough away from the fire. As life left the man's body, Duke held the man's blanket over his face to stifle the worst of the noise.

As he crept through the tall grasses back, he wished suddenly for the unnatural wolves who had come to his and Cheyenne's aid what seemed a lifetime ago now. It made his belly hurt to think of her alone there. But no. He set his mouth in a firm line and set to cleaning his gun. It was better this way. It must be.

Chapter 45

She spent her time vacillating between sadness and desperation and determination to take on the McLaurys without her magic. But she knew she couldn't do it without help, without advice. And even though she didn't have her father here, her grandmother was, and Cheyenne didn't know a wiser woman. That was where she could begin.

Her grandmother stood by the fire in the sitting room, and Cheyenne knew her elder's back would be straight even if not for the corset around her still delicate waist. Today, she was clad in a fabric that melted from blue to green, and peacock feathers adorned her hair. Cheyenne smiled. Even on the prairie, the woman kept to her routine and her creature comforts.

"Grandmother."

"I heard you stomping down the hall. What nettles you?"

"I've lost my power," Cheyenne blurted out. She thought that telling her grandmother would make her feel better, but the sense of panic and loss stung worse than ever. When her grandmother turned to look upon her granddaughter with her blind eyes, still green though, always still green, Cheyenne dropped her gaze.

"It is never lost," her grandmother replied.

"But…"

"It is never lost," the older woman repeated.

Cheyenne stood near the doorway trembling. She wanted to pout and stamp her feet and demand that someone else fix this for her, but she knew that she couldn't. She had to resolve this by herself, with her own wit, her own mind. So, she stood in the doorway and quivered because she didn't know how to proceed.

"Come, sit as you do." Her grandmother made her way to the couch by the window, and Cheyenne took her place at her grandmother's feet, resting her cheek against the smooth, cool fabric of the peacock dress.

"Tell me how it came to be that you believe you have lost your power."

"When Duke left…." she began.

"No," her grandmother interrupted. "Take a breath. Describe the scene. Details, feelings, what you saw, smelled, heard. Look at it as an outsider as you look inside as well."

Cheyenne closed her eyes and tried to do as her grandmother bade her do. "I woke from a dead sleep with a start, as though something had awoken me. Instinct or something of that manner. My power, perhaps. I ran to the window, drawn there by whatever woke me."

Her grandmother set a soothing hand on Cheyenne's head, and Cheyenne felt the woman send soothing waves into her. Cheyenne fell into a trance describing that morning in as much detail as she could muster.

"It was the greatest rush of power I have ever felt," Cheyenne said, still feeling the awe which she felt that morning.

"But it was tinged with your sadness, with your bitterness at Mr. Channing's leaving?"

The bitterness was with her even now. "It was."

Her grandmother hummed over that, placing both hands on her cane as she leaned forward on it.

"How do you account for it?" Cheyenne pressed. "Can I get it back?"

Frances did not say all that she thought. It seemed as though young Cheyenne had sent her power off to be with her man, to protect him on his long road ahead. Whether she was angry with him or not—and it certainly seemed as though she was—it was the ultimate gift of love to send one's power on with another. Duke would likely not know, though Frances knew he was a perceptive man.

"You can," Frances said carefully. "Come, help me stand. I want to be at the window."

Cheyenne helped her grandmother to the window, where they both looked out onto the prairie beyond, Cheyenne with her eyes and her grandmother with whatever sight she had—physical or spiritual. It stretched so far, Cheyenne thought. The prairie seemed endless, but she had heard of the mountains beyond, of their great snowcapped peaks and their awesome majesty.

"Duke must return for this to happen."

Cheyenne's heart fell. "But he will not, grandmother. He is long gone, and I may as well be Miss Goodnight again, so sure am I." But she was sure of their nights together, of his hot skin on hers under the full moon, under the stars. But that was all it had been to Duke Channing: hot skin against hot skin in the night. A fleeting affair that had left her here alone again. And she had wanted it to be so much more. She had wanted it to be everything.

"He is gone," she said again, her heart twisting as she said the words.

Frances did not press the matter. Cheyenne was young still, and she had not seen what her grandmother had seen when Cheyenne was not watching. Duke Channing would return for her granddaughter, of that Frances Goodnight was certain.

Chapter 46

Near the border to Texas, he began to pick up more traffic. Wagons and cattle trains gave him cover in his exhaustion. Had he needed to travel much further, Duke didn't think he would have made it. He would have unquestionably slipped up and fallen asleep that night or the next. The three lone McLaurys who were left drifted further and further behind him. They would know the reputation of the Texas Rangers. If they followed him over the border, there would be more trouble for them than a travel-weary Duke Channing.

Gaunt and full of dust, he crossed the border into Texas with relief that he could no longer see the men trailing him—if they still followed him at all. If he could just make it to the next outpost, he would find reinforcements. His horse was lame, and it'd been at least three days since the poor beast had thrown two shoes when they scrambled through a dry creek bed trying to elude the stubborn men following them. The next prairie dog hole would break its leg; he was sure of it. His horse deserved a long rest, and Duke was in desperate need himself.

He and his horse stumbled into the first dusty town he found as the sun was setting red and bloody in the west. Oppressive heat clung to him. He found a well-lit hotel that looked nearly full and got a room and ordered a bath. No one, not even the McLaurys, would be foolish enough to follow him here. If they were stupid enough to try and steal his horse—lame as he was—they wouldn't be counting themselves lucky for long.

Even for his exhaustion, sleep eluded him when he fell into his bed that night. Had the entirety of the McLaurys followed him, bent on his demise? He hoped so. But still, when he finally did fall asleep, it was uneasy. He had left Cheyenne behind unprotected. He had left her without telling her why. He had left her without saying any of the words he felt in his heart.

That thought woke up him fully. The words in his heart. What were they anyway? Were they the words that she wanted to hear?

What in the world could he offer Cheyenne Goodnight that she didn't already have in spades? That she couldn't conjure for herself if she wanted it?

Their nights together had been beyond anything he had ever experienced, and yes, she was a singular woman. But... what, then?

He should go back to her, make sure the town would be safe, but what then? Get stuck there? She would find a way, would be better off without him.

And he couldn't explain why when he finally drifted off to sleep, the knot in his belly only grew tighter. Unease chased him into his dreams...

Chapter 47

Time passed somehow. Cheyenne spent it restless, hating the heat and hating the shade, hungry until she ate, when the food soured in her stomach. If she wasn't speaking with the sheriff, and trying to make him take her seriously, she was on long rides across the prairie, at once looking for the rebels and wishing the wind and the sky would fill her dress like a sail and take her further west, up over the mountains which she pretended to see in the distance.

One ride, she came upon a group up on one of the limestone outcroppings where she herself liked to survey what was going on below. Though great stretches of the prairie were flat, this area offered hills and bluffs and rocky outcroppings where she could sometimes spot rebel camps.

These men didn't wear the buckles that the McLaurys did, but that didn't make her any less wary. That they stood at the edge of the outcropping did work to her advantage, though.

"Out riding alone?" one man asked. She thought she recognized him. He wore similar clothes to Duke, but his still retained some of their starch. And on his head was the same peculiar felt hat that Duke wore, though this man's was brown. Its stiff, wide brim would keep the sun off his face, a face which she thought handsome enough, though not as handsome as the man who had her heart.

Cheyenne gestured to the rifle strapped to her saddle. "Says the one cornered. But one is never alone with a firearm."

He laughed and Cheyenne realized that she did indeed know this man. Duke had spoken of him often, and her father had spoken of him as well.

"Major Brogan Taylor, yes?" she called out.

The man hid his surprise well. "How does someone such as yourself come to know of a ranger who keeps his business quiet?"

"Duke Channing," she said simply. "And I know him to be a marshal. You have no need to hide the truth from me."

They rode their horses closer together, but ever wary without her power, Cheyenne positioned herself so she could gallop away should any of these men have less than chivalrous intentions.

"And you are?" he asked.

"Cheyenne Goodnight," she said. Sorrow stabbed through her. No, she had no right to call herself Cheyenne Channing.

The man couldn't hide his surprise at that statement, but he didn't question her response aloud. The Goodnight name was known in the area, and if this man was who he said he was, he would know her father, too. "As you know me already, this is Roy and Daniel."

"Out scouting?"

"Something of the sort."

Cheyenne could hold her tongue no longer. "Was it you who sent Duke Channing south or was that of his own volition?"

The man raised an eyebrow at Cheyenne. "I will not speak of confidential matters."

"Not even to his wife?"

She saw the flicker of recognition, the connection of puzzle pieces, flit across the man's face. Magic or no, she could read faces, read body movements. He had heard of her, knew something.

"His wife would be privy to more information, though not all. Cheyenne Channing, then, is it?"

Cheyenne tapped her foot impatiently against one stirrup. "Lately, though perhaps not at all depending on your answer. Did he have orders to go south?"

"Last we spoke, it seemed he was on the precipice of petitioning to stay here."

That wasn't the answer Cheyenne expected. Not wanting Brogan and his men to see the emotion that welled up within her, she reached down and pretended to fix the blanket under her horse's saddle. Why had Duke left if Major Taylor thought he might stay? And what in the world would have given this man that idea? Every other sentence out of Duke's mouth had been a reminder that he was going to leave at the first opportunity. She hadn't thought he wanted to stay in the first place, let alone that he might've changed his mind over time. She gripped the reins until her hands hurt as she tried to school her face.

Brogan didn't say a word as she composed herself. Wise of him. She longed to ask if he *had* petitioned to stay, but why would Duke confide about her in this man, his superior? It was an emotional question, she knew, one fraught with the worry and anxiety and her own struggle to accept the truth. The hard kernel of it danced onto her tongue as looked back up at Brogan.

"Well, he is gone now. And he took a number of the

border ruffians with him. We must do without him and his sharpshooting. I know how to handle a gun, so…" Her voice cracked on the last words, and the tears she had held back slipped from her eyes as she wrestled for control of her emotions.

She turned her horse and pulled a handkerchief from her saddlebag to wipe her eyes. Crying in front of strangers! How untoward and graceless of her. Brogan and his men said nothing, did not move while she recovered herself.

"I propose we meet to speak of how we may aid each other in the coming fight," Cheyenne said when she had recovered herself.

"Isaac Goodnight has not yet returned?"

"No," she said. "Have you had word from him? Of him? It has been weeks since the last correspondence. I know that should not give me alarm, but to coordinate this by myself has been…met with resistance."

Brogan took in the woman who rode astride her great horse even for the voluminous skirts which she had tucked and folded artfully to be out of her way. He admired her guile and spirit, and he had no doubt that Duke Channing found her irresistible, as this was a woman who would not fall into line. The West was certainly the place for women like that. And Brogan knew well that the West called upon both sexes to do that which they might otherwise not be inclined. The West called upon them all to dig deeply into the deepest reserves of their courage.

"I have not," he said, his reply measured. He had word that Isaac Goodnight had departed Boston some months gone now. Anything could waylay a man between here and the east just as anything could kill a man between here and there.

As sturdy as this woman looked, he kept his mouth shut. It would be better that way. And it seemed Duke hadn't told her that he had ridden into the McLaurys' encampment and set it aflame before he rose south. Also interesting.

Brogan needed to have a longer conversation with this woman, see what she knew, find a way to help her in her father's absence. That was something the entire region would benefit from. That and the rumor that Isaac Goodnight had quite the supply of guns and ammunition. Perhaps Ms. Goodnight would be so inclined to confirm that for him. "Have you time now? We're due for a lunch break."

"I do. Will you come to Molly's place in town?"

Brogan assented.

They rode toward town as they spoke strategy, and Brogan seemed to be even more accepting than Duke of her input and suggestions. But she spoke nothing of magic. She trusted that Duke had kept her secret from this man, and she trusted herself to do that same. While the West was the place for those outside of society's usual decorum, magic was still another thing altogether.

Chapter 48

Once in town, they sat down at Molly's place below her family's quarters and spoke until the candles burned low. Brogan agreed that Cheyenne needed to be backed by their support, and publicly.

Cheyenne found herself soothed by Brogan's presence. He kept his eyes appropriately off anything below her chin and he waited for her to sit before he took his own chair. It seemed there were other gentlemen in the West after all.

"Do you have siblings, Miz Cheyenne?"

Miz Cheyenne. Interesting that he would not call her by either her married or former name. As wild as the West was, this was a man who knew when to step carefully in conversation. "No sisters. And I have not had the pleasure of having a brother, Mr. Taylor. I should think I was more than enough for my father to handle on his own."

Brogan gave a bark of a laugh at that. "Though not having known you long, I'd be inclined to agree."

Cheyenne smiled and sipped her whiskey.

Brogan settled back in his chair. "What do you know of the rebels' movements?"

"You would take the advice of a woman?"

"You live here, do you not? You see them move about, come into town on occasion, I would think."

Cheyenne crafted her answer for a moment. "I know they have been stockpiling supplies and arms for months now. With more urgency than they had. They are kidnapping more than ever, too. But a frightening number of them followed Du...Mr. Channing out of town. I know not why. I suspect the fire had something to do with that, but I cannot know if lightning or some other organic means started it."

"There was an ambush of supplies on the road that leads out of town not long ago," one of the men with Brogan said. Roy, Cheyenne thought his name was.

Brogan sent him a sharp look but didn't reprimand him.

"When would this have been?" Cheyenne asked, trying to keep the urgency out of her voice.

"A fortnight past."

Cheyenne tried to keep the panic from taking her right there. Surely that wasn't the same men who had ridden after Duke. Surely he wasn't...but no, she couldn't think that. If she thought that, she wouldn't have the strength to keep going.

Brogan was speaking. "...but they took no one and nothing that we could tell. Like they'd gotten spooked by something and kept riding. Or kept chasing."

"I think it a fair assumption that they will return eventually. My scouts tell me that they have left a few behind to guard their camp. They suspect there are traps waiting on the prairie should we get closer."

"Your scouts?" Daniel asked.

She heard the skepticism in his voice, and it nettled her. "Yes. *My* sheriff. *My* scouts. With my father on the road and Duke...absent...I am the only one who might keep the town in one piece by the end of all this."

Brogan wisely kept his mouth shut until he could form a statement that wouldn't get him the business end of a gun. Yes, it was very easy to see why Duke Channing found this woman captivating. "Well, I appreciate the head's up, then. We wouldn't want to go rushing in to take out the last of them and get caught unawares like that."

Cheyenne narrowed her eyes at him, uncertain if he was employing sarcasm or some other unsavory device. She decided that he wasn't the type of man to do that.

"They know me," Cheyenne said, "but I am still a woman, and their minds are mostly made up about my species. I think they are humoring me for now, but I do not know for how long."

"Well have some posters printed up for a meeting, then," Brogan said before sipping at his beer. "You'll introduce us, sit next to us, and I'll introduce our strategy."

Cheyenne scoffed and took a long swallow of the whiskey in front of her. It smoothed out the rough edges of her day, though she felt the eyes of the men with Brogan on her. Let them see her shoot whiskey, she thought. Let them wonder about her.

"And make them think it your idea," she finished.

Brogan sighed. "Well..."

"Well, yes," Cheyenne said. She sighed herself. "But fine. I'll take the blow to my pride. If it means securing the permanent safety of the town, I'll let them think it a man's idea."

Brogan held up his glass. "To ridding the world of ruffians."

Cheyenne picked up her own glass. "Indeed."

And they toasted to it.

A glimmer of hope sparked inside her. Though the flame

was small, she felt protective of it. Perhaps, just perhaps, they could do this without Duke. And without magic.

Chapter 49

When Duke had gathered his strength, he ran to Fort Worth, and Cheyenne's green eyes followed him. He saw her in everything, every woman he spoke with to try and forget her. And yet, speak was all he did. The moment he thought about stepping foot in a brothel, it nearly made him sick. He lost at poker and got his lip split for the trouble. He got trampled in the ring by a bronco that never would've unseated him in the past. Sore, bloody, and wishing for whiskey, he dragged himself to bed each night only to wake and seek the same poker games and endless strings of bulls and broncos and cheering onlookers.

Then the real trouble came.

Once they knew he was a sharp-shooter, they came to challenge him in a never-ending stream of drunken swaggering, of posturing with their tall frames and short ones and thin and fat ones. And they all told him they were reaching for their guns before they did.

And he felled them every time.

And he knew as he'd known even years ago, that someday this would all catch up with him. And he had the feeling that that day was drawing nearer. And that would be for the best, he thought, what with his heart sore all the time from thinking about Cheyenne and wondering if she was well.

On the final night of the summer, Duke stumbled back to his room under the watchful eye of the nearly full moon. Because it reminded him of Cheyenne—as nearly everything did—he cursed at it as he walked. Even for the drunk, he could feel her silken tresses between his fingers, those cool strands where he buried his face while he buried himself in her. He saw her lying in the prairie grasses, body hot and wanton against his. He heard her voice on the Texas wind, the whisper of want, her hot breath at his ear.

With a hoarse cry, he covered his eyes with his hands. He knew what honor was, goddamnit, and he knew he'd marred both his and hers in this. But he wasn't ready to apologize, and he paid for it with another restless night.

He hadn't slept a wink the night before. Sand and grit caked his eyes when he woke. His left eye hurt like a bitch. Likely bruised, he thought as he felt around it. That asshole the night before had landed a sneaky one on him. But there was nothing to do but move on, move forward, keep going. Black eyes would heal. He wasn't so certain that his heart would. And nothing he had done would close it up now that it had decided it needed to be laid bare.

When he went down the stairs for some breakfast at the bar, the air didn't feel right. It was too quiet in the dining area. This time of morning, it should have been bustling with patrons angling for a bite to eat before their day's work. At the top of the stairs, still out of sight for whatever awaited him below, he adjusted his holster and wiped his hands on his shirt. With a great, silent sigh, he adjusted his hat to sit a little further upon his head and started noiselessly down the stairs.

At the sixth stair, he saw that there was no barkeep or anyone in sight except three men sitting around a table playing with a deck of cards. Duke drew the hammer back on both pistols slowly, so slowly, that they didn't make a sound. He could see from here that the card game was a farce. Half the cards in the man's hand nearest him weren't even facing the right direction.

And he recognized the dirty blonde hair of the McLaury boys, specifically the three who had tailed him into Texas all those days ago. So, they had tracked him here. He assumed it was by simply dumb luck that they had, though. They weren't smart enough to track him the way he could track, but he hadn't exactly been trying to conceal his path there, either. He'd been overtired, not thinking clearly.

And now they were near him, and he was short on sleep. Well, let them come, he mused. Better here than back in Kansas territory with Cheyenne.

Duke took a long breath in and set a final booted foot onto the last step of the wooden stairs, where it landed with a thud.

And then time slowed.

All three men began to stand at once.

Duke watched as they rose. All three carried two pistols, so he would have to shoot two clean and get a third round off before each of them could get to their pistols if he had a chance at living. He sized them up as they stood. Whichever one was slower than the rest would get shot last.

There, the smallest of the bunch moved the fastest. He was slim and athletic, practiced. Not nearly as good as Duke, but here they were, all the same. His heavier brother moved slower, but only just. He would be second. The third was young, and it seemed he wanted to put his hat on before he grabbed his gun. He would get the third bullet.

But no, the youngest wasn't putting his hat on. He was throwing the rest of the cards into the air. A distraction. Duke spared the fluttering cards half a blink before he reached for his pistols.

Duke fired first, second, third before the first two men had a chance to pull their triggers. The third got a round off and missed him completely.

Before the entirety of the cards hit the floor, he'd put a bullet into each of the men before him. They all slumped to the floor.

Duke finally breathed out, surveyed the carnage. The three ruffians before him didn't move. He stepped closer, ready for an ambush, but none of them moved. Pistol cocked, he dug a rough toe into each of them. Nothing.

Three more McLaurys down was better than none, he reasoned. And these looked to be the men who had left him at the border. That only left a hundred or so to kill. He huffed at the thought.

Then, he checked his side. Ah, so he had been grazed by a bullet from the third. It hurt like a bitch. Blood seeped through his shirt, but he didn't think the wound was grave. He'd need to clean it, bandage it, but it wouldn't be the death of him. But he'd have to do that later. However these men had cleared out the place, it wasn't going to last forever, especially now that shots had been fired. He ran back upstairs to grab his bag.

When the sheriff showed up, he was already gone. He left payment for the destruction on the bar and headed to the stables, saddled his horse, and rode out. He had a hard few days ahead of him, but it wasn't like he wasn't used to that already. It was what he deserved, he figured. Duke winced when he urged his horse into a canter and the wound in his side complained. Yes, he deserved all this and more.

Chapter 50

She had begun doing things without magic. If she could be without her father and without her husband, though she was loathe to call him that, then she could find a way to be without her magic too. She could hold a gun. She could ride a horse. And she could fight for the place which had become her home.

Brogan's idea worked, though it left something of a bad taste in her mouth. But if they needed a man to outline the plan, so be it. They all wanted the same things: The ruffians gone. A peaceful existence on the prairie. To feel safe where they lived.

When the time came, the men of the town were ready to defend. The women were ready to keep their children and the elderly and infirm out of harm's reach. And Cheyenne was ready to ride out with the men.

She had taken to wearing men's trousers under her prairie skirts, and she could divest herself of the skirts quickly when the time called for it. Her silks would be waiting for her when this was all over.

Sounds far off had her scrambling to her feet. At the window, she gaped as she stared off toward the setting sun.

A huge dust cloud rose from the prairie. It had to be twenty, thirty riders, maybe more.

Terror gripped her only for a moment. How many of them were there? Cheyenne could only see the cloud of dust that the large group was putting up into the air. Cheyenne reached for the firearm and checked the pistol Duke had left behind. She steeled herself, tightened her grip on the gun. She could do this.

Then, another hard look at the group revealed Brogan on his horse at the front. Reinforcements!

A nervous-looking Deputy Walker appeared at the door to the sitting room.

"May I?" he asked.

"I have not the slightest idea what decorum dictates any longer. Yes, please do. You have news?"

"Nothing good, I'm afraid."

"Well, speak, then. Quickly."

"Major Taylor is arriving with a group."

"I saw that. What else?"

"Behind them is what appears to be the entirety of the McLaury camp."

Fear was a vice on her heart. Cheyenne wrestled it under control. She wouldn't let her emotions cost her anything this time.

"We will mount a defense of this town. With or without help from the fort." Cheyenne felt Walker's incredulous stare boring through her.

"Miz Cheyenne, it is not done," the deputy said gently.

"I do not care if it 'is not done,'" she mocked. "We will make certain this is done. This is my town until we have elected otherwise, and I will not let it be taken or influenced by a pack of wild dogs." She squeezed her hands around the gun, feeling the hot metal threaten to burn her hands. This was what she was meant to do. Protect that which she loved.

She would still protect Duke, she knew. And despite his abandonment, she loved him still. Loved him more for knowing him, for the time they had together. And it angered her. Oh, it angered her. But she would die protecting him just as she would die protecting this town if it was called upon her to do it.

"Come," she said to the deputy. "Let us go meet our reinforcements."

With Deputy Walker behind her, she rushed down the stairs and out into the street to greet the riders and their cloud of dust. As Major Taylor's horse pulled up near her, she grabbed its bridle and extended her hand for him. He gave her hand a hearty shake.

"Brogan! What's all this?"

"Reinforcements," he said simply.

"The army allowed it?"

The man gave her a tight smile. "The Rangers allowed it."

"They're coming, aren't they?"

Brogan nodded.

"Then we fight," Cheyenne said, then pointed toward the gathering hall where the munitions waited for them. "Come. We have arms enough for everyone."

Arms were tossed into waiting hands. Bodies scrambled for hidden perches without going out into the street. She and Brogan tethered their horses around the side of a building from their own hiding place, prepared to leap atop them once the enemy made it into town.

Let them come, she thought. They had arms and ammunition

even if she did not have her magic. This was the way it was done in the West.

She felt hardened against it.

Brogan knelt next to her, his own guns ready. "You are certain you wish to be here for this?" he asked.

"Let them come," Cheyenne growled, and hitched the rifle up to her shoulder.

Chapter 51

Bruised, broke, and bleeding, Duke pointed his horse toward New Mexico Territory. He'd sworn he'd never go back there, but he was out of choices. And he'd be damned if he admitted that he was brokenhearted over Cheyenne. Telling himself that didn't stop the damn ache in his chest, didn't stop the thoughts of her which plagued him night and day.

But he was Duke Channing, he reminded himself, best sharpshooter west of the Mississippi, and perhaps east as well, and a man who made certain others were obeying the laws of the land. He was a marshal, in command of himself and his hand each time he pulled the trigger when the lawless stood before him. He took comfort in that. But that didn't stop the ache when he called his own bluff.

And still, he ran from her.

But still, she followed him. Her memory, her scent, her laugh, her sharp green eyes. The way she sighed when his hands found her hot skin, the way she moaned when he drew a finger along the arch of her foot. The soft delicacy which was her inner thighs, always ready to receive his kisses.

He gripped the reins and dug his heels into his horse's side, pushing him into a gallop, as though he might still run away from the woman who welcomed him with open arms, who seemed to understand, accept him without question.

Now that was madness, he decided. Nothing in this harsh world was unconditional.

The desert welcomed him as he knew it would. It waited with open arms to swallow him and his horse alive. Humid days gave way to arid, bright days and freezing nights. His side ached and seeped, the wound not healing as it should.

One day all he saw were mountainous pillars of red rock rising from the land. Red dust-coated him and his horse. He fashioned a gauzy piece of fabric over his horse's eyes and nose to keep the worst of it out. He covered his own head in his second shirt. Near noon on the second day, he passed the large earthen scrapings of whatever natives lived nearby. This desolate place, the markings, told him that he was moving in the right direction.

And still, all he could think of was her.

She might've been wilder than he—how had she taken this all in stride? How had she accepted her fate to be wed to him when it seemed all she wished was to practice her magic unimpeded on the open prairie? She needed no man for that. And she certainly didn't seem the kind of woman who only thought of marriage and children.

That she might have come to love him or feel attached to him in any way was a possibility that he did not want to entertain. It made what he had done to her all the worse, no matter that his initial intention had been to help her by his leaving.

The desert punished him for his transgressions and took no pity on his wound which grew worse by the day. He hadn't taken the time to prepare as he should have. He'd filled his largest canteens and a small cask that was tied at the back of his saddle, but one never took enough water into the desert no matter how much one packed. He went as long as he thought he could without water, giving his horse the lion's share until he could find a cactus or some hidden spring to steal some moisture from.

And still, she followed him.

What had it been about her that he had admired so much? He had felt it, had commented on it, but had he allowed it to come inside him, to fill him?

Of course, he hadn't.

But there alone in the desert, losing his mind to thirst, he let himself think it. Her dark hair and sharp green eyes were always before him. And so was her sharp wit and intelligence. That was what he admired most. Certainly, she was the fairest woman he had ever known, but that she matched him in thought and mind struck him more deeply. And her courage. That she flew into battle beside him with nary a thought to the fear that should inspire struck him deeply.

If he could only ride for a few more days, he would reach the old ranch. As he drew closer, he felt the dread settle in his belly. He'd been a young man when he'd left, and what had he come back as? Was he now less of a man for the things he'd done?

A curious dizziness took him when he thought his journey might be near its end. A look at his wound told him that it had festered without treatment. It was just as well, he told himself. He no more deserved to reach his destination safely than he did to have Cheyenne back after what he had done. But he soldiered on as he had done before. He would reach where he was going, or he would not.

Chapter 52

He must've been dreaming. Or dead. That was more likely, gauging by the impossible sight that spread out to the horizon before him.

Duke rode up the newly graveled drive, unbelieving eyes taking in the lush green grass they'd somehow gotten to grow here. A sign announced his family's property. New fencing shone in the bright sunlight. Sleek horses ran in fenced pastures that went on as far as he could see. Sheep and cattle dotted the landscape. Crops grew in other fields separated by more fences, a far cry from the kitchen garden he grew up with.

And there, the house he'd grown up in. That was the same, rising out of the landscape as it rose out of his memory. It was red adobe in the style of the natives, who knew how to live in the heat. Duke knew it would be cool and inviting inside the house, and he yearned for it with a desire he'd not known had been brewing inside him. The rooms within waited for him, watching him even now as he drew nearer.

The world began to sway before him, the blue sky and green fields and stone walls of his home blurring together. Or was he swaying in the saddle?

A tall, broad-shouldered man and a small woman waited out on the expansive porch. The knot in Duke's belly grew larger. What was he thinking coming back here? Was opening the wounds of his past worth adding to the guilt he already felt?

He had never felt this kind of anxiety before, this worry about what others might think of him. He was clearly going soft as he aged.

And then, he knew he must be dead, for out the door rushed his brother and sister. They were just the same as he remembered them, wearing the clothes they'd died in and all. But they called his name and rushed down the drive toward him, jubilant, excited, happy to see him.

The world tilted, then, and stabbing pain in his side made his vision waver. His siblings disappeared, but he could still hear their laughter. For twenty years, he'd missed that sound. But there on the porch, his parents stood, side by side, waiting for him to come greet them.

He opened his mouth to call to them, but no sound came out, and nausea gripped him. The world tilted again, grayed.

Duke slid from his horse, and the ground rushed up to meet him.

Chapter 53

He was a child again, lost in the fever which had taken his siblings from him. Darkness and flames rushed up around him, alternately illuminating and then plunging into darkness the worst days of his life. The day his siblings had been lost in the rushing waters. The day he had left Cheyenne, not knowing what fate had come to her in his absence. His demons. His mistakes.

Dark horses made of burning wood galloped through his dreams, their preternatural screams punctuating his own groans of pain. They, too, shed light on the scenes which played over and over again in his mind. Death, fear, rushing water, the cries of a woman at once both pleading and angry.

Images of Mary and James as they dug in the creek, first as children, then as the adults they would never become. Their governess, her skin purple and white when they found her body, bloated and open-mouthed. The terror he'd felt when they found her, the pain he felt when they never found his siblings, blurred together as the images fell over him like the water had on that day.

And then silence. Darkness. For a time, he simply floated, somewhere between living and death, not caring which way the current took him.

When he opened his eyes, the quiet around him was painful. He was propped up against soft white pillows, a thin quilt and sheet pulled up to his chest. Sweat poured from nearly every part of his skin. And his skin itched. Every square inch of it, his side especially. He clenched his hands weakly, fighting the urge to peel his skin from his body and be done with it.

He stared at the ceiling for a long time, tracing an old crack with his eyes as he had when he was a boy, then moving across the support beams, seeing the age and smoke stains that were new to his eyes. Light came through the drawn curtains, spearing through the dust motes in the room.

A silent maid came in—a small, older woman he did not recognize. When she saw that he was awake, she stole back out without a word. Despite his grogginess, Duke sighed and pressed back against his pillow. They would know he was awake now, and there was no delaying the inevitable at this point. What would he say? What *could* he say? He had amends to make, apologies to speak, but he didn't know where to start.

And then his family was in the room, still looking the same, though it had been twenty years. It was as though age had not touched them. And all he could do was stare at them as they stared back, both unbelieving. He saw himself in his father's face now, and he had most certainly gotten the color and texture of his hair from his mother.

And then his mother burst into tears and hugged him hard. In his weakness and her jubilance, he felt faint with the strength of her embrace. His father, stone-faced, came near and set a hand on his shoulder.

"Your mother said you would return any day, and I didn't believe her. We've thought you dead for some time, you know."

Duke didn't know what to say to that. An apology was still stuck somewhere between his heart and his head. He settled for casting his eyes away from the steel ones which matched his.

"This place has changed," Duke said as darkness swam before his eyes. Then, fearing he had been out for too long, he said, "How long have I been asleep?"

"Only a day," his mother said. She looked the same to him with her dark hair and dark eyes and her white woolen shawls which floated around her like clouds in the deepest part of spring. Duke felt a child again, and he said nothing, afraid of what might come out of his mouth. His fever dreams clung to him like the sheet over him.

"Senna will come back to help you," his father said. "Seems you've had a run-in with the wrong end of a gun."

Duke winced when he tried to sit up more. No one had landed a hit on him like that since back in '49. And they wouldn't again, he thought darkly.

"The ruffians who ambushed me won't be talking about their wounds," Duke bit back sharply.

His father replied with a laugh and ushered his mother out of the room. "Ah, there is the whip-smart boy whom we knew all those years ago. Get moving, come around to the dining room when you're ready. There's food aplenty for you there."

The same older woman who had been in his room before came in when his parents had left.

"Senna?" Duke asked.

"Si, senor," she said quietly. "Your bath is nearly ready. Follow me."

Though small, the woman was strong, and she helped Duke stand and shuffle to the bathing room down the hall where she left him in the care of other staff. The household had grown in his absence, and he felt a quiet pride for his family and what they had built here in the desert. The halls and rooms were immaculate and lit with the light of soft flames behind amber-colored glass. He remembered running down that very hall as a child, skittering on the sand which collected there. But now the floor was continuously swept, and one could walk silently down the cool hallways.

In the quiet of the bathing room, Duke sipped on water while a bath was drawn, and a maid fluttered in and out, leaving fresh clothes, a bar of soap, a towel, and a glass of wine. He was weak, his muscles betraying him as they had not since he was young as he trembled his way down into the tub. The hot water stung his wound, and he hissed as he slid down into the water. Duke noted the fine furnishings in the room, though they were of a style he knew would not be found anywhere in the East.

Soon clean and his wound tended and bandaged, he felt slightly more alive. He donned the white shirt, belt, and pants that were left for him. New socks, too, he noticed gratefully. Those he pulled on, then his boots, which were all beat to hell from his journey. They'd been new for his wedding.

That thought spoiled any good mood that the bath had given him, and simply the act of dressing had taken most of his energy. Everything came back to his family and Cheyenne.

Cheyenne *was* his family now, he realized with a start that sizzled through him.

And look how he had treated her.

Shame heated him more than the fever had.

He made his way slowly to the dining room, touching walls and his mother's decorations as he went. It felt surreal to be here again, to walk the halls which now felt so much smaller than they did when he was a boy.

In the dining room, he took the seat which was his place now as an adult. That, at least, was different.

His father joined them at the table when food was served, and he was composed and quiet. Duke had expected an explosion that never came.

Duke slid a bite of hot cornbread and tender veal into his mouth and felt his childhood rushing back to him. This was a kind of magic all of its own, a balm for the hurt which swirled inside him. Food on the trail was what it was—sustaining—but this was nourishing. These flavors soothed him as nothing else could have for these last twenty years. Something in him loosened, and he relaxed another notch. The wine and food were working.

"Cook is still here," his mother said softly.

"I wondered. It tastes just as good as it did then. It seems everything else has changed, though."

"Others have joined the household. Especially after the treaty was signed," she said.

His father nodded. "Much has transpired since you left. They fought a war here, and I signed the treaty which followed after."

The world was changing. Duke knew it. He had seen the push west, had seen the wagons laden with goods and people heading for their doom or fortune. There was a rush for gold in the mountains in the far west of the Kansas territory. Would others eventually populate this area? He could not fathom it. It was too hot, too dry, too far from anything resembling society.

But his family had made it.

"Why did you choose this place?" Duke asked suddenly.

"You know I have traveled," his father replied. "The world over. I have seen the desert of the far east, and it is a much more inhospitable place than this. Yet it is far more populous."

"Certainly, but why here?"

"I love the desert," his mother said, and Duke saw his father smile at her. Smile at her in a way that he never would have noticed as a child. It was a look that he knew he had given Cheyenne a time or two when he had let his guard down, when he had simply let himself feel good in her presence.

"I always have," his mother continued. "And you father was too flighty to pick a place himself. We perhaps would have settled in the mountains, but the winters are too hard. Here we know what to expect, know how to handle the clime. And we have good help, have made good friends with those who live around us."

His mother reached out and smoothed a hand over his head as she had when he was a boy, and the rush of shame that filled him was too much. He pulled away. She looked so small there in her dress and shawl.

"You have found someone," she said finally.

"Aye, I have." He didn't ask her how she knew. Having seen what Cheyenne could do, he suspected there was more magic around him than he knew. Perhaps his mother had it, too, or something like it.

"Why are you not with her?"

"It's a long story."

His mother cuffed him gently on the ear. "We have nothing if not time. Come, have some more food, some wine. Tell me your story."

And so he did. Over more food and water and wine, he

249

haltingly told them about his time spent scouting, about finding the little hamlet that was Warren, in the Kansas territory. He told them about Cheyenne and how smart and sharp she was. He told them of her unrivaled beauty while his heart pounded when the words made him miss her so much it squeezed his chest. And when he mentioned Isaac Goodnight's name, his father laughed.

"So that's what's become of that old man."

"He said he knew your name. I was unaware of your close acquaintance," Duke said, holding back a snide remark about Isaac Goodnight's proposal that Duke could not have helped but accept. Duke needed to swallow any of the sour feelings that remained from that. It was past time.

"We were together on some grand adventures in my youth. He is a good man."

"I am married to his daughter," Duke said quietly and watched as his father's eyebrows shot up. He didn't dare look at his mother.

"Oh?" was the little noise that finally came from his mother.

"Goodnight had to ride back to Boston, to get reinforcements. He did not want Cheyenne unprotected."

"It is an honorable man who keeps his own protected when he leaves. He was a good judge of character then. What do you think of him?"

Duke felt the stone in his belly grow heavier. He would have to tell them soon.

"He was...is a good man. Fair, though he drives a hard bargain. I found I couldn't tell him no," Duke said, and as he said it, he knew it was the truth.

His father laughed. "He sounds the same man I knew. And what of the trouble around the town? It sounds Isaac has found his calling on solid ground finally."

"There are groups of men near the border who try to sway the elections. They do not want the Kansas territory to be Free. They have been organizing lately, growing their numbers, beginning to use more strategy."

His father made a sound of disgust. "I will never understand people who hold those notions. If a man can hold down a job and gets along with his fellow man, there is no need to separate him from the rest of us. You've heard, I'm sure, what they're doing with the Indians."

"Sadly."

"It should be a crime. So this town you were in, it fell to the ruffians? And you had to leave?"

"They were great in number," Duke said. "Many of them chased me from town. I assume whatever of them were left went back to the town after I gave them more trouble than they wanted."

"And they had overtaken it when you returned? Or not?"

Duke felt his shame growing over him, crawling over him with the sticky feet of a grasshopper, of a scorpion. "I have only just stopped running now that I am here."

His parents were quiet as they absorbed what he had told them. His father stood. "I have duties to attend to, but I would like to speak with you about all of this again. In greater detail," he finished, and Duke knew what he meant.

He felt his mother's eyes on him when his father left the room, but he could not meet them. She would see through his lies, just as she had when he was a boy.

"You left her there?" His mother's voice was soft, but he caught the surprise, the sadness in it.

Chapter 54

Duke cringed. "I didn't know what else to do with the ruffians about to descend upon the town. I had to draw them away."

"But you did not return?"

Duke had no answer for her.

"This woman thinks you have abandoned her?" his mother asked, though it sounded more like a statement.

"It is better for her that way."

"How is that?" His mother's voice never grew louder, but it did have a touch of a chill to it. No matter if she hadn't seen her son in years. She would make certain he knew that he needed to go back to this woman who had captured his heart. She had seen it in his eyes when he spoke of her, the way he said her name with reverence.

"I had to draw the rioters away. And she deserves so much better. I know I am an arrogant sonofabitch."

"Watch your tongue. She told you this?"

"She didn't need to."

His mother cuffed him on the ear, harder this time, and then he did feel like a child again, like the boy who lost his siblings in the raging arroyo. "I taught you better than this. Why did you truly leave?"

Duke didn't want to say what he felt in his heart. It was too painful, too raw, too vulnerable. He had not saved his own hide and kept his own self safe on the prairie for this many years to be torn open by a woman. But he had. He had been torn open, and he needed to be if he had any chance of getting Cheyenne back.

His mother would have none of his silent deflections. They moved to the sitting room, where large windows showed off the great beauty of the landscape outside. "Tell me why you have truly left. Is this about Mary and James?"

Duke looked away from his mother and out the windows past their corrals and the scrubby desert to the mountains beyond. Their land stretched all that way, and between the house and the mountains was the arroyo which had taken his childhood from him.

"I am not the same person I was that day. I am hardened from it."

"You have done that all on your own, then."

"It is how it is."

"Duke Voltaire Channing, I taught you better than that. Look at me."

Duke did, and his mother watched him with fiery eyes. "It is only how you choose it to be. I lost two of my children that day, but I did not lose all of them. I could have spent my life in mourning, and parts of me mourn still, but I could have chosen to never pick myself up and continue living. But I did. For my husband, for my children, for myself. Why have you not chosen the same?"

"Because it was my fault." And the pain of it ate away at him inside even now, the hard ball of it which felt like lead in his belly after so many years of adding on his guilt and his shame.

"You summoned the rain?"

"Of course not."

"You are God and know what weather comes miles and miles down the road from where you stand?"

"I know that the arroyo floods when there is rain. I should have gotten them out of there when I smelled it in the air."

"And perhaps I should have kept you all inside that day, for fear of rain. For fear of snakes and scorpions. For fear of the sun. Perhaps we should not have moved here at all. Perhaps one of you would have been run over in a busy street had your father wished to stay in New York."

"Mother!" Shocked, Duke stood and paced to the window. "Tell me that it isn't true."

Duke said nothing, but his heart beat fast while his mind whirled around what his mother had said. Could it be that he'd wasted all these years? The horror of that thought warred against the guilt which was crumbling before him. It was true, and he couldn't argue with that any longer.

"Mother, Cheyenne has…certain skills that I want to talk to you about."

His mother drew her woolen shawl more closely about her despite the heat of the late afternoon. She would need it once the sun went down, when the cool settled over the desert and the coming rain chased the heat away. "This is why you have truly left her? Tell me about them."

Duke felt his mother must understand. "No, no not at all. She can do magic."

His mother took the words without surprise on her face. She sat in the rocking chair near the window and looked out. "Is it the magic of ancestors long gone?"

"Yes, it is. She told me where it came from, about the people who came over a land bridge centuries...thousands of years ago. I want to know...I didn't know if maybe you..." He let the thought hang.

His mother laughed gently, the lines on her face crinkling up beautifully on her tanned skin. "No, I do not. It is true that I come from much different stock than your father, but I do not pretend to be able to do more with my body and spirit than my own ancestors could. You are not frightened by her... skills, you call them?"

"No, never once. She is made to live in the desert, on the prairie. I do not know how she lasted so long in a city."

And as his mother continued to ask questions, to make him speak of Cheyenne and what he had learned about her in his time in Warren, he began to understand what he was missing, what he had left behind. Yes, he had felt guilt, but the feeling moving over him now felt different. Bigger, somehow. It filled his heart just as being with his family did. And he knew what he had to do.

Chapter 55

The sun set brilliantly here, the sky just as vast as the prairie, and just as on fire with brushes of red and orange and pink and purple. He stared at it from his bedroom window as the day left in fire, and the stars winked into existence as deep indigo and black crept into the sky.

He had spent the better part of his day speaking of her, and with the vastness of the desert before him and nothing else to do in the moment, he thought deeply of her. Of what might be in his heart for her.

And every night, he dreamt of her.

He woke with a yearning for her that was so great, he had to touch himself.

Her hair, her face, those smart green eyes, the heat of her soft skin against him. Never in his life had he known a woman could be so soft, could feel so right against him.

He came with a quiet moan that he felt to his very core. And when he was finished, shuddering, he wanted her even more. He lay there gasping for breath, and he knew what he must do.

It took him days to finish recovering from his injury and his journey there and to learn what he had missed in his time away.

His family had taken him back into their fold without so much as a negative word. Would Cheyenne take him back so easily?

There was one final conversation he needed to have before he left. He found his father in his study, a cool breeze coming in the open window.

"Father."

"Son."

"I have to go back to the Kansas territory."

"I am not surprised."

Silence hung between them.

"Will you go back to your woman?"

"And go back to assess whether the ruffians are holding the line or not. They need to be driven out."

His father seemed surprised. "And to beg forgiveness and tell this woman—Cheyenne—that you love her? What is a man if he cannot tell the woman he loves that he loves her?"

"Why should I?" Duke asked. Thinking that perhaps he loved Cheyenne and being confronted about it appeared to be two different things. Why should he give his father the satisfaction of hearing him say it? Wasn't it enough that he felt it?

"You sound like a boy. A man would face her head on and tell her how she feels."

"As you do with mother? I have never once heard a word of love come from your lips." He didn't see the hand before it struck him across the face. Eyes watering, a hand rushed up to his lips. The bottom one had been split by the force of his father's hand. His fists immediately came up to the defense, but his father was already stepping back out of range of Duke's fists. And Duke saw himself in the man. Their fighting stance was the same, both ready with their fists and sparkle in their eyes.

"I never thought I'd have to strike you once you were a man. I see now that I was wrong." His father shook out his hand, relaxed back a few more steps. "Your head is so hard, though, it's no wonder no sense has made its way in there."

It took an immeasurable amount of control for Duke to drop his fists. Though he wanted to plan a fist in his father's face he pulled the handkerchief from his pocket and held it to his lip. His ears still rang from his mother's cuffing, and now this? His anger and confusion bubbled together.

His father's eyes were hard. "I love your mother more dearly than anything else in my life save God above. God can take my military career, he can take my riches, can have this ranch and everything that I have worked for. But he cannot have her. I would die for her," he said, a fire in his eyes that Duke felt mirrored in his own heart for Cheyenne.

"I had no ide…"

"Do you love the woman you left behind?" His father interrupted

Duke knew now, could say it without hesitation. "Yes."

"I understand that you left to keep her from harm, but it sounds as though you kept running when you should have turned back and gone to her. Is this true?"

"Yes." That truth hurt even more than his throbbing lip.

His father sighed and sat on the edge of his desk. The heat of the late summer would have stifled the room without the breeze coming through the windows. It smelled of rain coming in the night. Duke's eyes wandered over the shelves of books and the exotic items his father had brought back with him from his travels. The skulls of monkeys and a strange reptile, the feathers from jungle birds, the ancient fossils and chunks of amber.

"I have gone too far to make amends."

"God does not take away his mercy just because we have sinned again, my son. He never takes away that offer of mercy."

"I have not found much of God on my travels. You see what they are trying to do in Missouri, what they are trying to bring to the Kansas territory? It is abominable."

"Could you bring your woman here?"

Duke sat on that for a moment, imagining Cheyenne trekking through the desert. She wouldn't complain, he knew that, and with her skills, they might have a more comfortable trip, a less dangerous one. He imagined her as she had been on the day she had worn a man's clothes to fight beside him. Yes, she would do it, if only she would leave the town she had come to love.

"If she would part with the town her father is founding, yes."

"No one said you would have to stay forever. You are young yet, and I am not ready to give up the ranch to you. But one day it will be yours."

"It should have been James," Duke said quietly.

His father nodded, then sighed. "At one time, yes. But that choice was taken from him by God."

"How can you say that and not hate me?" Duke asked, voice raised. "How can you simply say those things and not feel like your insides are boiling?"

"I miss him, but it would not do to dwell. It has been twenty years, and you are alive, Duke Channing. You are alive and well and full of fight. Do you still wish to plant a fist in my face?"

"Of course."

"That is a good thing."

"That's insane."

"I am just glad you are here."

A quiet fell over the pair as Duke absorbed everything. Perhaps, just perhaps, he had been wrong to take on all the blame. He could not go so far as to say that it was God's will. No, that he would never believe. But something loosened inside him.

His father left him there to sit and stew after a while, called to chores on the ranch which he chose to do, though he had the staff to handle all of it.

And where did Cheyenne fit into all this?

But he knew. He knew, though he had not let himself think it, had not allowed his heart to even feel it. Her great love for the prairie, for the West, her fight and spirit and sharp tongue—they all mirrored his feelings for the West. Would she ever leave that dusty town in Kansas?

Not without her father.

A pain seared straight through him. Her father. She would surely know by now that he had passed or would suspect that something was very wrong. And what then? She was capable of taking care of herself, but that didn't mean that she needed to be alone. The thought that when he offered himself and she rejected him made him feel sick, but he couldn't run from it now. He would go to her, and she would accept him or not, but he couldn't live with not knowing any longer.

He packed now that his strength had returned, and his family offered a fresh horse and bags laden with supplies. Their goodbye was heartfelt, but not forever. They both knew he would return.

And for weeks after, he pushed his horse on the trail with almost no knowledge of the terrain that passed beside him. His focus was singular, and he would not rest until he was back in Warren. Back by Cheyenne's side where he belonged.

Chapter 56

Cheyenne's sleep was restless. She had slept for years alone, and yet now, without Duke by her side, the room felt empty. It was the damnedest thing. And even as exhausted as she was, as ready as she was for the next day to come and for them to drive back the McLaurys once and for all, she only slept in fits and spurts.

But when she did, she dreamt he visited her. He stumbled into the room, bruised and bloody and covered in dust from the trail. He fell into her arms where she held him as tightly as she could. He had been shot, carried with him the bullets which he could not avoid.

She could almost believe that he was there with her, sharing her bed again. And he was just as she remembered, all hard muscles and hot skin that smelled of hard work and hard days on the trail. And he was rough with her, taking her with the passion of missing each other.

Cheyenne woke knowing something was wrong. Duke's apparition, the smell of him still in the room, got her quickly out of bed and on her feet. But what could she do?

She sat down on the edge of her bed, the exhaustion of the last week weighing on her. She still missed Duke with a fierceness she couldn't shake.

When Brogan met her for breakfast, he looked as tired as she felt.

"This is the day?" she asked cautiously.

"One more good push and we'll have them," Brogan said confidently.

Molly served them coffee which roused Cheyenne when she thought nothing might. She shot the woman a look over where she stood behind the bar. "Molly, dear, what did you put in this?"

And Molly, ever the clever one, just smiled and winked at Cheyenne. "A bit of extra. It's Molly's Magical Mixture. Do you like it?"

And while she didn't think there was actual magic in it, Cheyenne did find she was ready to face the day, whatever it might bring. But she did taste a hint of chicory root. And a number of other roots and herbs which she herself had never thought to put together. While the other woman might not be a witch in the true sense, she knew how to work her own kind of magic in the kitchen.

Brogan downed the last of his coffee and stood while he finished off his toast. "Molly. Thank you kindly for the food. We'll be needing the energy today."

Molly waved him off. "Just go finish off those ruffians. They're bad for business."

When Cheyenne was back on her horse, she realized just how saddle sore she was. Riding for pleasure, galloping for the fun of it was one matter. Riding into battle, maneuvering to save one's life, holding on with just her legs while she shot a rifle—those were other things entirely.

Brogan must've heard her moan because he stifled a laugh.

Cheyenne shot him a look without malice. Were he Duke, she could have threatened to turn him into a rabbit to get a laugh from him. And a look in his eyes that shone at the challenge. She missed him. God, she missed him. She was seized with the sudden emotion that clawed up the back of her throat and squeezed the breath from her lungs. Damn Duke Channing for ever coming into her life. He was likely dead somewhere on the trail and she'd never know. Never have the satisfaction of actually turning him into a rabbit for leaving her here alone.

"Saddle sore?" Brogan called.

Cheyenne tried to shake the feeling. "Yes, quite. But it is a small price to pay for ending this."

"Spoken like a true soldier," Brogan said.

And then they rode. Under the early morning sun, when dew still stuck to prairie grasses, they rode onto the prairie in a wide arc that would take them up to the McLaury camp a different way today. And a way that had been cleared of traps and snares. Johnny Tanner's horse had found a bear trap lying in wait in a thicket just off a path that led to the camp. The poor beast had to be shot by Johnny himself before they were found out. As it was, men came running to the commotion, and Johnny barely got away with his skin.

As they drew near, Cheyenne took a deep breath and raised her rifle.

Chapter 57

Smoke and flames made the day nearly unbearable. Gunshots rang through the air, most missing their mark. The sound of shattering glass in town became but another background noise to the stampeding of hooves and the cries of men down the street. Try as they might, they had not been able to keep the McLaurys from town, but their enemy's numbers were dwindling quickly.

Cheyenne, under her wide-brimmed hat and in trousers which allowed her to be less encumbered on her horse, rode opposite Brogan. And though he treated her kindly, he did treat her as a man might another man. Exhaustion rode closely with her all day, and her muscles ached with lifting the gun time and again. Brogan was fair but expected her all, and while she was used to giving that with her magic, it was another thing altogether to give it with her physical strength and a sharp eye. Her admiration for what Duke could do grew even as it made her heart ache and tremble.

Brogan rode up next to her, their horses bumping hips. He grabbed her arm to get her attention. "You recall I said one more push, and we'll have them?"

"I do," she said, feeling something well up within her, a last burst of energy that would carry her through.

"This is it!" Brogan said. And with his men behind him, they drove forward into the last of the rebels. Cheyenne rode in with Duke's pistol, hitting her mark once, twice, thrice, and fairly trampling a fourth man whom she was certain would not get up again.

It was a dirty, awful day, and when the dust finally began to settle, Cheyenne surveyed the damage before her. Her town, though it was scarred, still stood. Her town.

Brogan rode up and clapped her on the shoulder. "Will you petition for sheriff next, Miz Cheyenne?"

Cheyenne laughed with what little energy she had left. "Perhaps tomorrow. Today, I'll spend celebrating."

Her ears rang as she rode back toward the stable. Her horse would need to rest for many days after what she had asked of him. *She* would need to rest.

She looked up at the sky once she was on her way back to her quarters, stumbling with exhaustion. *Duke, if you're out there, I wish you could have been here. You would have loved this skirmish. And Father...Father, please come home. I cannot do this without you.*

Chapter 58

Duke rode into the forsaken land between Mexico territory and Kansas territory. He rode as laden as he could with provisions and bits to trade along the way. And he rode as fast as he could, beginning his day before the sun rose and riding long into the night. All in all, it would take him a month of hard riding to get back to Cheyenne.

And his heartbeat said the same thing over and over again as he rode. *Cheyenne, Cheyenne, Cheyenne.*

There was more traffic on the Santa Fe than he'd ever seen before. Wagons loaded with men and families headed west. Men on horseback with their saddle roll, taking little with them except their hopes. He'd heard that there was gold to the west, in the mountains, but that sounded like a hard, cold life. Duke much preferred the heat. The heat of the day in the desert, the sand and rocks nearly scorching to the touch. The heat of the day on the prairie, where it hurt to have the sun in your eyes. And the heat of Cheyenne, her hot, flushed skin under him. Her warm hands and feet next to him in bed. Her eyes flashing with heat when he teased her too much. All of her was warmth to him, and he knew now that he needed it. Needed it like man needed fire in the winter.

She was with him with every thought.

His mother and father had both told him in their own way that he must apologize for what he had done to her. But how was a man supposed to do that? The worry of it ate at him as nothing had before.

Suppose she didn't take him back? Suppose she had…no, he couldn't think that. He couldn't think that she had perished if the McLaurys had been able to reorganize themselves and invade the town.

He didn't know if he liked this new way of looking at things. It made everything too bright to look at, made him worry and wonder and think about the future. And thinking of the future while living in the West was a dangerous business on the best of days.

But either the ruffians he saw on the way back weren't looking for trouble or they saw the wild look in his eyes, but he was unmolested on the trail back through scrubby desert where mountains rose in the distance to his north and west, and through the great vastness which was the western prairie. Rolling grassy hills gave way to the flatter prairie. As he rode, he wondered if people would ever come to populate this place, if someday a train would roar through this wild land. The stars stretched from horizon to horizon when he bedded down at night, and the only sounds were crickets and the far-off calls of coyotes. During the day, great herds of buffalo roamed and grazed. One day, he watched from afar as natives hunted down a great buffalo. The hard beauty of it squeezed his heart.

He imagined living among these grassy plains.

But he *did* live in them. In a place called Warren, where a sultry witch waited for him.

He followed the sun in the morning and let it chase his back well into the evening. He rode into Wichita feeling as though he may have become part of the prairie while he was out in it.

He stopped in Wichita, and there was drink and song below him well into the night. In the morning, the current sheriff stopped him to chat, mentioning their own opening for deputies. Duke's reputation had followed him here, it seemed. And did he want to run for deputy or sheriff in the next free election? They could use men like him, Wade said, could use a firm but fair hand in a city that was wild and needed taming.

But no. He had business north, a job to do. He did want to come back through someday, to see what there was to see in this raucous, dirty town rising out of the prairie. Like Warren, Wichita had found a river to build itself by, so perhaps it would survive. Perhaps trade would come through here like it did up north.

He left later than he wanted that morning and felt he was running out of time to get back to Cheyenne. He should never have left. And he felt cracked open, like God had watched his ride from far above the clear sky. What was honor and trust and loyalty if one broke a promise like the one he had given to Cheyenne?

Selfish is what he had been. Selfish and scared. He could admit that to himself, but could he admit that to Cheyenne, her father?

Chapter 59

When he was close to the city, he began to feel that something was amiss. He had ridden into plenty of ghost towns during his time as a marshal and a ranger. Towns that had been emptied because the occupants had all simply left for one reason or another—lack of food, famine, bad water, sickness, trouble with the natives—were common in the west. Most people weren't equipped to begin life out this way, didn't have the necessary skills to survive or thrive.

But sometimes he came upon a town where there had been bloodshed. That happened for a number of reasons as well.

He saw the blood, but there were no bodies. Had they all already been dragged away by animals? But no, even animals left traces of their kills, and the bodies had been picked up from the spot where they lay. There were no marks to suggest they had been dragged. So, humans had picked up the bodies. To burn or bury. He hurried on.

He rode up to the river to see if there was a bustle or even someone to speak with. But the ferry drifted out near the middle of the river. It looked as though no one was aboard. A thrill of fear lanced through him. Warren was small, but it was bustling. Now he saw no one. Smoke not far distant, the kind of smoke which came from a building fire, rose above the trees. He spurred his mount faster.

The town ahead was smoking, smoldering.

He rode into town with a feeling of growing horror. Here, too, no one was around. Several outbuildings and the farthest town store were burned-out husks, still smoking. Windows were broken out down the storefront walks and doors hung open. Paper and debris tumbled down the street. He saw no bodies, for which he was thankful, but the sight he saw was bad enough. Had the McLaurys simply ridden everyone out of town? Had they taken them somewhere to slaughter them? That did not sound like their way, but better men had done worse for far less.

Spurred by the thought, he hastened his horse on toward the other end of town and Cheyenne's residence.

He knew he'd drawn the McLaurys away. He had. They had chased him all the way to the Texas border, then harassed him nearly all the way to Fort Worth. But how many had it truly been? He'd killed near a dozen in the skirmish leaving town and while they tried to track him. Then there were the three in Texas, but how many were there left behind?

He walked into the restaurant below the Goodnight rooms with his gun drawn. But no one was here either.

And he'd lost track of time. How long had he been gone? As long as he'd been running, he wasn't certain. The time at his family's ranch, which seemed to exist outside of time, where he had to regain his strength, was already a blur of days and nights and days and nights.

The grand doors which led to the Goodnights' spacious quarters upstairs were barricaded with all manner of chairs

271

and furniture. Feeling fueled by the certainty that Cheyenne was near, he tore through the barricade like a man possessed. The closer he got, the more he swore he felt more powerful, nearly indestructible.

The hall beyond was quiet and dusty. A window at the far end was broken out, the fine lace curtains blowing in the breeze. The place felt deserted, haunted. Though he wasn't Catholic, he still crossed himself, feeling as though he had both stepped onto sacred and hallowed ground. He prayed it was not a graveyard too.

If he didn't know better, he would have said that the hush over the place was simply bated breath, waiting for something so it might exhale. As though everything would spring to life once the trigger set the world into motion again. If this were some kind of magic, he didn't want to tangle with it unless he had Cheyenne by his side.

He pushed his way into her rooms, terrified of what he might find.

Chapter 60

And there he found her. Huddled into a corner in the upturned sitting room, her clothes torn and dusty. The rooms looked as though they hadn't seen a maid in weeks. Good God how long had he been gone?

He ran to her and gathered her into his arms, too glad to see her to even wonder if she was unhurt. She mewled and weak sparks flew from her fingers. They hit him like static electricity and didn't hurt. He puzzled at it.

Was she so exhausted that she had nothing left?

Duke pulled her against him, feeling overwhelmed with something he had never felt before. It was kin to the feeling he had felt when he realized his brother and sister were no longer alive, but this feeling was bigger somehow, fiercer.

He touched her hair, her arms, every part of her he could reach. Was he truly here with her? Or had they both died, and this was their purgatory? Her eyes fluttered open, confusion giving way to surprise, and then she was hugging him back, her own hands feeling over him as though she didn't believe what she was seeing.

"Where is everyone?" Duke demanded frantically. "When I rode into town and it was deserted, I thought...I thought you were dead. I thought the worst."

"Everyone is at the church celebrating this evening. I couldn't. I am so tired, Duke. I…" Cheyenne grabbed his arms to steady herself, and then his hands were everywhere at once. Dear God, she was so happy to see him. She'd never been happier to see someone.

And then her strong, steel man was burying his face in the crook of her neck."I'm sorry," he said. "I have wronged you. There is nothing I can do to take back th…"

"Shhh," she admonished, tears pooling in her own eyes. "You are here now. You are here now."

"But…" he began.

She silenced him with her mouth. He tasted of dust and salt and riding long and hard across the desert, the prairie. He tasted of guilt and remorse, and she was reminded of their first night together, when they lay in their sweat in the dirt and the grass, and the night sang around them. It was still seared in her mind, as she knew it would be forever. It would be one of the many moments she would treasure.

And as he pulled her closer into the kiss, opened his mouth for her eager tongue, a great wind arose, circling around them both. Spirits whispered within it. And the power which ignited between them bound them close, and a vapor passed from his mouth to hers.

She pulled away when she felt it enter her and looked up at Duke in shock, her hand coming up to her mouth. There was a great turbulence within her and she felt her power rushing back, the magic coursing through her as pure and true as it ever had been. And more than before. A hundredfold, a thousandfold. It ran through her veins with such joy as she had never experienced before. She felt renewed and whole again.

"Duke," she whispered, her hand at her lips still. His steely eyes never left hers.

"I think you sent something along with me," he said.

"I didn't…I didn't mean to."

He chuckled softly as he leaned in to press his cheek against her, his stubble rasping gently against her skin. "Yes, you wouldn't have given that up willingly for the world. But it kept me safe until I returned to you."

"My bad man," she whispered in his ear, catching his lobe between her teeth.

He hissed softly as she continued her gentle assault with her teeth. "My witch," he said breathlessly.

"Will you always call me that?" she asked with a laugh, then set her teeth against his neck, which drew a louder hiss.

"As long as you're enchanting me with those damn eyes of yours. And those teeth," he groaned, driving his hands into her hair. Those glorious silken locks spilled through his fingers, trailed down her back. That she accepted him without berating him, that she opened her arms when she had every right to shut him out, it touched him.

"I will spend the rest of my life apologizing to you," he said, catching her eyes with his. "I am a fool for what I have done. I don't deserve you, and I'm sorry."

The ghost of a teasing smile pulled at Cheyenne's lips. "Perhaps you don't, but I want you all the same. You ran from what you did not know," she said carefully, "though you broke my heart for it."

"Can you trust me again?"

She buried her head in the crook of his neck and breathed deeply. Man, horse, sun, wind, desert, prairie, they were all part of him. Her wild man. Her rebel. "I can," she said. "With time and patience and love."

"Love," Duke said, feeling the word in his mouth. Had he even told his own mother he loved her when he was a boy?

"You do not have to say it," she laughed softly. "But I must feel it to be happy. It is more than words, anyway. It is how you treat me, how you treasure me."

Duke gathered her close, stroked her hair. "How I touch you?"

"Yes," Cheyenne sighed, closed her eyes. "That too."

There was a slow building, of a story told with their hands. His were hesitant at first, seeking. She gave willingly, opening herself to him, letting herself be vulnerable, to believe that this was what she had been waiting for her entire life.

He discovered her again, learned her shape and her curves, found again the spot where her neck met her shoulders that made her gasp and sigh. But slowly. Slowly so that he would remember it forever. Forever and until the next time he touched her, which he already wanted. Already yearned for the next time.

"I want to hear your story," Cheyenne said.

Duke cringed. "It is not a happy one."

"Good," she said with another laugh. "I would not have expected it to be. But I want to hear it soon."

"I saw my family," he said. "I went back to them. I had not seen them in twenty years. They live deep in the desert on a large ranch there. I was not always a rebel. I was once only the first son of a wealthy man."

So he had done much atoning since he had been away. She hoped that there had been healing in it for him, too. She yearned for him to be able to see the world, to experience it without thinking only of his ultimate demise. She wanted him to live.

"You are more than that, and I think you know it. But they welcomed you?"

"They did. They did not have to."

"They did because they love you," Cheyenne said. "Love washes away everything."

"You sound so certain."

"I am more certain than I ever have been. You have come back to me. I feel I could fly for the happiness within me."

Duke pressed his cheek to hers, unable to ask her about her own family, to see if Isaac had returned or if the truth of it had finally come to her.

Her dress rustled as she slid her arms around him, and warmth filled him. He was here. He was back. And he wasn't going to let this woman go ever again. "I love you, Cheyenne Channing."

Chapter 61

When he drew her closer to him with a hand at the small of her back, she arched into his hand, bent like water and flowed to him.

She tipped her head up, and he dipped his own to take her lips. This time, he savored, holding the wild woman still against him. And there she trembled while he took what he wanted, possessed her with his lips, his hands.

When they drew apart, she was breathless and there were stars in her eyes.

"You're really here," she said.

"I am."

"To stay?"

"If you'll have me."

She answered with her mouth, drunk on being once again filled with magic and with the sight of him.

Duke guided her to her bed and pressed her back on the edge so her legs hung over the side. What a fool he had been to even leave those beautiful legs behind. What a fool he had been.

"Duke!" she cried out.

"Yes?"

"Whatever are you doing?"

"Pleasuring my wife," he said.

A noise of satisfaction left her that sounded like a plea. "Your wife?"

"That's what I said."

Cheyenne let out a little laugh and collapsed back onto the bed. If this were a dream, she would die here in it, she felt so happy.

He knelt between her legs and pressed his nose into the crease of her thighs. He could get drunk on the scent of her, could lose himself in that heady scent. He gently moved his nose side to side through the patch of hair at her mound, teasing her, tickling her, relishing in the 'oohs' and 'ahhs' he got out of Cheyenne.

And when he spread her lips and pressed a light kiss to her most sensitive place, she gasped and arched her back.

And then he took her in his mouth, flicking his tongue over the rosebud glistening with her want for him.

She bucked against him, and he reached his arms under her legs so he could hold her against his face.

There against him, so vulnerable and open, she felt the last of the previous weeks slip away into the face of pleasure.

Cheyenne rode him until her pleasure crested, as swollen and golden as the sun rising over the prairie in the summertime. Wave after wave of it rocked her until she didn't know which way was up.

Duke slowly crawled up into the bed with her, pulling her further into the soft confines of its space.

"I'll have you now," he said huskily as he knelt above her, the scent of her still filling him.

She looked beautiful splayed out beneath him, her hair all a

279

mess and her dark skin begging to be kissed again.

"Yes," she breathed, her eyes still closed. If she didn't open them, then she couldn't find that she was dreaming, simply imagining that he was here with her, that he had come back to her. "Yes, please."

And so he did, lifting her up hips so that he could rejoin her completely. She cried out when he entered her, when he slid into her wetness and claimed her as his own again.

"Duke, my God!" she cried breathily.

"I am not so certain your God would approve of your thinking," he said and leaned into to take her tantalizing mouth. Her mouth hung open and wetness glistened on her lips. He had to have her lips on his, to mingle the taste of her, from above and below.

And when they were both spent, Duke pulled his woman against him, pressed his face into her hair, and slept.

Chapter 62

I t would take weeks to set the place aright, but every able-bodied man and woman was pitching in to help get the town back on its feet. He was pleased to see Molly shining up her bar the next morning. Come to think of it, he was pleased to see any other people the next morning. After his fear that Warren had become a ghost town, he had to concede that while he still didn't like people, he did like it when he knew they were near.

But there was one thing weighing heavily on him still.

Cheyenne had not mentioned her father yet. Had she accepted that he was dead? Or had she simply refused to believe it? He did not think her naïve enough to not understand what now must be true.

He broached the subject to her gently as she sipped on tea and nibbled at toast late that morning.

"I have feared the worst," Cheyenne said, tears of true sadness welling in her eyes. "When I saw his favorite horse in the stable…" She didn't need to finish that sentence.

"Have they looked for him?"

"Of course. But not as thoroughly as we could now that the McLaurys have been beaten back. The surrounding prairie is safe once again. I should go out and…"

"No," Duke said. "Allow me. Whatever I find, you do not need to be part of that search party. I won't allow it."

Cheyenne cast her eyes down, for once not arguing. This was something she hadn't been ready to face. And in the absence of a battle to be fought, there was not much else she could think about.

And Duke had to know for himself.

This was only the beginning of his atonement. And if it took him the rest of his life, he would keep doing whatever he could for Cheyenne. He got on his horse and rode out onto the prairie, through the tall grasses and tangled thickets. They had found Isaac's horse, but not the man. And the months Duke had been gone? He would be lucky to find bones, but there was water and plenty of hiding places near where they had found Isaac's horse. Men had survived on less if they wanted to live badly enough.

He fixed Isaac's horse up with a bridle, secured the reins to his pommel, and trotted out of town. The poor horse wouldn't be going on long rides or journeys any longer, but he'd recovered from his split hoof enough that he could pull a plow or serve as a gentle first horse for some young boy or girl.

The day drew on, hot and humid. It was surely the last of the sweltering days, he thought as he rode his horse through the scratchy prairie grasses which were dry and crispy in the heat.

As he rode, his faith grew. The horse had returned, but the man and the charm did not. The McLaurys would have gloated about either kidnapping or killing such a man as Isaac Goodnight, yet Cheyenne said she had heard nothing of the sort.

He hadn't told Cheyenne that while the bag that had contained the charm had returned, the charm hadn't. Isaac Goodnight still had his daughter's charm with him. Duke had to believe that. He had to believe that the power that had followed him all the way to Texas and the desert and back could also sustain a man on the prairie for eight weeks or longer.

The horse whickered and pulled to the east. Duke untied the reins and threw them over the horse's back, letting him go where he would.

He urged his mount into a lope when Isaac's horse disappeared into a grove of trees just beyond the limestone field. One couldn't call it a forest, but it would offer cover to anyone wishing to get out of the sun and not be seen.

He hurried into the shade, feeling pulled as the horse had been.

And there was Isaac Goodnight, relatively unharmed in some scrub north of town. He was sunburned and in desperate need of a shave, but he otherwise appeared unharmed. Duke cursed with relief. The man should've been dead. In one burned hand, he clutched something. Duke's skin prickled. Isaac Goodnight was damn lucky to be alive.

The two stared at each other for a long minute. Duke dismounted and walked closer, wary still.

"How long have you been out here?" Duke looked around the little camp Isaac had been living in. It was sparse but utilitarian. The bones of small animals—including many rabbits, Duke noted—were in a neat pile beside the banked fire that Isaac surely would have died without.

"Weeks. Months. I do not know how many days I lost before

I began keeping track." The man's voice cracked with disuse.

"How have you survived? What happened?" Duke couldn't fathom what had kept the older gentleman alive these long, hot days. The creek looked cool and clear, but how had he hunted?

Isaac said nothing as he opened his clutched hand and showed Duke what was there. Duke felt his heart leap in his chest. He recognized the protective charm which Cheyenne had made for her father before he had left on his fated journey. It was a braided and woven leather loop neatly holding several colored stones and what looked like feathers and grasses.

"I cannot account for it except the protection my daughter sent with me," Isaac finally said. "But my leg was broken when my horse threw me. I thought I would die out here. I heard the great commotion over the last weeks, then silence. If you are here, the town must still stand."

Duke stared at the man, unbelieving. When he finally recovered his voice, he found it gruff, and hot tears stung his eyes. The love Cheyenne had for her father was humbling, and he was humbled that she shared some of that love with him.

"It does. Let's get you home."

Duke helped Isaac to his feet, and they shuffled slowly to the second horse.

"You seem certain you would find me."

Duke didn't want to tell the man that he thought him long dead and picked clean by vultures and all manner of predators.

"I could not think of any other outcome. I don't know how Cheyenne would have taken the news."

Isaac grunted as he got situated on the horse. He was hurt. Badly. His leg would have to be rebroken to be reset right,

Duke saw. That alone could kill a grown man. That he had not succumbed to infection or animal attacks in the night was a miracle.

"We may still have a battle ahead of us. Cheynne…" How could Duke tell his father-in-law what had happened?

"Is she well?"

"She is. I will let her tell you the tale." And Duke turned them slowly toward town, hope and relief growing within him with every step.

Chapter 63

Cheyenne told the tale, and Duke listened with held breath.

She described the battle, how she had worked with Major Brogan to ready and fortify the town. Isaac and Duke both felt appropriately angered for the lack of support they had gotten from the fort until their victory was certain.

"And where were you while all this was happening?" Isaac asked Duke pointedly.

"He had driven away a good number of the McLaurys so that we might be able to take on a smaller number." Cheyenne held Duke's eyes as she said it, but spoke nothing of his abandonment.

"Is that so?"

"They chased me all the way to Texas before they finally gave up." Which was the truth, though the rest of his truth still sat uneasily within him. He would atone for that for as long as necessary. He knew now what he had almost lost, what he had almost given up by running away.

"And what of that group?"

"They came back in pairs and threes. We were able to pick them off them the help of Brogan and his men. The fort never gave us an official contingency, but Brogan and the Rangers lent their help."

Isaac sat quietly with his tea and whiskey, looking contemplative and finally relaxed.

"I shot a gun, father. Well," Cheyenne said. She lifted her chin. She would be proud for her entire life of how she had defended the town, even without her magic.

"I am sorry to have missed the excitement. I should have been here," Isaac said, shifting uncomfortably. His leg ached from being rebroken and set straight, but he felt already that it would heal right this time. Thanks to Cheyenne, his mother, and the doctor, he would be walking again in a few weeks' time.

"I'm proud of you, daughter," Isaac spoke softly to his daughter. "And you, Duke. I am thankful that you stayed."

When Duke opened his mouth to tell Isaac that he hadn't chosen the right path, Cheyenne set a hand on his arm to silence him. "We are all thankful that Duke is here. And that you are returned to us in one piece, Father."

Isaac Goodnight nodded, and upon seeing what appeared to be a growing love between his daughter and Duke, decided to say nothing else on the subject. It seemed they had worked things out after all, and for that, he was pleased. If his daughter was happy, he would be as well.

That evening, Cheyenne found Duke at the lookout point where they had so often met before. The sun set in blazes of red and orange in the west.

Together they stood while the greatness of the prairie stretched out below them. It was as vast as the ocean and more beautiful in Cheyenne's eyes.

"I worry I am not good for you," Duke said

Cheyenne reached out and threaded her fingers through his. "A woman who shoots a gun and wields magic would be a bad woman to some."

Duke turned a grin on her. "Then they shall leave you alone, and you will be all mine."

She saw him go broody again when he turned back to the setting sun.

When he spoke, his voice was so low that Cheyenne almost didn't hear him.

"I don't want to lose you. I don't want you to get hurt again on my account. For any reason."

Cheyenne set a gentle hand on Duke's strong back. His muscles relaxed under her tender touch. "My mother lost her life giving birth to me. That doesn't mean that we must throw our futures away simply because we have lost that which was closest to us. It does not mean we should not love. If anything, it means we should love more. Harder. With more passion."

"I cannot stay in one place. It would not suit me."

"I have always wanted to see the desert West, the mountains which I hear are full of gold."

"Cheyenne," Duke began.

She shushed him gently and drew him against her ."Come. Hold me as the sun sets."

He did, sliding his arms around her from behind to pull her close. Her skirts rustled against him. She was bedecked in her finery again, and he found he liked that just fine. She could be both his wild prairie woman and the gentlewoman witch in her finery.

And what was he?

He leaned his chin against the side of her head, and she made a little noise of pleasure and leaned her head against his.

"My bad man," Cheyenne said, without any heat, as though she had heard his thoughts. "You are my rebel cowboy, my man of the Wild West. You are my man."

"I like that just fine," he replied.

"I'm glad," she said with a contented sigh. "I'm glad."

Forthcoming from Autumn Storm...

After *The Rebel & the Witch* is...
The Widower & the Witch
Catherine and Brogan's story

Chapter 1

It had been a good summer for Warren but an awful one for Brogan Taylor.

Brogan heaved a deep sigh, glad that he was alone for the moment with his thoughts and the early evening sun. The sunsets on the prairie were hard to beat, but he loved the moments before them the best. When the light changed from day to not-quite-evening. When every living thing paused for a moment to recognize that the day would soon end.

He should count himself lucky, he knew. If not for Duke Channing and Cheyenne Goodnight and her father, his summer would have been much worse.

As it was, he found himself a widower, adrift with half a house built and no one to help make it a home.

"Bethy," he said to the early evening sun. "I'm so sorry."

And because it was too much for him to bear, he turned away from the sun, trying to curse and fight away the tears of grief that still followed him everywhere he went. It had been a year, goddammit, and he hadn't even known Beth anymore, not after how long he'd been gone. But she had been constant, had been kind and tender to him in her letters; the perfect wife. On paper, at least.

And when any thought of wanting something more from the marriage had crossed his mind, he squashed it down. Gratefulness was what he needed, not wanting more when he had everything that should make him happy.

It didn't stop the thoughts from continually coming around, though.

"Leave it alone, man," he admonished himself.

Below him on the newly graveled road, a heavily laden wagon made its way toward Warren. The team that pulled it labored hard in the heat of the waning day, pulling to the left and then to the right, as though an inexperienced driver were at the reins.

Brogan clucked at his mount and spurred him down the hill toward the road. Something wasn't right about that wagon.

As he got closer, the scene confused him even more. A woman sat on the wagon seat, face red from the heat, her bonnet dangling behind her, its laced snarled into her still pinned hair. She wore clothes he had only seen in Kansas City, or on Duke Channing's wife when she wasn't riding the prairie.

The woman driving the wagon swayed dangerously in the seat.

The team shied away from Brogan when he rode up next to them, with no help from the driver who appeared to not have noticed him.

"Pull over!" he hollered over the road noise.

And then the woman did notice him, her eyes growing wide with fear. She yanked back hard on the reins,

Brogan finally grabbed ahold of the bridle of one of the front horses and stopped the wagon slowly.

"Just what do you..." And when he turned to the woman in the wagon, he was stunned to find himself looking at the barrel of a very old, very ornate gun. Its wood handle shone in the fading light of the day, and the engravings on the metal plates that adorned it glowed with recent shining. The derringer the woman held must've been years older than she was.

"Don't come any closer," the woman slurred. The hand which held the gun shook.

"You need water," Brogan said, frozen with one hand still hanging onto the lead horse and the other resting near his own firearm. Sweat ran down the back of his neck and under his collar. This had taken a turn he wasn't expecting even from the first unexpected turn at finding a woman of means driving a wagon alone on the prairie.

"Am I close to Warren?" The woman asked. Not a man who normally noticed such things, he wondered at how artfully her hair was arranged for how obviously alone she was. And how unmarked her clothing and hands were. If she were truly alone, how had she made it so far and so kept together? Brogan's mount shivered under him, a ripple and a twitch of the horse's skin that started up near its ears and that Brogan could feel roll under the saddle.

Brogan reached carefully for his water bag, keeping his eyes on the woman's the entire time. He didn't think that she could hit the side of a barn from five paces with the ancient thing—if it was even loaded—but there was a first time for everything. And he wasn't aiming to get shot by a woman with a derringer today.

"You're near enough, but it's getting dark, and from the look of things, you've not had water in a time."

He watched the woman debate answering him.

"If you don't guide me straight to town, I'll shoot you."

"That's fair," Brogan said as he tossed his water bag to the wagon seat.

The woman caught the water bag neatly despite her condition and lowered the gun slowly, keeping her eyes on Brogan. "Who are you?"

"Major Brogan Taylor."

The woman's green eyes (which looked oddly familiar), narrowed. "The fort or the..." she waved her hand around. "The...I don't know."

Brogan caught her meaning. "The fort. In the free state of Kansas."

The woman visibly relaxed, uncorked the water, and drank deeply. Brogan was at a loss for words as he watched her drain the last of his water. Droplets escaped her lips and ran down her neck, coursing over her skin and under the neckline of her dress. Feeling his face heat with impropriety, Brogan averted his eyes. "Are you traveling alone, ma'am?"

"I'll not answer any other questions until I see my cousin," the woman said. Her eyes were clearer now, though she still looked heat-stricken from the sun. And no wonder, if she was as alone as she appeared!

"Your cousin?"

"Cheyenne Goodnight. She lives in Warren, and if I'm almost there, I'd like to see her before night falls. How close am I?"

Brogan tried to hide his surprise. So that's where he'd seen eyes like that before. He took in this woman with that information in mind and saw a passing resemblance in the dark hair, the striking eyes. He had a strong respect for Miz Cheyenne after their dealings together with the McLaurys. Without her keen eye and sharp wit, Brogan wasn't certain where the town might be today, if it was still a town at all.

"Come, then," he said with one last look at the woman who claimed to be Cheyenne's cousin. "We'll need to go now before the dark catches up to us."

Chapter 2

Cheyenne was being chased around the couches in her sitting room by her darkly mischievous-looking husband. No matter that she held one sock and one boot captive in her hands while he had to tromp around with only one boot on trying to catch her.

She had just leaped around a footstool and cleverly evaded Duke's hands when there was a loud knock at the door. Startled, Cheyenne paused for just long enough for Duke to catch up to her. He wrapped his arms around her and pulled her into a blistering kiss. Happily caught, Cheyenne let herself be swept up in the kiss.

"I win," he said, the dark grin still on his face. Cheyenne couldn't argue with his tactics.

"Come in!" Cheyenne called when she had caught her breath.

Jonathan slowly opened the door, pretending, of course, that he hadn't heard the ruckus the pair were causing.

"Major Taylor is here to see you," Jonathan said.

Duke wrestled the other boot and sock from Cheyenne while her attention was on the door. "Did he say why?"

Jonathan made a noise in his throat. "Pardon me, but not you, sir. Mr. Taylor is here to speak with Mrs. Channing."

"Jonathan, you're to still call me Cheyenne. Did he say what he wanted?"

"No, Mrs. Channing. Only that he bid you come down to the street quickly."

Cheyenne looked to Duke, fear spearing through her. Though the month behind them had been blessedly calm, they both lived with the worry that someone else might come to take the McLaurys' place and disturb their peace.

"I'll go with you," Duke said quietly.

They both finished dressing and hurried down the stairs. Cheyenne rushed out the door toward where she saw Brogan's horse next to an exhausted team of wagon horses. Confusion replaced her fear.

"Brogan, what…" And she stopped dead when her shoes reached the edge of the street. Brogan was helping a woman from a wagon, but not just any woman. A woman who had been a girl last Cheyenne had seen her. A woman who could not and should not have been there at all.

But there she was, getting handed from the wagon as though it were the flashiest carriage, right onto the dusty street below her. When she saw Cheyenne, her face lit up in a grand smile.

"What are you doing here?" Cheyenne looked back at the wagon, as though she expected other people to jump out of it. Namely, a male chaperone, likely her uncle. But no one did.

Catherine brushed the dust from her dress. "If you're looking for someone else, there's no one there."

The look on her cousin's face was priceless. "You came alone? Or some terrible misfortune befell your chaperone along the way?"

The heat in Catherine's gaze matched that in Cheyenne's. "I left alone. I traveled alone. I arrived alone. Seems simple enough."

"Miz Cheyenne, your cousin is lucky she arrived here safely

at all, why it's only been a year since Elizabeth…" But the rest of the thought became caught in Brogan's throat.

The look Cheyenne gave him wavered between empathy and cool calculation as only Cheyenne Goodnight—Cheyenne Channing, now—could give.

"I am thankful such a gentleman was able to steer me right, cousin," Catherine said. "I'm astounded at the rudeness you're showing toward someone who saved me from certain death on the trail."

"Oh, no," Cheyenne said. "You will stay away from Brogan. And you," she pointed at Brogan, "will stay away from my cousin. She's going back home shortly in any case."

Brogan put his hands up. "I have no intention of…"

"You can't tell me what to do!" Catherine interrupted.

"In the absence of a chaperone or other adult, I surely can, and as soon as I can get you to a train, you'll be on it back home."

About the Author

Autumn Storm is a paranormal romance author from the United States. She first got into paranormal romance with The Parasol Protectorate series by Gail Carriager. Autumn loves both historical paranormal romance and contemporary paranormal romance. Wolf shifter romances have been some of her favorites to write, and she can't wait to explore more avenues in the paranormal and supernatural worlds!

You can connect with me on:
🌐 http://www.autumnstormromance.wordpress.com
📘 http://www.facebook.com/autumnstormromance

Also by Autumn Storm

Available Late February 2022!

 **Her Protector: A contemporary wolf shifter romance**

A wolf shifter romance about a human woman struggling to find herself and the man she meets who is more than she ever could have imagined.